With Love from Poland

With Love from Poland

Linda Lee Keenan

Dedicated to my amazing daughters,
Kristyn and Tammy

Acknowledgments

Writing this book has been an interesting journey. There are many people who helped me along my way – past and present.

This is a historical novel, so first, I owe a debt of gratitude to my amazing history professor, Dr. Eric Roman, now Professor Emeritus in the great beyond. You motivated me to write what I loved and what I wanted to know more about. You, being a critical teacher, have served me well in the writing of this book – thank you!

To my parents, Bev and Dave who read my chapters as they were "hot off the press" – thank you for your comments, suggestions and especially for the questioning that prompted me to be the best that I could be – words are not up to the challenge of matching my gratitude but thank you!

To Karen Bruno Roos, a giant THANK YOU for augmenting my ideas, listening over and over, and for finding Helena's doll, Katrynka. You're amazing!

To Ellen Herman and Rosemary Hughes, my best friends forever –thank you for staying close to my heart.

To my faithful companions, Clancy and Max – thank you for helping me write this book. You two made me keep a toehold on earth by reminding me when it was dinnertime!

To my husband, Bob - your endless patience was very much appreciated while I was partially absent during the writing.

INTRODUCTION

Jeszcze Polska nie zginela means Poland has not yet perished. It is the first line of the National Anthem of Poland. The lyrics describe fierce protection of the Polish homeland and culture. Poland's history is one of waging successful battles against Teutonic Knights in the 15th century, the Swedes in the 17th century and then against the Turks in that same century.

The 20th century would once again visit wars upon Poland. First in 1918 against the Russian Bolsheviks from which Poland would emerge an independent state; then again in 1939 when Hitler's army attacked Poland, an event which precipitated World War II in Europe. The world was in shock. It had been a political atmosphere of appeasement regarding Hitler's aggression.

Hitler had been covertly clever. Germany signed a nonaggression pact with the Soviet Union on August 23, 1939, with a secret clause wherein the Nazis and the Soviets agreed to divide Poland between them. Britain had promised military support to Poland. However, Hitler's next tactic would baffle and confuse all of Europe. He staged a mock attack on Germany, using his SS army wearing the *Polish* uniform. This allowed Hitler to swear that his massive attack on Poland was a defensive one. And so, on Friday, September 1, 1939, at 4:45 A.M., 1.5 million German troops invaded Poland along its borders, advancing 140 miles into its heartland within the first week of fighting. Poland had been preparing for such an attack, but the element of surprise severely compromised their military capabilities. The Polish cavalry on horseback was no match for the German panzer tanks.

On September 17th, Poland's fate was sealed when Soviet troops attacked its eastern border. The next day, the Polish government fled, leaving the Nazi and Soviet governments to claim their formerly agreed upon zones of occupation. Later, a Polish Resistance Movement would rise with the assistance of their exiled Polish government.

With Love from Poland merely touches on what was taken from the people of Poland, what was lost, what could never be found, and ultimately what *was* found. It is a work of fiction, a labor of love, intertwined with historical facts.

Other than historical figures, the characters are fictitious. Their names are chosen at random and meant to represent groups of people. This is a story of humanity, of people helping people in life and death situations within the very dark days of the Second World War. *Jeszcze Polska nie zginela!*

Table of Contents

A Meeting..1

Helena...9

Jan..21

Acorn Park 29

The Spring Social...37

Family 61

1939 - Before the War...67

June 1939...75

First Meeting...89

The Organization 101

Acorn Park Preparations...115

Summer's End 1939 129

The Last Week of August 1939..149

The Arrival of September 1, 1939..157

After Cracow..179

Leaving Paris 191

Plymouth Naval Port...203

Leaving England 213

Autumn of 1939..223

March of 1940...229

Epilogue..239

Chapter One

A Meeting

By 1920, the Industrial Revolution in Europe had been underway for more than sixty years. Both the Jasinski and Pawlowski families were engaged in the prosperous textile industry. Jan Jasinski met the beautiful, fair-haired, emerald-eyed Helena Pawlowski on a sunny day in March of 1920 in Cracow, Poland, while delivering cotton to the mill where her Papa worked.

It was most unusual that Helena should visit the mill. However, her Papa had forgotten his lunchbox on that fateful day. She welcomed the chance to take a pleasant stroll around Acorn Park to deliver the forgotten lunch.

Jakob Pawlowski was delighted to see his only daughter and happy to have his lunch moments before the noon whistle sounded. After Helena handed him his lunch, Jakob threw his arms around his daughter and thanked her for her kindness.

Helena blushed and smiled. She kissed him on the cheek and then turned to enjoy the short walk home.

She had barely turned on her heel when she was knocked off balance by a cart being commandeered by a brash young man with fiery red hair and brilliant blue eyes. He'd been rushing all day trying to get his deliveries made early because his Mama had promised to prepare his favorite meal for his birthday that evening – *golabki*, better known as stuffed cabbage.

Helena was shocked and angered by the thoughtless young man. She had every intention of ignoring him and escaping quickly to avoid further assault. But Jan simply stood there, staring and blocking her passage. If she had not been a lady, she'd surely have smacked him with her empty burlap satchel.

Instead, she stared right back at him and waited for an explanation.

Jan was spellbound by the immediate connection he felt with Helena. Never had he imagined such magnetism from another human being. It was as if he'd known her forever, but how could it be?

Helena experienced an equally compelling reaction, but in a different way. She became anxious. She wanted nothing more than to run from this stranger. It was all she could do to appear unaffected.

Helena was the first to speak. She asked him what was so important as to cause him to be reckless with his rickety cart piled high with cotton.

Jan saw Helena's lips moving, but he was so mesmerized by her voice that he was helpless to respond, for he'd dreamed of an angel with that melodious voice just the night before. He had to remind himself to breathe.

His world stood still. He had no idea how much time passed before he did the only thing he could think to do. He spoke to her from his poetic heart and said,

> Oh, my lovely lady fair,
> pardon me for not a care.
> Should you forgive my thoughtlessness,
> my grateful heart will beat in bliss.

He watched as her eyes softened almost imperceptibly. Her crossed arms dropped to her sides. Now *she* was mesmerized, not knowing how to react.

He waited for some response.

Finally, she spoke. "Where did you find that poem?"

"My own heart wrote it, for you, just now," he said with a self-satisfied grin.

Her eyes narrowed in suspicion. "I doubt that."

"Maybe this will convince you then." Without hesitation, he said,

> Please believe all I say to you
> is from my heart and fully true.

Softly, he asked, "Shall I continue?"

"No! I must hurry to meet my little brother to walk him home from his violin lesson. He's only six years old and tends to wander away to catch frogs if I don't catch him first." She realized she was rambling but could not stop herself. She felt self-conscious and shy with this interesting stranger staring at her. And still, she did not move.

She began wishing she'd worn her blue frock instead of the ragged yellow smock she'd put on to work in the garden that morning. At least she'd braided her hair neatly and added a pansy clip she'd fashioned that morning on a whim.

Once again, Jan surprised her. He said, "Catching frogs! Well, that's just about the most fun boys can have! Let's go get your little brother! What's his name anyway?"

"His name is Jozef and as I said, he's six years old and he doesn't like strangers either. So, if you'll excuse me, I'll be going now."

Jan had no intention of letting this beauty escape without at least planning to meet again. He was thinking of the angel who'd appeared in his dream with that alluring voice. What was it she said before she floated into the night? Oh yes, he remembered…

"You will know me when you meet me first by the music of my voice and then by the sea green of my eyes. I will fill the places in your heart that you did not know were empty until they are overflowing with love and joy."

Helena heard her Papa. "Lena, why are you still here? Jozef will be wandering off if you don't hurry now."

He eyed the boy with the cart. "Do you know this boy?"

Jan cringed and bravely answered the strapping man's question. "I was just apologizing, Sir, for knocking into her, then I thought maybe I met her somewhere, but can't remember just where exactly."

"That is not likely. Helena is at home taking care of her brothers or in the garden most of the time. Please Lena, go ahead now."

Just as she turned to go, the noon whistle shrilled, startling the three of them. Helena obeyed her Papa and hurried off.

Jan was left by himself. He had to act fast if he was to see Helena again. Otherwise, he would not know where to find her.

He yelled a little too loudly, "Sir! May I ask you a favor?" The workers who'd gathered in the courtyard for lunch turned toward Jan. Helena's Papa knew Jan was addressing him.

Jakob turned, took three giant steps back and stood directly in front of Jan, to be out of earshot of the others. He hissed, "What is it that you want, boy?"

Jan squared his shoulders, drew in his breath and with all his courage said, "I would like your permission to sit with your daughter one week from today at 11 A.M. on that park bench right over there." He pointed to Acorn Park where there was a bench beside the duck pond across from the mill. Tulips lined the pond and stood as tall as the ducklings, looking as if they could be their silly umbrellas in case of rain.

Now it was Jakob's turn to stare at Jan. This boy reminded him of himself when he was young. When he met his wife, Marta, for the first time, his entire being had been captivated. Yes, he believed in love at first sight just as this impetuous young man apparently did.

Jakob thought of the times he'd caught the lonely look in his daughter's eyes over the recent weeks and months since her best friend Julia had moved to America with her family. Lena was seventeen years old and should have been thinking of beginning her own family rather than hiding in her garden pretending to be content.

Leaning closer to Jan, Jakob spoke quietly, "What is your name, Son?"

The reply came a little too forcefully and when Jan spoke, it sounded more like a croak. "My name is Jan Jasinski, Sir. I live on the west side of the shipping canal north of town. My Papa runs the mill that I work for and he's teaching me the ropes so I can run the mill one day. My Mama is a music teacher. I can play the harpsichord, the viola and the flute too!"

Jakob interrupted him, "I suppose you'll just go on talking if I don't consent to allowing my daughter to meet you, right, Jan? It *is* Jan, right?"

"I apologize, Sir." Holding his breath, Jan asked, "Are you saying yes, Sir?"

"What I am saying is I give my permission, but I cannot speak for my daughter. She has a mind of her own and it does not seem to me that she is very interested in meeting up with you again. I will ask her if she will meet you on that bench by the duck pond next Monday at 11 A.M. I cannot promise she will be there. I *do* have a strong feeling that even if she does not show up, we've not heard the last of you, Jan Jasinski! Good day to you now."

Jakob shook the boy's hand and gave him a wink, letting him know that he hoped Helena would show up as requested. He then joined his co-workers for lunch.

Jan fairly leapt for joy; he felt certain that Helena was the angel of his dreams, quite literally, and he meant to make her his girl. Suddenly, he remembered why he was there and did a fast turn to deliver the cotton in his trusty old cart that had led him to have a happy accident.

Leaving the mill that day, he took a lingering look at the park bench where a bright new chapter of his happy life would surely begin.

To LODZ

CRACOW 1920.
(Fictional Rendering)

N

WIEŚNIACY DOMY
(Villagers' Homes)

POCIAG STACJA
(Train Station)

MLYN
(Mill)

LAWKA
(Bench)

GENERAL SKLEPS
(Stores)

KACZKA STAW
(Duck Pond)

MIESO SKLEP   RYBA SKLEP
(Meat Store)   (Fish Store)

BANK
(Bank)

ZOLADZ PARK
(Acorn Park)

PIEKARNIA
(Bakery)

LOD DOMY
(Ice House)

OGROD PIWO
(Beer Garden)

KOSCIOT
(Church)

SZKOLA
(School)

STARY DAB DRZEWO
(Old Oak Tree)

Chapter Two

HELENA

As Helena passed Acorn Park, she noticed the bench beside the duck pond. The bench was empty except for the harbingers of spring looking for food in the wet soils after the previous evening's rainstorm. The ducklings quacked happily as they played "catch me if you can" on the sparkling pond. Helena stopped and giggled at their antics.

Her attention was drawn to the bench. She saw a boy and a girl sitting together, holding hands. They looked so happy and unaware of anything else.

Then something amazing happened...they disappeared! She wondered if she'd really seen them at all.

Helena was not given to fantasy. In fact, she was quite practical. Her friends and family called her "Logical Lena." Aloud, she thought, "I must be more tired than I thought. I hope we don't have a rainstorm that keeps the children awake again tonight."

She dismissed the incident and walked a little faster until she arrived at the far side of Acorn Park, where she knew Jozef would be waiting for her.

As she rounded the last curve on the pathway, she was relieved to see Jozef walking toward her with the violin case in his hand, which was just about as big as he was.

Jozef was small for his age. He'd been born with a small heart, so Doc Kaminski said. That did not stop the little dynamo from going off on impromptu adventures at every opportunity. When she reprimanded him, he would look appropriately mournful just for a moment, then flash that freckle-faced grin, and the trouble would simply be forgotten. He would then jump into his sister's arms and tell her how much fun he'd had that day. His enthusiasm was mightily contagious.

Lena had been the only Mama Jozef remembered. She had died in the influenza epidemic that struck all of Europe in 1918.

Marta Pawlowski was thirty-eight years old when she died, leaving fifteen-year-old Lena to care for her two younger brothers, Jozef and Franz.

1918 was a horrible year in Cracow from beginning to end. The epidemic randomly and thoroughly ripped families apart, , leaving unbearable heartache.

Jakob Pawlowski had no time to grieve the loss of his beloved Marta. He'd promised her as she lay dying that he would carry on as if she were still living. "Let me live in your heart, my darling Jakob," she begged him. The moment she was assured that he would comply with her last request, her grip on his hand relaxed.

The children had been kept from their Mama since she'd become ill just days before. It was a miracle and a blessing that they escaped the dreadful consumption.

Jakob believed completely that his Marta lived in his heart for the rest of his life. It's what kept him living.

After the health workers gently took Marta from the bed where she loved her husband and gave birth to their babies, Jakob bravely went to his children.

He held his boys in his lap with Helena at his side in front of the hearth where they'd enjoyed their meals, sung songs together and recited poetry.

Jakob told his children their Mama had been healed by the angels and allowed to go to Heaven and before she went, her heart had been divided into four equal parts. Now, each of them had a part of her heart in their own heart.

He went on to tell them they could talk to her with their heart anytime and she would always hear them.

Helena tried desperately to comprehend what her Papa said. Jozef was four years old and Franz was two years old. They simply looked at Helena's puzzled expression. She knew her little brothers would need comfort from her and so she put on a brave face. Her best friend, Julia, called it her pretend face.

Little Jozef wanted to know if Mama could talk to him from Heaven. Jakob answered with total confidence. "Yes, Jozef, Mama asked me to tell you, her smiling boy, that she will talk to you and if you really believe and if you are very quiet, you will hear her." Jozef grinned.

Jakob then looked at Franz, who was too young to understand and said to him, "Mama says to tickle you every single day, Franzie." With that, Jakob tickled the toes of his youngest child. Franz laughed so much that they all laughed with him. It was a much-needed release of emotion.

A thoughtful look came over Jakob's face. He knew Helena would miss her Mama as much as he would. Marta had known it too. Through her pain and weakness, Marta managed to say these words to her husband that she wanted her daughter to know, "You, my sweet Helena, are so like me, it's as if we know what each other thinks before we say it. I promise you I will be with you when you marry, when you birth your babies and whenever you need me. I will be your Guardian Angel, and I thank you for taking care of your brothers. Just think of me whenever you have a concern, large or small, and you will know what to do. Keep your faith."

Helena listened intently. Somehow, she knew everything would be alright. She believed every word her Mama had said.

***

Later that day, as Jozef practiced his violin lesson and Franz was taking his afternoon nap, there was a knock at the door. Helena answered, wiping her hands on the smock she wore while harvesting peas and carrots from the garden for dinner.

When she saw the uniformed young man, she hesitated, but then saw he was holding an envelope for her. The postal carrier had a letter from Julia.

Julia had left Cracow with her family to start a new life in America. The two girls had what they called their last supper sitting under the Old Oak Tree beside the schoolhouse on a cold and dreary night, many weeks before. They vowed never to lose touch with each other and to travel to visit each other every chance they got, and as soon as possible. This was the first letter Helena had gotten from Julia since then.

Helena thanked the carrier and eagerly ripped open the envelope even before the door was closed. The envelope was postmarked six weeks before and was dirty and crumpled from its journey across the Atlantic. She rushed to sit on her bed to read it. She reached into her smock and pulled out the doll her Mama had placed in her cradle when she was born. It was a special doll, for it was given to Helena's Mama by her Mama. The doll wore a navy print dress and matching kerchief with a red vest and a little white apron trimmed in pink. She was made from flesh colored fabric hand-stitched together. Helena named her Katrynka just because she liked the sound of it. The doll had long golden braids, sparkling blue eyes, rosy cheeks and a heart-shaped mouth that looked like she had a secret. She sat Katrynka on the quilt that she helped her Mama sew. She began to read.

15 February 1920

Dearest Lena,

I hope you are well. I miss you so much that my heart hurts! I put a tiny drop of perfume on this letter. It's the perfume you gave me as a going-away present. As you know, it's our favorite fragrance. If you hold the paper to your nose, it will almost be like we're together!

There is so very much to tell you about our long journey and about America. The beginning of our trip was by rail. We were only allowed to take one large trunk per household and one train case each. I packed my favorite green sweater, three cotton dresses, woolen socks and one night gown. We all wore layers of warm clothes as journeying in winter is brrrr cold! And of course, I had a little pocket in my train case for my perfume, hair combs and the bracelet my Babula gave to me. I kept the letter Kazi wrote to me in the pocket of the apron I wore. I read it every single day. He even said he sealed it with a kiss; imagine that! He promised to find me here when he and his family come to America in June. I hope it with all my heart, Lena. If you see Kazi at Sunday Mass, please tell him I'm waiting for him and that I have met his cousin, Jozef, here in Yonkers at a church social. Goodness gracious, those two could be twins. For a split second, I thought it was Kazi sitting at that table, talking to all the girls. He certainly is a flirty sort, unlike Kazi.

Back to my journey…the trip by rail was long but not terribly uncomfortable. I can still see you in my mind, waving with a pretend smile on your face as the train left you and Cracow behind. It was soon dark, and I quickly fell asleep. By morning, we arrived in Budapest and changed trains to go to Zurich. The scenery seemed so like home with the snow-capped mountains, lakes and rivers, and I was already homesick. It was many hours to Paris, the most exciting city I had ever seen. If only we could have had more time, I wanted to see all the sights again, like when Papa took us on holiday to Paris when I was twelve. As it was, we had only time to have dinner at a restaurant near the train depot before the next train to the Port of Le Havre. Once again, I fell fast asleep on the train. You know me, I can sleep anywhere!

A giant ship stood in the Port of Le Havre. It looked as big as a city, right there on the water! When it was time to board, I began to feel like I was almost to America. The Captain greeted passengers. Papa introduced us, speaking French, of course. He later told me that the Captain said there were 1,142 passengers on board and they were mostly from Spain, Italy and France. Some were traveling back to their homes in New York City after having spent the Christmas holidays in Europe.

Most of the passengers were in 3rd Class. Thankfully, we are among the few with 2nd Class accommodations. Looking out at the ocean on the few fair-weather days, it seemed we were not moving at all. I kept myself busy talking with other teenagers, but only after my tutor said I was through studying for the day. I do enjoy learning from Miss Milewski. She makes everything seem fun and interesting. In exchange for tutoring me, Papa paid for her passage to America, where she will apply for a job teaching at one of the schools in New York City. She is so brave to go all alone to America without her family. But her Papa insisted she would have a better life here than she would have in Cracow.

As we crossed the Atlantic Ocean, we took a more southern route than the Titanic took eight years ago. Thankfully, we did not see any icebergs. I was worried about that as I knew Mama was. Papa did not say, but I suspected he was a little bit concerned too.

It was a huge relief when we saw the entrance to America at Ellis Island. We had been on the ocean for weeks and we were exhausted and past seasick. Some whales escorted us to port and they seemed as excited as we were! It also looked like they were traveling faster than our ship. It made me wonder if I should have traveled by whale!

Miss Milewski said I should learn American History on the way to our new home. I had to write an essay about Emma Lazarus. She was the poet who wrote a collection of poems to raise money for the base of the Statue of Liberty. The statue was given to the United States by France in 1884. Miss

Lazarus wrote about the terrible things that happened to the Jewish people in Europe, including Poland. I was so excited to see that statue. But my, oh my, when I saw Lady Liberty standing strong and proud as we neared the harbor, I cried along with the other passengers. We would finally be free to be, free to practice our religion and free to be proud of our Polish heritage!

Disembarking was another adventure. All passengers had to show their citizenship papers at Ellis Island. The lines were long and some people were asked to step aside if they were ill. I asked Papa why. He said if someone was sick, they would have to go to the Ellis Island health facility until it was determined that they were not bringing disease into America. I even saw a couple of children being carried off the ship on stretchers and it did not look like they were alive. I did not ask about them. I did not want to know for sure.

When Mama, Papa and I got to the head of the line to be admitted to New York, Papa took the lead and spoke in his broken English. He had to confirm what our citizenship papers said, which was our full name, date of birth, race, our last residence and the American friend or relative who sponsored us. Then the agent wrote the name of the ship we arrived on, the arrival date and the line number we were on. He stamped our papers and we were finally in America! We forgot that we were bone weary!

We had already said our goodbyes to Miss Milewski and she was somewhere behind us in line, all alone. She told us her cousin Stanley was meeting her and would escort her to her temporary residence offered by the Polish Women's Alliance. While there, she will be working at the orphanage to earn her keep until she is able to get a teaching job. We gave her our address in Yonkers and arranged to be together for the Easter festivities a few weeks later.

Although the journey was long, we did arrive at the expected time, and so our sponsor, Father Michalowicz was waiting for us with a car. We knew him because he said he would be carrying his white terrier puppy named Buttons when he came to meet us. While Papa loaded our trunk and train cases into the car, Mama related the details of our crossing to Father Michalowicz. I put my hand out to pet that cute little Buttons and he jumped right into my arms! I almost did not catch him, but he caught his back legs in my coat pocket and saved himself! He licked my face and then laid his head on my shoulder, perfectly content.

Buttons sat on my lap for the car ride to Yonkers, north of New York City. We arrived within an hour or so. Along the way I saw a train in the sky! And there was really tall brick buildings called skyscrapers, a very good name, by the way. We didn't look at the roadway, we only looked up. So much that our necks started to hurt! Lena, wait until you see this amazing place!

Yonkers is magical. We could see the great Hudson River and suddenly I was homesick again, remembering the Vistula River that we used to sit and look at from Wawel Hill. Our own Wawel Castle looks a lot like the church here overlooking the Hudson.

Father Michalowicz arranged for us to rent a lovely home next to the university where Papa will teach science. The Polish National Alliance is helping us to get settled. They also give us news from home as soon as they receive it.

There is so much more to tell, but it's Saturday night and we go to church early tomorrow, so I must sign off. Oh, one more little thing. When we first arrived in Yonkers, Papa had a present for me. That cute little Buttons who greeted us at Ellis Island is MINE! We are inseparable! Buttons and I send you butterfly kisses. I promise to write again soon and I will be waiting for your letter. Be sure to tell me when you will visit me, I will count the days! I miss you, Lena!

Fondly and truly,
Julia

Buttons
1920

Helena mopped her face with the corner of her smock and blew her nose with the hand-embroidered handkerchief. She picked up Katrynka and held her close. She imagined Julia in her new home, going to church and school, and looking at the Hudson River, seeing instead the Vistula River in her mind's eye. Once again, she smelled the perfume on the letter and sighed deeply.

Suddenly, she realized she no longer heard the squeaks and creaks of Jozef's violin. That could only mean one thing…he must be in the garden looking for frogs or some other creepy crawly critters to show her. She carefully folded Julia's letter and tucked it into her smock along with Katrynka and promised herself she would read the letter again after the boys were in bed that night. It was Monday, Papa's night to go to the church meeting, then to the Beer Garden, but of course, he did not tell her that part. In any event, she would have time to herself to read the letter again and to write one in response.

As she passed Franzie's bed, she saw he was just waking up from his nap. He grinned as he saw that his sister was looking at him. Helena went to him and tickled his toes. They laughed. She washed his face, then gently sat him on the kitchen floor by the hearth to play with his wooden blocks. It made him happy and unlike his brother, he could be trusted to play alone.

Just as she suspected, Jozef was in the garden picking up grasshoppers with one hand while trying to catch butterflies with the other. It was a comical sight. She left him in his Adventureland and went back to preparing dinner for her family, her mind on all Julia had written.

Chapter Three

JAN

As Jan burst through the garden gate and directly into the kitchen, the aroma of golabki momentarily prompted him to forget what he was about to tell his Mama. She was not surprised by his exuberance, but she was startled when he nearly knocked her over with a bear hug. It was the second time that day his energy had gotten the better of him.

He always looked forward to family birthday celebrations, whether it was his or not. His Mama put her own special touches on what she called "the celebration of yourself." She spent long hours preparing and cooking the golabki and even longer making the piernik. Mary Jasinski had come from a family of bakers of Torun in northern Poland, where the medieval confection was famous. She was proud to announce at every opportunity that Torun was the birthplace of Copernicus. Her family pretended to be impressed with this information as if they were hearing it for the first time. Piernik was something between a cookie and a candy, individually molded with just the right combination of ginger, cinnamon and nutmeg and was enjoyed with alcoholic beverages. Now that Jan was of an age to drink with his Papa, it was an extra special treat.

Jan had chosen his Mama's tort piaskowy, also known as sand cake, for his birthday dessert. The simple recipe using potato flour was made delicious by the orange-almond icing that smothered every morsel.

Just as Jan was about to tell her all about the angel of his dream, delivering cotton to the mill, meeting a real-life angel, and seeing her again next week *and* that he intended to marry her, there was a pounding on the sturdy oak door. He was exasperated by the interruption and reluctantly opened the door without peeking through the little window first.

His Uncle Stanislaw stepped in and picked up his favorite nephew as easily as if he were a bundle of cotton. Jan was laughing and yelling at Uncle Stan to let him down. Watching the interaction between her brother-in-law and her son, Mary Jasinski was reminded how very fortunate her family was to enjoy festivities together. Stanislaw and her husband, Jan, were the only Jasinski boys who'd survived World War I. They had supported the war effort at home in their respective professions.

Stan had made special arrangements to attend Jan's birthday celebration. He worked six days a week at the Wieliczka Crystal Rock Salt Mine, which was a short distance from Cracow. Since he was a foreman, he took the liberty of taking half of Monday off to surprise Jan. He carried a gift for Jan hidden in the wooden box that his own Papa had given him for his eighteenth birthday. When Jan tried to snatch the box from under his uncle's arm, he found himself on the floor without the coveted box.

The three of them laughed and hugged all at once. Mary told her son to wash up for dinner and offered Stan a beverage before dinner. They heard the mill whistle; it signaled that Big Jan would be home soon.

Not unlike his son, Big Jan burst through the front door knowing it would be an eventful evening of fun and merriment. Stan had settled into the overstuffed chair in front of the fireplace with a tall goblet of vodka. He jumped up to greet his brother. The two men embraced and clapped each other on the back. One was as big and burly as the other, strong and proud Polish. Mary was certain their voices could be heard blocks away, but she was so happy that they were together; she did not bother to quiet them. She finished up the sauce for the golabki and when Jan came back into the kitchen, she asked him to set the dinner table. He gladly did so, listening to his Uncle Stan and his Papa trading work stories.

Uncle Stan was telling of the statues of the Virgin Mary and of the Last Supper that had been sculpted by miners in the underground chapels of St. Kinga and St. Anthony. Entire chapels are carved from the crystal rock salt, including the chandeliers and the murals. The salt that is brought up to the surface with the help of horses is quite precious and referred to as white gold.

It took a certain kind of man to be a miner and Stanislaw Jasinski was one of the best. He used his years of experience and knowledge, along with his keen intuition, to keep his crews safe from harm, although the previous spring he lost six men. They drowned when groundwater flooded a cavern, almost instantly forming a lake in one of the mine shafts. No one could have predicted the flood, but Big Stan felt responsible. He insisted that he be the one to inform the wives and children of his men of their deaths. After a visit to the home of each man, he retreated to the underground Chapel of St. Anthony. A day later, he emerged and returned to the job fully prepared to bolster the morale of his crews and to keep them safe.

Neither Stan nor his younger brother Jan was a stranger to loss; their family lost five boys to World War I. Shortly after the war ended, the flu epidemic claimed two younger sisters and Stan and Jan's Mama and Papa.

Big Jan and Mary had also lost their twelve-year-old twins, Piotr and Henryk, to that dread disease, leaving sixteen-year-old Jan an only child. Thus, they all knew how to be forward-thinking, no matter how difficult. Looking backward served no purpose and was far too painful.

Big Jan told his brother how well young Jan was doing learning the ropes at the mill. In the short time Jan worked with his Papa, he'd been promoted from maintenance to the mailroom, to dispatch, to the order department, and most recently, to the local delivery department. He was learning the textile business literally from the ground floor up. Young Jan was grinning from ear to ear. He loved working with his Papa and loved even more that his Papa was proud of him.

Mary Jasinski rang the dinner bell, signaling all was in readiness for the birthday dinner to begin. The Jasinski household had a round dinner table, so everyone had a seat of honor, so Jan's Mama said. But tonight, Jan had a special place – the seat with gifts next to it.

The four of them said a prayer of thanks together and the giant bowl of golabki was passed, followed by sauce, and everyone's favorite side dish—pea patties. Steaming hot bread, fresh from the oven, came next, along with Hawthorne berry jam from the cellar, having been canned late last fall. They ate to their heart's content, complimenting the cook over and over.

Jan's Mama noticed he was not eating as much as usual and asked him why. It was the perfect opportunity to tell the news of his day. He said he was very excited to have met a wonderful girl when he delivered goods to the south mill.

In an effort not to appear silly, he did not tell the angel's message in his dream the night before, or that he literally ran into the unsuspecting, wonderful girl with his cart. He said her name was Helena and she had beautiful golden hair with flowers in it and emerald eyes that sparkled when she spoke to him. He also did not mention how those eyes flashed angrily when his cart struck her. He stretched the truth when he said she'd been delivering her Papa's lunch box to him just as he arrived, and then her Papa introduced them. He further embellished the actual events when he said her Papa, Mr. Pawlowski, suggested the two might like to get to know each other and meet again next week in Acorn Park. Jan had said he would be delighted and Helena agreed right then and there! They were to meet at the bench next to the duck pond at Acorn Park next Monday at 11 A.M. Jan also thought it wise not to get into details of the poetry he'd spoken to Helena.

At that point, Jan's Papa spoke up. "Son, do you realize who Jakob Pawlowski's daughter is?"

"What do you mean, Papa?" Jan had no idea what he was about to hear.

Big Jan continued. "She is one of our most accomplished violinists. She performed for King Poincaré of France, King Gustaf V of Sweden and even for the Holy See in Rome! Why, she's practically royalty! I've not laid eyes on her, but I hear she's quite beautiful and charming!"

Jan was about to chime in, but his Mama was practically bursting at the seams to comment about the young lady who'd caught the eye of her precious son. "Good Heavens, Jan! Marta Pawlowski brought her five-year-old daughter, Helena, to my class when I was teaching at the Academy of Music more than ten years ago! That little girl impressed me with her natural talent. She learned to play on a magnificent, borrowed Stradivarius. Some say that her music comes from the great Stradivari himself!"

Now they were all talking excitedly. No one voice could be heard until Big Stan's voice boomed above the others with, "That's my boy! You know how to pick 'em!"

Jan felt so many emotions at once that it was difficult to complete a thought, much less a sentence. His most pressing thought was that there was every possibility that Helena (he now imagined her playing a harp) might not meet him again. That thought terrified him. What would he tell his family then?

His elders stopped talking and were looking at him for a response to something he had not heard.

Jan's Mama interrupted his inner turmoil, "Jan, did you hear me? I said that Helena's Mama died in the horrible flu epidemic two years ago. Since then, the poor girl has cared for her family and all but quit playing her violin, at least in public. Such a shame to lose your Mama. All the church women loved Marta Pawlowski. She sang solo in the choir, you know. At our Christmas Pageant three years ago, she sang 'Silent Night' and there was not a dry eye in the church!"

Jan sighed. "Mama, I remember being at that pageant and hearing that pretty lady sing. She was amazing; I can still hear her voice."

Suddenly, Jan was stunned! He was certain the angel's voice in his dream was the voice of Helena's Mama. This was getting very strange indeed. Jan's Mama had often told him he was what people called a "sensitive" but he'd never had such a vivid dream. Being a sensitive accounted for his poetic heart, and for the ease with which he was able to play music by ear. But hearing angel voices in his dreams was unusual.

Uncle Stan broke the silence. "Well, my favorite nephew, will you open your birthday gifts now that we've devoured this wonderful meal so we can dig into that luscious birthday cake?"

"With pleasure, my favorite uncle!" Jan reached for the wooden box. "I will open this one first!"

Jan lifted the brass clasp on the old wooden box and picked out an eight-inch figure carved from crystal rock salt. He knew it was from the mine where his uncle worked. He turned the figure over and over, marveling at the finite detail and how the light bounced off it. It took him a minute to realize it was carved in the likeness of his beloved Grandpapa. When he looked up, his Mama, Papa and Uncle all had tears in their eyes. Jan got up from his chair, went to his Uncle and hugged him with all his might. "Uncle Stan, this is the best gift I ever got! I will keep it with me always. Who created this masterpiece?"

It was a day of surprises. Uncle Stan said, "Why, I carved it. I figured if my workers could carve entire chapels and murals, that I could carve a single figure! I am pleased you like it."

Looking at his brother, Stan said, "You know Papa loved this boy best and I could think of no better way to honor their relationship than to create his likeness for Jan." Big Jan nodded silently, pressing his fist to his heart in agreement and remembrance.

Mama gave her son a large, wrapped gift, hoping to lighten the mood. Jan accepted it, thinking there was only one thing that could be in this unusually shaped package. He ripped the wrapping off and revealed a beautiful violin! He'd been wanting such an instrument for a long time, saving as much as he could from his weekly wage, but not having nearly enough yet. Jan loved playing the viola but thought he now wanted a violin for some reason, and now he had it.

By way of thanks, he jumped up, violin in hand. He applied resin to the bow, tuned its strings perfectly, and played Beethoven's Symphony No. 7 Sonata for violin and piano. He'd heard it played once or twice and now captured every note with precision and confidence. Before he completed the first stanza, his Mama recognized the tune, sat at the piano, and joined him in joyful playing.

When they finished the piece, Jan gently set his gift back into its red velvet-lined case and hugged his Mama. "Thank you so much to you and Papa for this beautiful violin. It's more than I could have hoped for. And thank you again, Uncle Stan. I am so happy you are here with us tonight."

Jan's mama announced it was cake time. They sang the traditional z okazji urodzin (birthday) song. Jan was flushed with happiness. As soon as they were served ample portions of the special sand cake, they dug in and thoroughly enjoyed it.

Yes, Jan thought, this was the beginning of a bright new chapter of his happy life. He was not sure how he would be able to wait until next Monday at 11:00. Maybe he would fill his spare time by practicing a song to play for Helena. Now there was a good idea!

As soon as Uncle Stan took his leave, promising to come for dinner two weeks from Sunday, Jan began to practice a song to capture the heart of Miss Helena Pawlowski.

Chapter Four

ACORN PARK

On the next Monday, both Jan and Helena awoke before dawn on opposite sides of Cracow, hearing the same clap of thunder. Jan thought, "Oh, no rain today of all days!" Helena thought, "Oh good, a reason not to go to Acorn Park to meet that red-haired nut."

Helena's Papa pleaded Jan's case to his daughter the day after she was accosted by him, as she put it. He explained that young Jan Jasinski was not just a delivery boy. He was the son of Jan Jasinski, the Manager of the prosperous mill north of town. Jakob told her what Jan had confidently told him after Helena had left the mill that day. He did note some interest when Helena heard Jan's Mama was a music teacher and that Jan played the harpsichord, viola, and the flute. Her interested look was followed by a wistful one. Jakob understood because she had not picked up her violin in many months.

"Lena, Jan would like to sit with you next Monday at 11:00 on the bench next to the duck pond in Acorn Park. I think you would enjoy getting to know him. I said I would give my permission, but it would be up to you to decide if you would meet him."

Helena twirled the end of her braid as she gazed out the window, pretending not to listen to her Papa. Despite herself, when she heard he'd given permission without speaking to her first, her head snapped up and before saying something she would regret, she took a big breath.

After the mental count of three, she said, "Papa, I am not interested in seeing this boy again and I don't care who his family is. I am very happy to take care of you and the boys, tending to the garden and reading. Why, I don't even have time for him with all that I am involved in!"

Jakob interrupted her. "Lena, kochanie, please do not be upset with me. I know how you feel, and I know you have been lonely since Julia left. You keep yourself occupied, but it really is time for you to have some fun with boys and girls your own age. You are only young once you know. Don't let this time go to waste. Just tell me you will consider meeting Jan, even if you only stay for five minutes. I do not think you will be disappointed. Tell me you will think hard about it, Lena."

To placate her Papa, Helena agreed to think about it. In her own mind, she'd already decided *not* to meet Jan, and there would be nothing to change her mind. She smiled and gave her Papa a peck on the cheek, then she went to her room to read before she went to sleep. He seemed satisfied with their agreement, thinking he'd made perfect sense to his Logical Lena.

Helena fell asleep almost immediately, book in hand. She dreamed of her Mama sitting in the same chair that her Papa had sat in while trying to convince her to meet Jan. What was her Mama saying to her? It was not too clear, and it was not even her Mama's voice. It was her Papa's voice and his words, coming out of her Mama's mouth. The same words had an entirely different effect on Helena in her dream, with the presence of her Mama. It was as if her Mama was telling her it was right to meet Jan.

Aloud, Helena said, "Oh, alright, what have I got to lose anyway? Like Papa says, I can stay only five minutes if I want to, or I would say even less." So it was decided.

When Helena told her Papa the next day at dinner that she'd decided to meet Jan the following Monday, he was very pleased and he was more than a little bit proud of his powers of persuasion. Now, Jakob was another person who could not wait for Monday at 11:00.

Finally, it was Monday morning, it was raining, and Jan headed off to work whistling a happy tune. Helena hummed a silly tune she'd heard but did not know where or when; each of them was busy with their respective tasks. The morning hours slipped by one by one. When the clock struck ten, the rain stopped, the sun broke through the clouds, and a rainbow stretched from the north side of town to the south side of town.

Jan thought, "Oh, good, the rain has stopped and the rainbow is good luck for me!" He went on whistling a happy tune.

Helena thought, "Oh no, now I will have no excuse not to show up at that dumb bench, and I have less than an hour to look presentable!" With that, she took Katrynka out of her smock pocket and looked at her as if the doll would tell her what to wear. When that did not happen, Helena put the doll on the bed and found her best blue dress. She argued with herself all the while she dressed. She thought of wearing her smock for the two-minute meeting. But she continued to put the blue dress on. She put freshly cut pansies in her hair, then took them out. She did not need to impress Jan Jasinski!

At 10:45, Helena began her walk to Acorn Park from the south, and Jan began his bike ride from the mill, north of town. They arrived at the pathway to the bench at the same time. They stopped. Jan grinned when Helena curtsied, holding the fullness of her sky-blue dress. He thought he should respond in kind, so he jumped off his bike, allowing it to drop to the ground. He went to her and bowed. "I am so glad you could come to meet me, Helena. Let's sit and watch the ducklings for a while."

"That would be nice, Jan. Thank you." Helena was pleasantly surprised as she realized how comfortable she felt.

She breathed an audible sigh of relief, which Jan pretended not to notice. He smiled to himself.

They sat on the bench for two full hours, talking and laughing as if they'd known each other forever. They talked about silly things, about important things, and they were unaware of passersby. It was as if they were in a bubble and no one else existed. They did not notice the antics of the ducklings trying to catch minnows and bugs. They did not even hear the noon whistle from the mill across the road. Nothing else mattered.

When Jan reached for Helena's hand, she let him take it. The bubble burst at one o'clock when Jozef came running up to the bench with his violin case, yammering on about how many frogs he caught at the other side of the duck pond. Helena completely forgot she was to meet her little brother to walk him home after his violin lesson. She was upset with herself for forgetting him. Jozef was thrilled to have time for an adventure on the other side of the pond, and he could see his sister, so he did not wonder where she was.

Jan reluctantly released Helena's hand and reached out to shake Jozef's muddy little hand. "Well, congratulations! How many frogs ya got there, little man?"

Jozef ignored the fact that this boy called him "little man." He announced, "Whall, I 'spose I got least hundreds of 'em but I lost count cause I knew Lena would make me throw 'em back, so I did. But I had fun! And I could see you two from aaaalll the way over there," he said, pointing to the far side of the pond. "You din see me cause I was hidin' hind that big tree. You din see me, did ya?"

Jan and Helena laughed at her mischievous little brother. Helena asked Jozef if he got a good grade on his violin lesson. He changed the subject by asking Jan who he was, and that was her answer. She decided to talk to him about his grade later. She did not think he'd practiced his violin lessons enough.

Jan was just about to tell the precocious Jozef who he was when Helena said it was time to go home. She really did not want Jozef to tell everyone all about her meeting at the park. The sooner he forgot it, the happier she would be. He talked too much but was easily distracted.

Helena jumped up and took her little wanderer by the hand. She thanked Jan and walked toward home.

Jan only had time to say, "It was my pleasure, Helena." He headed toward his bike, still lying beside the path, when he stumbled on something. A rock had tripped him, then saw something shiny beside it. He bent to pick it up. It was a heart-shaped key. He thought it must belong to Helena. He dropped the key into his pocket, hopped on his bike, and pedaled around the pond toward Helena. At first, he did not see her. She must have been walking very fast, he thought to himself.

Jan heard an excited voice by the big tree Jozef had pointed to earlier. He looked in that direction and saw Helena dredging something out of the pond that looked like a rat. A soaking wet Jozef was next to her.

Once again, Jan let his bike drop to the ground and rushed to help her. As he neared, he saw Helena had scooped a tiny gray kitten from the pond.

As Helena handed the sopping little thing to Jozef, she saw Jan. In the excitement, Jozef had dropped his violin case, so Jan picked it up and gave it to Helena. She gave him a grateful look and brushed herself off. Jan pulled his handkerchief out of his pocket, and out popped the heart-shaped key. They both looked surprised.

Before either could speak, Jozef ran over to show the kitten to Jan. He said, "Hey! Did you see the kitty drownin' too? I saw him when I was by the big tree catchin' frogs and he ran away from me, he musta climbed the tree. But he's too young to climb so I guess he fell in, but I rescued him, din I, Lena? I guess he din listen to his Mama bout not climbin' no trees! I would never climb *that* big tree." He crossed the fingers of his free hand because it a little white lie.

Jan tousled Jozef's wet hair. "Well, looks like you're not such a little man after all! I'll call you Jozef the Hero, how's that?"

Jozef, with the kitten, leaned into Jan's side, enjoying the warmth. He giggled and said, "Tha'd be real good, that's me - Jozef the Hero! Right kitty? I wonder what's his name. Lena! Lena! Can I keep the kitty? Can I, can I? I promise to feed him and make him a bed near mine and to clean up after him, just in case he does, you know, make a mess."

Helena took a minute to answer, thinking she did not want something else to take care of. Jozef saw the hesitation on his sister's face and took the opportunity to pour on the charm. He walked over to her, kitten in hand, knelt in front of her and placed his little hands together, which looked very funny as there was a kitten in the middle of his prayerful hands. Jozef the Hero said, "Lena, if you let me keep him, cross my heart, I will practice my violin lessons every single day and then I will play music as good as you and I just know you will be so proud of me!"

Jozef saw her resolve crumble, and he jumped up and kissed her hand. "Thank you, my best sister! You will not be sorry, yu'll see! And I already know his name. Do you want to know whut it is?" Jozef looked at Jan and Helena. As they both shook their heads, half in consent and half in curiosity, he proudly announced, "Froggie! Isn't that funny? Ya know, cause I always look for frogs, now Froggie an me can go froggin' every day." He hesitated for an instant and said, "That is, after I practice violin fer shure! Ya see, I'm already keepin' my promise!"

Jan and Helena could no longer contain themselves, they both laughed. It was a moment that would be remembered. The three of them, plus Froggie, were already making memories.

Jozef asked if he could borrow Jan's handkerchief that Helena was using to dry Froggie. She handed it to him and he walked over to the big oak tree, plopped himself down and began to dry his new best friend.

Jan's bike was still on the ground and he was holding Jozef's violin in his left hand and the heart-shaped key tightly in his right. He turned to Helena and again, it seemed as if they were in their own private world.

Jan cleared his throat to give himself time to gather his thoughts a bit. Helena looked at him warily. He stepped forward, showing her his open hand with the key in it. "Helena, I think you dropped this next to the bench just now."

Helena was confused. She'd kept her hope chest key hidden in Katrynka's apron pocket. She could not understand how it got into her blue dress pocket. Then, silly as it sounds, she realized when she asked Katrynka what she should wear, somehow her magical doll made the key appear in the dress she decided to wear!

Many unusual things had happened to Helena since her Mama had died. Helena was afraid that if anyone knew those things were happening, she would be labeled "Lena the Lunatic" instead of "Logical Lena!"

There was an ongoing dialogue in her head that seemed to last for a long time. She remembered when little Franz was sick last year and they all thought he might die. She'd stayed up with him around the clock for days and was exhausted when one night, she saw her Mama's rocking chair moving back and forth next to Franz's bed. She blinked and clearly saw Mama with Franz in her arms. She looked at Helena and put her finger to her lips as if to say, "Quiet now, he is alright." Helena blinked again and Franz was sleeping peacefully in his little bed and the rocking chair was still. Helena believed her Mama's last words to her, that she would always be there when she needed her. Finally, she dragged herself to her own bed, and as her head hit the pillow, she fell into a peaceful sleep.

Helena felt a hand on her shoulder. It was Jan. She released thoughts of the past and came back to the present, in Acorn Park. "Helena, is this your key?"

She said, "Why yes, Jan. I did not realize I dropped it. Thank you for bringing it to me."

Jan gave her the heart-shaped key ever so gingerly, and as he did, he leaned in and gently kissed her cheek. She felt his breath on her face as he whispered in her ear, "Will you go to the Spring Social with me on Saturday, Helena?"

Helena nodded. "Yes, Jan. I would be happy to go with you."

Just then, Jozef and Froggie bounded up to the couple. "Lena, Froggie says he's starving, can we please go now?" He looked at Jan, "Whut did ya say yer name wuz?"

"My name is Jan and it is very nice to meet you. Go ahead now and get Froggie some food and please make sure he does not climb any more trees. Here is your violin. Can you handle it with your kitten too?"

Jozef puffed up his chest, hugged his kitten under his arm and reached for his violin case. "Of course, I am Jozef the Hero! Remember, Mr. Jan?"

Helena touched Jan's hand and gave him an admiring look. Jozef skipped ahead, wanting to get home ahead of his sister to show Froggie the garden where they would be hunting.

Jan said goodbye, picked up his bike and rode back toward the bench on his way home.

Helena waved and followed Jozef.

Jan rode at a leisurely pace, reliving the past few hours. As he passed the duck pond, he saw a young couple sitting on the bench holding hands. They were unaware of anything or anyone. In the next instant, they disappeared. He was only momentarily taken aback. He understood.

Chapter Five

THE SPRING SOCIAL

The next five days were filled with preparations for the annual Spring Social at the church, south of Acorn Park. Every member of the congregation was involved in some way. The ladies tended to join the decorating committee, or the food committee and the men joined committees that called for setting up the stage, dance floor or dining area. The young people volunteered to help on any committee that needed more hands, but many of them preferred to join the games committee.

Since Helena could sew, she always volunteered to repair last year's costumes or make new ones if needed. This year, she made herself a new costume with her favorite colors of aquamarine and pine green with ivory lace trim. She pieced together material from a dress of her Mama's, a vest of her Papa's, and the lace trim from a tablecloth her aunt had tatted.

Mrs. Kaminski asked her just after the last social if she would make her little girl, Sophia, a costume to fit a four-year-old, for the next year. Helena knew that the Kaminski family had lost their baby to the flu epidemic around the same time her Mama passed. She was honored by the request to sew for the cute little girl. Helena grew nostalgic for a moment, remembering Spring Socials with her Mama. It took all of her will to come back to the present. She was happy to be busy.

Jan and his Mama served on the music committee. Every night during dinner that week, they talked about the music that would be played and the songs that would be sung. Jan was working on the music he would play for Helena. He'd been practicing in semi-secret.

Early on, Jan had the idea of getting the town's youngest musicians together to show off their talents. After meeting Helena, he realized Jozef was in the group of twelve boys and girls ranging in age from four to six. It was a cute rag-tag group of little violinists, flute, harmonica and cymbal players and even a drummer. Oh, and little Sophia Kaminski was to play the bells. The children had practiced very hard to learn their two-minute song. Jan truly loved children and encouraged them to have fun as they learned and to laugh at their mistakes. They all loved him and were anxious to please him. There was only one tense moment when the smallest musician, Michal, refused to play his flute because he said he did not want to sit next to a dumb girl. Jan kept a straight face as he told Michal that Sophia was not dumb and he could sit on the other side of the drummer and not look at Sophia. He begrudgingly agreed to move and the crisis passed. One look at Sophia told Jan she was just as happy not to be distracted by the finicky Michal. Jan marveled at how male-female relationships continued on the same track throughout life and how it kept life interesting, albeit somewhat dicey at times.

Big Stan Jasinski contributed his skills and enlisted the help of his brother Big Jan to carve an ice sculpture that would not be unveiled until the evening of the social. Meanwhile, it was kept in the icehouse next to the beer hall.

Helena and Jan hardly saw each other that week. Every time they thought they'd have a minute to talk, someone would interrupt them, and they'd each be off to their respective tasks.

Jakob Pawlowski could barely contain his excitement when Helena returned from meeting young Jan Jasinski the previous Monday. Over dinner, she asked if he minded if she went to the Spring Social with Jan. Jakob said, "Mind? Do I mind? Of course not, Lena. I will be happy to see you two having a fun time together!" He got up from the dinner table and gave her one of his famous bear hugs, and she laughingly tried to escape. She was somewhat hesitant to tell her Papa about the invitation and now realized there was no cause to be nervous. She realized how excited she was, not only to go to this year's Spring Social, but with someone special. She thought, *Mama would be happy for me too.*

Jakob caught the nostalgic look on his daughter's face. "You know Lena, your Mama would be very happy for you." Helena looked at her Papa. Both had tears in their eyes. She could agree only by shaking her head. It was a bittersweet moment. Helena busied herself with clearing the dinner dishes and serving up the apple and nut pie she'd baked. The boys were too busy trying to gobble up their vegetables so they could have pie, to notice anything that was said between Helena and Papa.

Finally, Saturday arrived, and it was an unseasonably warm sunny day for late March. As everyone in the town started coming out of their homes, excitement filled the air. It was as if you could grab a handful of joy. But there was no need to. Plenty more excitement was to come before the town clock would strike eight that night.

Precisely at 1:45, Jan opened the front gate to Helena's house. It was the first time he'd visited her home. He looked forward to seeing her Papa, Jozef and Froggie and to meeting little Franz.

As Jan lifted the iron door knocker, the door flew open and the knocker with it. Of course, it was Jozef who had been looking out the front window, waiting for Jan to arrive for Helena. He shouted, "Hey, Lena! Mr. Jan is here to walk you to the Spring Social, so hurry up and stop lookin' in the mirror!" As he was yelling to Helena, he was dragging Jan by the hand to show him the garden where he and Froggie hunted. He was not about to let this opportunity go by. He wanted to show Jan his adventure sites. As they went through the kitchen door and entered the garden, Froggie pounced on Jozef's head. The fearless kitten had climbed a vine to get on top of the fence just to surprise his master as he walked by. Yes, Froggie and Jozef were meant to be together. Jozef took it all in stride, as this was not the first time his kitten had played the prank on him. Jan was momentarily startled. Then he laughed heartily.

Helena appeared in the kitchen doorway. Jan thought she was beautiful before, but now he thought she was almost too beautiful to be true. She was dressed in a flowing aquamarine dress topped by the richest pine green material he had ever seen. Ivory lace accented her tiny waistline, her wrists, and her delicate neckline. She wore her hair in the traditional single braid of a maiden. She had added flowers to her hair.

Jan walked to her and kissed her hand. "Helena, you look very beautiful. Did you make your costume?"

Helena was spellbound herself. Jan looked unbearably handsome in a white silk shirt with the customary tie and suspenders that happened to be the same shade of green as Helena's bodice. He wore light-colored tan pants and his favorite brown boots. He had his ceremonial hat in his hand, which he would not put on until the first dance of the Spring Social.

She said, "Thank you, Jan. Yes, I made my dress. And you look most handsome on this beautiful day that we have!" For a moment, they simply stood smiling, admiring each other, once again forgetting all else.

Froggie broke the magical moment when he scurried between them with Jozef close behind, laughing and calling his mischievous kitten.

Helena's Papa heard the commotion from the time Jozef yelled for his sister and decided to remain out of sight for a few minutes. As Helena and Jan came back into the kitchen, Jakob met them, holding Franz in his arms. Jacob was grinning like a schoolboy himself. He shook Jan's hand as he said, "Well, well, it's good to see you again, Jan. I am glad to see that you and Helena are getting acquainted. You are sure to have a grand time together at the Spring Social. You have made quite an impression on young Jozef too. He has not stopped talking about you for one minute since Monday!"

They all laughed.

Jan said, "Thank you, Mr. Pawlowski, it's good to see you again, too. Jozef is delightful. And who is this young man you have here? Could this be the little Franzie whom I have heard so much about?" Jan reached out and tickled Franz's cheek, making the child giggle.

Jakob said, "Yes, this is our happy little boy who likes to build cities with his blocks all day long. Isn't that right, Franzie?"

The child smiled and buried his head in his Papa's shoulder. Franz said, "Down please, Papa." Jakob walked over to the hearth where his son had left his blocks. He put him down to let him play. Franz would be staying at home with his babysitter, Miss Mary from next door.

Jakob said, "Well, you two had better go kick off the social…it's nearly two o'clock. We'll see you later, have fun!"

Jan and Helena gladly took their leave, but not before Helena grabbed the green cape she had made to match her costume. She accepted Jan's offer to drape it over her shoulders as they walked out the front door for their stroll to the social. It was their first real date. She was not aware that she was walking. She thought perhaps she was floating. What she did not know was that Jan felt the same.

From the moment they stepped out onto the walkway toward the church, they could hear people talking and laughing, dogs barking, and the town band playing. They could see the banner hung high up in the trees that told of the day's event. They arrived at 1:59 amid the curious stares of the townspeople who had not seen this couple together before. Jan and Helena tried not to notice. But showing up at a public social event together was like sending out a message from the Vatican!

Thankfully, their arrival was pre-empted by the church bell announcing the opening of the Spring Social at precisely 2:00. Everyone cheered. Dozens of red, blue and yellow balloons were released into the air. There was a slight northerly breeze that gently sent them floating over Acorn Park. It was a beautiful sight. Helena wondered what the ducklings in Acorn Park thought of the balloons floating over their pond. The band played a lively tune and the festivities began.

The crowd walked counterclockwise around the grounds, looking at the many tables of crafts, baked goods and the exhibitions that had been set up overnight. The centerpiece of this year's social was on display next to the bandstand. It was a quilt the ladies' guild had sewn in honor of the parishioners who died in the flu epidemic. The background was pure white with an evergreen tree embroidered on each corner and had a four-inch red border all around. The nine-foot square quilt was comprised of eighty-one twelve-inch squares — one for each family affected by the epidemic. Each of those squares featured a surname embroidered in gold metallic thread with the first names of family members who had died, also embroidered. The color of the thread for the first names denoted which generation they were from. Yellow was for grandparents and great-grandparents, blue for parents and red for children and babies. The squares were arranged in alphabetical order by surname and were littered with all three colors. There were 192 names in total. The quilt was a memorial, in addition to the numerous monuments in the church cemetery. It was a humbling sight. After the social, the quilt would remain on display under glass in the church vestibule.

Helena and Jan approached the quilt together, holding hands. They saw the Jasinski square at the same time and paused to read the names of Jan's beloved family. They perused the other squares, remembering the grief that had befallen Cracow. Helena saw her Mama's name even before she saw the Pawlowski name. Jan saw her face and was surprised to see a smile on her lips, even though there were tears in her eyes. Helena was hearing her Mama's voice saying, "My little Lena, your life begins again on this day, enjoy it with thoughts of me and be happy." Somehow, in the look that Jan and Helena exchanged, Jan heard Helena's Mama's voice too. It occurred to him that he was getting used to this kind of communication since meeting Helena.

It was then that Helena felt a tug on her skirt. She looked down to see little Sophia Kaminski, dressed in her festive costume.

She said, "Miss Helena! Look at me, I so prit-tee!"

Helena bent down, hugged the precious child and said, "Why, yes, Sophia, you certainly do look very pretty!" Sophia was eyeing Jan to be sure he also saw how pretty she looked.

Jan was doubly charmed by the sight of the two before him. The song he would be playing later that day, the one that he'd practiced for Helena, came to mind and he realized anew how appropriate it was for this event.

Mrs. Kaminski joined the threesome. "Sophia, there you are, I did not see you. I should have known you'd be wherever Miss Helena was. Oh, and Mr. Jan is here too. How are you two?" She looked from one to the other, sized them up as a couple and seemed pleased.

Jan and Helena greeted Mrs. Kaminski simultaneously with, "Fine, Mrs. Kaminski, thank you for asking, and how is Dr. Kaminski?" Mrs. Kaminski laughed. "Oh, you know the Doctor, he always keeps busy, especially with all the new babies these days!

"I will say goodbye for now, it's almost time for the young musician's show, you know. We will see you later. It was nice to see you both." She gave a little wink in Jan's direction as she took Sophia's hand and headed for the music tent.

Jan squeezed Helena's hand and they went to see some exhibits before going to the young musician's show. As they strolled around, they saw people gathered around each of the exhibits watching the craftspeople making willow baskets, decorating wooden eggs or making paper chandelier ornaments. They also saw some fine embroidery on all sorts of linens. A little further along, they watched men carving wildlife statues from chunks of wood. The favored statues were of deer, bear and rabbits, and of course eagles, the emblem of Poland. The wood carvers also made little square trinket boxes with different symbols on the cover. It was fascinating and inspiring to see what could be created with one's hands.

Jan asked Helena if he could buy her a trinket box. She nodded and he asked if he might choose it for her. She said, "Yes, Jan, thank you."

Without hesitation, Jan chose a box with a heart engraved on the lid and handed it to Helena.

She said, "Jan, that was the box I wanted. How did you know?"

The wood carver had been watching the couple. When Jan asked how much the box was, the carver said, "This is a special box that I carved just this morning. It's the only one that has a heart on it. Usually, I carve an animal into the lid. I now see why I was led to carve a heart on this box and I would be honored if you would accept this as a gift for you to give to this beautiful young lady." Both Helena and Jan were delighted. They thanked him and gratefully accepted the carver's generosity. It was nearly three o'clock and time to go to the music tent. Helena put the precious trinket box into her small satchel, knowing that the tiny heart-shaped key for her hope chest would be kept in the box. She leaned close to Jan's ear and softly said, "Thank you very much, Jan. I will treasure this box." Jan was very pleased and said, "You are welcome, Lena. This is only the first gift from me to you, there will be many more."

They arrived at the music tent in time for Jan to get his little musicians situated for their performance. Helena stood just off to the right where she could see Jozef and he could see her. He looked so grown up in his white shirt, tie and suspenders. He was not too pleased to wear short pants and high socks but that was the custom for young boys, so he relented without much argument. At his age, it was proper to wear the ceremonial hat. His hat had a red feather in it which he said was because he was "Jozef the Hero."

Jan rang the big bell in the music tent to signal the young musicians' performance. He waited for a couple of minutes to give everyone time to step into the tent to hear the music. The song Jan had taught the children was a simple A and B March. It was just two notes written primarily for beginning violinists. But Jan arranged it to allow for the flute, harmonica, cymbals, drums and the tinkling of Sophia's bells to be heard in unison with Jozef's violin.

Jan stepped in front of his little musicians, baton in hand. He had told them that when he raised the baton, they were to be ready to play the first note, and when he brought the baton down, they would all begin to play in unison. He hoped they could all stay focused during the short arrangement.

Jan raised his baton, looking at them. The crowd had hushed. Suddenly, a crash was heard. The cymbal player was so anxiously awaiting the down stroke of the baton that he dropped both cymbals and was scrambling to pick them up before the down stroke. Almost immediately he popped back up, sat on his chair and was ready for the first note. He seemed unconcerned that he'd caused a ruckus, just as Jan had taught them. There were a few giggles from the crowd, but the moment quickly passed, and the music began.

For the next two minutes, the musicians played their little hearts out. They were surprisingly in time with each other and you could actually discern some of the A notes from the B notes, amid some out-of-sync players. But what mattered most was that this was their first performance in front of the entire church, and they were proud of themselves.

As the song ended, clapping, laughing and cheering was heard for the little performers. Jan turned and took a bow, then turned again to his band and clapped for them along with the crowd. Everyone agreed it was a wonderful addition to the Spring Social and that it should be continued annually.

Since there was so much noise, Jan gathered the children together by signaling them and, with Helena's help, had them put their instruments away before greeting their families. The children talked to each other, and Jan took note that Michal was even talking to Sophia. Apparently, they were now friends. Jan smiled to himself.

The band went in different directions and Jan looked for Helena and Jozef. He found them talking to their Papa. Jan headed to where they were standing and Jozef saw him before the others. He ran up to Jan, hugged his knees and said, "Mr. Jan, Papa says we are a real band now and that I played very well and I should thank you. Thank you, Mr. Jan!"

Jan reached down, hugged Jozef and said, "You are welcome! You *did* play very well, Jozef, and I am very proud of you! Now, shall we find some good food to eat?" Helena and her Papa agreed it was time to eat. The four of them walked past the exhibit tables and followed the aromas to the food tent.

The very first thing they noticed in the center of the food tent was the massive ice sculpture that Jan's Uncle Stan had painstakingly worked on every night over the weeks. It was a beautiful oak tree very much like the one in Acorn Park. It was sculpted in one-quarter scale, which made it about ten feet tall. It was perfect for the social. The ice tree was shielded from direct sun but reflected light from the stained-glass windows of the church, creating changing shapes and colors on its graceful limbs. It was truly a sight to behold. Jan and Helena stood in awe of Big Stan's masterpiece.

Finally, they stepped away to allow others to get a closer look. They walked around to the first buffet table.

The assortment of foods was spread out along a twenty-five-foot-long table. Diners walked along either side to serve themselves. It was a feast, just like their sumptuous Easter feasts.

Jozef's Papa helped him with his platter so he would not take only salata z kartofli (potato salad) and paczki (jelly-filled fried dough). Helena and Jan walked along the buffet side by side, discussing the foods as they went along. There was bigos (hunter's stew), pork schnitzel, kotlet mielony (ground meat cutlet), golanka gotowana (pork hock), ryba po grecku (Greek-style fish) kluski slaskie (special potato dumplings) and pyzy (dumplings in the form of knobs). To round out the main courses, there was mashed turnip, fried carrots, stuffed kohlrabi and split pea fritters. Beside the stacks of potato pancakes was an assortment of pierogi. Little handwritten signs told of the fillings: meat and onion, sauerkraut and mushroom, ruskie (potato, cheese and onion), curd cheese and even bilberries.

There was a separate buffet section dedicated to desserts. Some of the favorites were Cracow tort, along with almond torte, spice cake, almond babka, paczki and of course sand cake.

Helena learned that Jan's favorite food was golabki and Jan learned that Helena preferred bigos as it had a balance of fresh vegetables, sauerkraut and beef. They both loved sand cake and shared a slice for dessert.

Jan checked his pocket watch. It was 3:45. He was to perform at 4:00 so he would see them later. He walked back to the music tent and spotted his parents. As he approached, both of his parents complimented him on the young musician's performance. His Mama beamed with pride. He thanked them and said, "I would like to take a moment by myself before I play my piece. I will be right back."

Jan stepped behind the tent to calm his nerves. By now, he knew the score of Chopin's Fantasie Impromptu as well as he knew his name. But he was nervous because it was so important to him that he play flawlessly with Helena listening. He had spent hours practicing this special piece for her. He decided this was no time to falter, so he took a deep breath and walked onto the stage. As he passed his Mama, she kissed him on the cheek for luck. He was as nervous as she'd ever seen him. She still did not know which piano piece he would play. He had asked her to have the Erard piano brought from the church to the music tent for his performance. This sparked her curiosity as to what song he'd chosen. The Erard was the best instrument Cracow had to offer. Jan had gotten special permission to practice on it at the church when no one was around.

Jan walked on stage at 4:00. He sat at the piano and felt his shoulders, arms and fingers relax in preparation for the opening allegro agitato tempo. Someone rang the big bell to let everyone know there was another performance set to begin. The crowd quickly gathered. Jan looked to his Mama to give him the signal to count three and then begin his performance. She gave him the extra bit of confidence he needed. His eyes were focused on his fingers and his ears were trained on the notes already playing in his head. His fingers began to fly over the ivory keys, his heart was pumping in time to the music, and his entire body was part of the piano. He had no need of sheet music, each note was embedded in his brain. With ease, his right hand played the semiquavers while his left played the triplets. He could feel the audience captured by Chopin's masterpiece. He loved the drama of it and when he reached the climax of the second movement, he heard gasps and murmurs from the crowd. The music changed tempo and tone, leading to the finale. The ending was no less dramatic, leaving the piece on a slow and mysterious C-sharp major.

Jan sat as if in a trance for a moment. He was totally mesmerized and still held by the emotions of this special music. It had a similar effect on the crowd and there was silence until Jan's Mama began clapping to let everyone know the performance had ended. There was uproarious applause, hoots, hollers and whistles for Jan's masterful piano playing. He turned on the bench to his right to face the crowd. Then he stood and bowed humbly. Clearly, he had played this difficult piece well. He imagined that Frederic Chopin, the famous Polish poet of the piano, was congratulating him on playing his beloved Fantasie Impromptu so well. He smiled to himself just as he saw Helena waiting for him. He bowed deeply again and headed to meet her.

The noise of the crowd faded as he walked to Helena's side. Jozef and his Papa were just behind her. They all looked at him with such admiration that he thought his buttons would pop with pride. Helena was the first to speak. "Jan, you played that piece wonderfully, it was very moving!"

Jan grinned widely and said, "I am very happy you liked it. I played it for *you*, Lena."

Helena could not respond for a second. She was honored that he would play for her.

Finally, she said, "Jan, you flatter me in a way that touches my heart. Words cannot express my gratitude. I will never be able to repay you."

Jan knew exactly what to say. "Lena, there is no need to repay me. However, I would be greatly honored if you would play your violin for me sometime."

Helena did not hesitate. "Jan, for you I would be delighted to play my violin."

Jakob Pawlowski heard the exchange between them he could not have been happier. Once again, he congratulated himself for helping the two get together. He could feel Marta's spirit standing with his family and he put his hand on his heart in acknowledgment.

Jakob stepped forward at the same time as Jozef. Helena stepped aside and watched her Papa and Jozef each give Jan a giant hug. Jakob said, "Jan Jasinski, you are an amazing young man and it is a pleasure to know you!"

Jozef chimed in with, "Mr. Jan! Mr. Jan! How did you get those fairies to dance above the piano while you played?"

Jan was charmed by Jozef's imagination. He said, "Well, Jozef, not everyone can see those fairies, so you got a very special treat!"

Jozef was thrilled with the explanation. He nodded and waltzed away toward the game tent, with his Papa following close behind.

Jan's parents broke through the crowd that was gathering around Jan to give congratulations. His Mama's tear-stained face said it all. She put her arms around her son. "Jan, you played as I have never heard. Better than I have ever played in my life or would ever hope to play. I am so proud of you!"

He looked behind his Mama and saw his Papa and it looked like there were two of him! He blinked and realized that Uncle Stan was there too. Big Jan allowed his brother to give Jan congratulations first. Uncle Stan said, "Boy, you played like the master himself, and I know who the inspiration for that piece was!"

Uncle Stan glanced toward Helena, giving her a knowing look. She smiled in a grateful response. They had not been formally introduced yet but it was obvious that he was Big Jan's brother who Jan had told her about.

Next, Jan's Papa threw his arms around Jan. Watching his son perform, he realized his boy was all grown up and would soon be leaving the nest to begin his new life, probably with a girl named Helena. He was choked with emotion and barely able to speak. But he said, "I love you, Son."

Jan looked around at the faces of the people who were so important to him and said, "Okay folks, the show's over! Let's go have a cold drink!" Everyone laughed, knowing the show would not be forgotten.

The schedule of events called for competitive games at 5:00. They had just enough time to grab a beverage, maybe a sweet treat and walk to the game field. They could not move too quickly as the whole parish had arrived and it was very crowded. Many parishioners worked on Saturday and were just arriving.

Jan saw the drink stand and asked Helena if she would like a cold drink. She said she would love a lemonade. He left her while he stood in line to get drinks. Surprisingly, it only took him two or three minutes to return. When he looked up from the cups he was trying not to spill, he saw Helena talking to a handsome young man. She seemed to be extremely interested in him. Jan's first response was to be jealous and to ask that whippersnapper just what he thought he was doing with his girl. His second response was to placate himself with the thought that maybe he was just one of her neighbors.

He pointedly stepped between the pair and handed Helena her drink, ignoring the interloper. Helena thanked Jan for the drink, looked over his shoulder and said, "Jan, I would like you to meet my best friend's boyfriend, Kazi Wolowicz. Kazi, this is Jan Jasinski. He is the one who just played Fantasie Impromptu for us. Did you hear him play?"

Greatly relieved and feeling somewhat foolish, Jan turned to shake Kazi's hand. He said, "Kazi, it is nice to meet you. Helena has told me about you, and about her friend, Julia, of course."

Kazi smiled broadly and said, "It's great to meet you too, Jan. I did hear your rendition of Chopin's great work. While attending the Warsaw Music Academy, I practiced it myself and could never keep up the tempo. You are to be commended!

"Helena was just telling me about the letter she received from Julia. She is settling into life in America nicely. I am very much looking forward to going to America with my family after graduation in June. Well, I will be going now. I plan to win the tug-of-war competition along with all my brothers! Helena, it was wonderful to see you. And Jan, it was a pleasure. I'm sure I will see you again. Goodbye."

Jan and Helena said goodbye and Kazi went with a friend to the game field. Jan's odd behavior toward Kazi initially, had not gone unnoticed by Helena. But she decided not to mention it. Whatever the reason, it seemed to have resolved itself.

They walked along, sipping their fruit drinks. Jan really needed it after pouring himself into his music. He surprised himself when he said, "I think I will enter the tug-of-war contest. Care to watch?"

Helena did not think it was a great idea to endanger his hands in such a sport, but she realized that his enthusiasm overshadowed anything she might say. Plus, she would not want to spoil his fun. So, she said, "That would be fun to watch and then we can join in the three-legged race together, okay?"

Jan loved that Helena was a good sport. He said, "Okay, first I will be on the winning tug-of-war team and then we will win the three-legged race together, Miss Lena! And then my reward shall be a kiss from the prettiest girl at the social!" Helena blushed slightly, smiled in agreement and gave Jan's shoulder a little shove with her free hand as he left. He grinned, once again, self-satisfied.

Jan was one of the last to join the tug-of-war. He made sure he was on the team opposite Kazi Wolowicz and his brothers. All the boys and men took a place at a large knot in the massive rope on their respective sides. As they waited for the gong to signal the start, the contest director announced the rules. There would not be much doubt which team lost, as they would be pulled into the large mud puddle that had been created especially for the game.

Jan was thrilled to see that both his Papa and his Uncle Stan were on his side of the rope. The three of them nodded to each other as if to say, "We got this one!"

Jan was momentarily distracted when he saw Helena in the front row beside the game field, watching him. Before he realized it, the gong sounded and he was yanked forward. This caused him and his teammates to react quickly and forcefully, pulling backward. The rope jerked forward and back again, each team getting dangerously close to the puddle of shame. Uncle Stan was at the very end of their side of the rope. He shouted above all the other voices, "Oh, no you *don't*...into the mud you go!" He gave a forceful yank of that rope with such suddenness that all his teammates literally fell back into his pull and the opposite team flipped into the mud puddle in a heap!

The crowd loved the spectacle and screamed for best two out of three. But the winners would have none of it. They'd won fair and square and they were rewarded with bragging rights — plenty of prize for them.

The sopping wet Kazi and his brothers greeted the Jasinski men to congratulate them on the win. Jan thought it was the best part of winning, although he didn't appreciate the dirty handshakes.

With a puffed-up chest, Jan joined Helena. Laughing, she said, "Okay, fancy-man, let's see how you do in the three-legged race!"

Jan said, "You'll see, together we can do it. And then... I'll collect the real prize!"

They turned to the field next to them and saw the couples tying their legs together, laughing and having a great time of it. Jan grabbed Helena's hand and they ran to the box of sashes to tie their legs together.

Helena grabbed a sash and they sat on the grass side by side and tied her left leg and his right leg together at the ankle. When they were satisfied the tie would hold but wasn't be too tight, they tried to stand. They toppled over and tried again, laughing so much that it was difficult to stand. On the fourth try, they stood and walked a few steps to get a rhythm that would allow them to go as fast as possible without falling. That was okay until they tried to turn around and go back to the starting line. Their legs got all mixed up, and down they went again. They looked around and all the other couples seemed to be doing better than they were. They really did not care, they were having such fun.

The two-minute warning was called and the twenty three-legged couples each chose a spot behind the starting line to wait for the call to begin to cross the fifty-foot course without falling. If a couple fell before reaching the finish line, they had to stay down until there was a winning couple who could cross the finish line without falling. If more than one couple made it, the first to cross the finish line would be the winner.

They heard the starter shout, "On your mark, get set, and GO!" Jan and Helena started out, not able to see that there were some couples who could not even cross the starting line without falling over. Then there were only fifteen couple competitors left. Jan and Helena egged each other on and soon gained on all the participants. They were in perfect harmony. It looked like they were sure winners. A couple passed them on the left, laughing as they went by. Then another couple passed them on the right, no laughing there, they were intent on winning.

Jan said to Helena, "Okay, Lena, are you ready to cross the finish line?" They'd regained the first position and could see the finish line just a few feet ahead. Helena said, "Yessirree, let's win!" She had a fair amount of competitive spirit too, and she thought this was the best fun!

Helena had tied up the skirt of her dress with an additional sash to keep it from tripping them. In the interest of modesty, she did not tie the skirt up too high. The sash took the last moment of the race to fall off, causing Jan and Helena to stumble. They did not fall and thought they would still win by crossing the finish line first. But that was not to be…the second couple gained on them when Helena and Jan stumbled.

Jan and Helena finished without falling, but in second place. They were out of breath and they laughed until their ribs hurt. The minute they crossed the finish line, they sat on the grass to untie themselves. They agreed it was a relief to walk on their own two legs again.

They collected the ribbon for second place and happily walked away hand in hand. Neither seemed to mind that their costumes were dirty and rumpled.

They found themselves walking behind the music tent where no one else was at that moment. Jan stopped and turned to Helena. "Lena, we did not win the race and I did not earn a kiss from you. But, do you think I might collect that prize anyway?"

Helena said, "Of course, Jan." With that, Jan lifted her chin and moved in for a kiss. Helena closed her eyes and allowed his gentle lips to touch hers. Their kiss lingered, and time stopped. Neither wanted it to end.

However, as luck would have it, they heard Jozef calling for them and his voice was getting near. He'd apparently seen the direction they'd walked in and followed them. Josef was hoping to show them the stuffed animal he'd won in the ring toss game.

Unfortunately, they could hear Helena's Papa close behind Jozef, telling him to stop running ahead. This was threatening to be an embarrassing moment and called for quick thinking. Helena and Jan had the same idea. They ran as fast as they could to get into the crowd so that her Papa and Jozef would not know they were sharing a kiss behind the music tent.

By the time her Papa and Jozef caught up to them, it appeared that they were simply walking along with everyone else, innocently enjoying the festivities. They shared a knowing look, both feeling relieved.

Jozef reached them first. He thrust the stuffed monkey in Helena's face, saying he had won the ring toss when nobody his age could do it. Helena said, "That's wonderful, Jozef. That must have been a very hard game to win." Seriously, Jozef said, "Yes! Lena, it was verrrry hard!"

Helena's Papa said it was time for them to go home and leave the young people to dancing and merriment. Jozef looked crestfallen. He said, "But Papa, I love to dance! Lena will keep me with her and Mr. Jan. Won't you, Lena?"

Helena was saved from having to disappoint her little brother when Jan said, "Jozef, if you promise to go home now and go to sleep early, I will take you and Froggie fishing tomorrow after church. How does that sound?"

Jozef's eyes lit up. He did not have to think about it. He said, "Okay! Can I put the worm on the hook too, Mr. Jan?"

Jan said, "Of course you may, Jozef."

Helena and Jozef's Papa thought that was a grand idea, and a wonderful way to entice Jozef to gladly leave the social. He took Jozef by the hand and said, "Thank you Jan, for everything today. You two have fun and I will expect you home by 8:05, Lena."

Jan said, "You are welcome, Mr. Pawlowski."

Helena and Jan agreed she would be home no later than 8:05 and said goodnight to her father and Jozef. The twosomes went off in opposite directions.

The rest of the evening was magical for the young couple. They talked and joked with friends, had another meal of their favorite foods and then it was time for the square dance.

The children and their parents had disappeared for the most part, after having a fun-filled day in the sun. The only ones left were young people who wanted to dance, the band, the square dance caller and a few curious onlookers.

By then, it was nighttime, and dancing would take place in the church hall which had been decorated with a spring country field theme — perfect for square dancing. The band could be heard warming up as couples began moving in through the double doors of the church hall. Spring had come early that year, bringing with it dogwood blossoms, daffodils and even some tea roses. The decorating committee took full advantage of Mother Nature's gifts by collecting all they could carry from parishioner's farms. They strung blooms together, hung blossoms from the light fixtures and placed milk pitchers of tiny pink tea roses on all the tables. The church hall had never looked so festive.

Jan donned his hat for the first dance. He and Helena joined a foursome as the side couple for a reel dance. They looked across to the other side couple and discovered it was Kazi. He had obviously changed into clean clothes. He was paired with his sister for the quadrille. The band began at a moderate pace and the caller's familiar monotone filled the hall. The head couple commenced the first dance. Then the do-si-do, promenade and pass-through calls got everyone following along, having great fun. Most everyone had learned the easy repetitive steps before but for beginners, there was a dance master to help them learn the calls. When the call came to "change partners to your left, then again," it meant Helena was partnered with Kazi. Jan watched them so intently that he missed swinging his partner and nearly stumbled. He quickly got back into the square, caught his partner and continued with the reel. Helena and Kazi pretended not to notice.

They danced to the Polish Reel, Duck for the Oyster, and the Pattycake Polka. One of the favorite dances invited all the dancers to a Contra, or Line Dance. The boys were in one line and the girls formed a line across from them. The couple at the far end of the line danced down the middle and joined the other end of the line. The next couple followed suit, and so on, until all had danced down the middle.

The dancing ended all too soon. It seemed as if it had just begun when the caller announced the last dance was a Round Dance. For this dance, everyone was in a circle and changing partners all around. It was quick-moving and everyone had become comfortable with the dance steps, adding to the fun.

The music stopped and the caller thanked everyone for joining in. He bid everyone a good night.

Jan and Helena stepped into the moonlit night. It was refreshingly cool after dancing inside for more than two hours. Kazi and some friends passed them and they exchanged goodbyes. Jan thought it would be nice when Kazi moved to America. Being jealous was a new and unwelcome experience for Jan. He hoped it did not show too much.

The gong sounded the end of the annual Spring Social. That also meant it was 8:00, and Jan knew he had better stay true to his promise to have Miss Helena Pawlowski home within the next five minutes.

It was a short walk to Helena's front gate. They arrived with three minutes to spare. As Jan opened the gate for Helena, the moon ducked behind a cloud, and Jan seized the opportunity to steal a kiss. Helena did not mind, and she kissed him in return.

Jan took Helena's hands in his and said, "Helena, this has been one of the best days of my life. I have enjoyed being with you and I hope you enjoyed being with me."

Helena smiled. "Yes, Jan. It was a beautiful day with you. Thank you."

"After Jozef and I go fishing tomorrow, perhaps you and I could have a picnic in Acorn Park?"

Helena said, "That would be wonderful. I will pack a picnic basket for us. Good night, Jan."

Jan was reluctant for the day to end, but he said, "Good night, Lena." He closed the gate behind him.

Helena gently opened the front door. She saw no lights and heard no sounds coming from the bedrooms. She tiptoed to her bedroom and did not turn on the light. She dropped her clothing on the chair, laid on her bed and promptly fell into a happy sleep.

Jakob listened for Helena to come home. He knew by the lack of sounds after her tiptoeing that she was fast asleep. He also fell into a happy sleep—to dream of his Marta.

Chapter Six

FAMILY

So much had happened in the months since the Spring Social that Helena found little personal time. Early one morning after she'd caught up on her chores, she sat at the dining table in front of the hearth with a pen and paper. She picked up the letter Julia had written to her just after she'd arrived in America. She'd promised herself she would write back to Julia and simply hadn't found time. She began to write.

22 September 1920

Dearest Julia,

Hello, I hope that this letter finds you and your family well and happy (and Buttons too).

First, I must apologize for not writing sooner. After you read this letter, you will understand and forgive me, I do hope.

Heavens! There is so much to tell you, I barely know where to begin. I so wish that you were still here to share everything that has happened in my life!

I know that Kazi and his family would have arrived in Yonkers in late June. I saw him at church just before they left, and he promised he would tell you all about our Spring Social and about Jan Jasinski. I gave him the biggest hug.

Just a few weeks after the social, my family celebrated Easter with Jan and his family. It was the most special day filled with church, music, singing and an Easter feast like we have never had! I am sure you had a similar feast in your new home with your family and probably with Kazi's family too.

Jan's Mama is a marvelous cook and she and I agreed that she would cook the main courses, and I would cook the side dishes *and* bake Jan's favorite dessert, sand cake. You know I love to bake and I've eaten the sand cake that his Mama makes and it's very good. My sand cake was topped with a sweet and savory salty lemon drizzle and everyone loved it.

Jan and I fell in love at first sight (almost). That's almost for me and instantly for him, as he says. After the social, we spent a lot of time together. Jan rode his bike to my house after he finished work nearly every evening. (He works with his Papa at that mill north of town. You know, the one we passed on our nature walks.) Jan and I would often cook dinner together and then he would join us, of course. Papa, Jozef and Franzie all love Jan.

Back to Easter evening after our feast. With the dinner dishes washed and put away, we all sat around the dining table in front of the hearth again.

The conversation went to music. Jan's Mama is a music teacher. You may remember her from our Academy of Music, where we both took violin lessons many years ago. Kazi probably told you about Jan playing Chopin's Fantasie Impromptu at the Spring Social. Jan also plays the violin, viola, flute and harpsichord—all by ear, I might add!

You know after Mama died, I put my violin away. I simply could not bear to play it without her listening. It hurt too much. Well, Jan inspired me to pick it up again and I have been playing my heart out and loving it. Jozef is doing quite well with his violin lessons and he likes to play his violin when I play mine. I am grateful to Jan for convincing me to get back to it.

Jan had brought his violin to our Easter feast. Our parents asked if we'd play a song together. We said we'd be delighted, and so we played a piece we'd practiced together. It was one of Szymanowski's violin sonatas. When we played the last note, Papa stood and clapped and said, "Don't these two make beautiful music together?" Everyone at the table agreed, even little Franzie, who generally keeps to himself.

Papa cleared his throat and continued, "I believe this is the perfect time to tell you all that I have given my permission to young Jan to take Helena's hand in marriage!"

Well, no one was more surprised than I! With all eyes on me, Jan knelt on one knee in front of my chair and took my hands in his. The look in his eyes nearly melted my heart. Here's what he said, "My dear Lena, you have made my life complete. My greatest hope is that you will consent to be with me for the rest of our lives, to be my wife and bring our children into the world. Will you marry me, Lena?"

Poor Jan was so nervous that I did not make him wait for my answer. I said, "Jan, you are the piece of my heart that I did not know was missing until you crashed into me that day in March!"

My unexpected humor broke the tension and we all laughed. Then I said, "Yes, Jan, I will be your wife and happily spend the rest of my days with you."

With that, Jan jumped up and said, "Oh, I have something for you, Lena." He fumbled in his pockets and finally found a tiny white velvet box. Gingerly, he opened the box, took something out of it and asked me for my left hand. Julia, he put an emerald and diamond ring on my finger that is breathtaking, and it fit as if it was made for me. He bent and kissed me and then he said, "Do you like it, Lena?"

"Jan, this is the most beautiful ring I have ever seen. I love it, thank you." It was then that I saw Jan's Mama crying. Jan looked at his Mama and back at me. He said, "Your ring is a family heirloom. It goes back three generations on Mama's side of the family. Now it is yours, my dear. You are the first with emerald eyes to wear this ring, so I've been told. You are more beautiful with it on, if that's even possible."

Once again, Jan began fumbling through his pockets for something. He pulled out a crumpled piece of paper and said, "Lena, I've written a poem for you. May I read it to you now?" I thought there could not possibly be any more surprises. I said, "Yes, please." I committed to memory the words he read to me:

> When I met a lady oh so fair,
> it was all I could do not to stare.
> Into her emerald eyes I fell,
> she cast upon me a lovely spell.
>
> When I heard her voice, my heart stood still,
> at once I knew my dreams she would fill.
> It seem'd I had known her before my days,
> so strange to think I knew all of her ways.
>
> She was charming, with a smile very sweet,
> a more perfect lady I ne'er thought to meet.

Emotions at a time like that are contagious. We all had tears in our eyes. That is, except my little brothers, who just looked perplexed.

Jan and I saw no reason to delay our marriage. We set a date of July 22nd and invited only immediate family. I wore my Mama's wedding dress, which was a perfect fit, and a hair wreath of my favorite flower—lily of the valley. Two days before my wedding, Jan and Papa went in search of the delicate little blossoms even though their season had passed. They went deep into the woods and found bunches growing under lush ferns, untouched. They gathered more than enough for my wreath *and* for decorations.

After we exchanged our vows, the soloist, Mrs. Kaminski, sang "Ave Maria." She sang like an angel and it reminded me of how Mama would sing that song at weddings for so many young couples. Mama's last words to me were that she would be with me on my wedding day and I felt her presence completely. When I looked at Papa during the song, he looked so happy and I knew he felt Mama was there too.

After our wedding, we came back to our cottage for a wedding dinner prepared by Jan's family. The first toast was given by Papa and of course, the traditional "Sto Lat" was sung by all because, as you know, it signifies one hundred years of good health for the bride and groom.

Now it's two months later and we've been so busy. We decided to live with Papa and the boys because they still need me and Jan thought that it would be a fine idea.

I've saved some of the very best news for last, Julia...just yesterday, Jan's Uncle Stan brought us a lovely cradle he made himself. We will need it in just seven months. Jan and I thought we would try to keep it a secret for a few more weeks, but his Mama took one look at me last Sunday and said, "My, Helena, you are glowing. Do you have something to share with us?"

Jan was in the next room and overheard. He came up behind me, hugged me and proudly said, "Yes, Mama. You, Papa and Helena's Papa will soon be grandparents!"

Papa and Jan's Papa had also overheard. Everyone surrounded us with a group hug. It was the first group hug for our baby too. I have no doubt that Mama knew she would be a Grandmama at the same moment I knew that I would be a Mama. We are a very happy family.

Julia, now you know why I have not written before now. Please know whether I write or not, you are in my thoughts. I miss you every day. Please write soon and give your Kazi a hug for me.

Always Love,
Lena

Helena re-read her letter and sat back thinking of Julia. They'd grown up together and shared everything. They could not have been any closer if they were sisters. Their Mamas had agreed.

Her attention was called to the mantel; she felt something drawing her to it. She got up and stood in front of the hearth for some reason she did not understand. She reached for the family bible and opened it. Out floated a compressed lily of the valley stem that she'd saved from her wedding day. It was beautifully preserved with its pure white tiny bell-shaped blossoms protected by its broad green leaves.

Helena picked up the sprig. The ceremony that had joined her and Jan flashed through her mind. She smiled.

She knew she was meant to place this memento in with the letter that she'd just written to Julia. She also knew Julia would see her marriage to Jan in her mind's eye when she held the lily of the valley that would float out of the envelope when she opened it.

Helena had learned that experiencing life with close family members from afar was a natural occurrence. After all, she sensed her Mama's presence often and it was the same sense she had about Julia. That's what families do. She smiled again, folded the letter, addressed the envelope, sealed it and stamped it just as she saw the postal carrier approach the front door. Perfect timing.

Chapter Seven

1939 - BEFORE THE WAR

Finally, Helena had an entire afternoon free. It was a rare pleasure since she'd become Mrs. Jan Jasinski and after having their children. She thought of how happy they were.

She giggled as she recalled Jan asking Uncle Stan to make a second cradle for their firstborns. The look on his face as he tried to get Jan's meaning that Christmas Eve in 1920 was priceless. As understanding dawned, he bellowed, "My favorite nephew and his Lena are bringing us twins! I think it will be a boy and a girl! Let us toast to this news!" With that, he raised his goblet of vodka and everyone joined him and shouted, "Hear, hear!"

The music and merriment in their cottage continued long after Helena retired that night. She'd fallen into a smiling sleep with her arms encircling her unborn twins.

On the first day of the New Year, Uncle Stan showed up with a second identical wooden cradle, except this one had a pink ruffle around the bottom. Jan's Mama had painstakingly and lovingly smocked the ruffle. It was exquisite. She was a master at embroidery and hand-sewing.

Jan and Helena looked at each other, both thinking, "What if we have two boys, or two girls?"

Uncle Stan caught the look and announced, "Don't worry you two, Uncle Stan knows these things! You are having a boy and a girl. I can see them now; baby boy with red hair and blue eyes, and baby girl with blonde hair and emerald eyes like the sea!"

Helena glanced at her engagement ring and its emerald glow seemed to wink.

Four months later, on May 7th, Piotr and Julia were born on the New Moon - an auspicious time to begin life. Their babies looked exactly like Uncle Stan had said they would.

The newest family additions were instant celebrities. One was as bright and inquisitive as the other and from the moment they were born, they looked out for each other. It was as if they shared one mind.

Now there were a lot of little people in the Jasinski-Pawlowski household. Even so, there was always room. Helena's Papa and Jan had made the attic into a sleeping loft for the older children. The potting shed attached to the kitchen, had been converted into a small den which doubled as a guest room whenever necessary. Helena's gardening tools found a place in a corner of their ample kitchen. The original two bedrooms were large enough that they were divided into two smaller ones. The four main bedrooms were for Helena's Papa, Jan and Helena, little Julia and the three Jasinski boys, after the new baby grew out of his cradle, of course. Jozef and his brother Franz were more than happy to sleep in the loft and thoroughly enjoyed their nightly ascent up the ladder into their own private quarters. Their cottage seemed magical with its ability to be transformed into whatever their family needed.

Seven-year-old Jozef adored the twins and was forever entertaining them with news of his latest adventures with Froggie. Each night at dinner, he would report what little Piotr and Julia had said to him that day. Jozef was convinced he spoke "baby talk" and that Piotr wanted to go on adventures with him, but Julia would stay with her Mama because "girls don't do adventures, you know," he'd confidently announced.

When the twins were five months old, Franzie entered kindergarten. After his first day, he ran all the way home because he couldn't wait to tell them about the giant building blocks they had at school. Everyone was appropriately thrilled for him. How he loved to build!

Helena's Papa had taken an active role in helping with their expanding family. He loved walking his grandbabies in Acorn Park on Sunday afternoons after church. All the townspeople called him Grandpapa in those days. The acknowledgment made him beam with pride.

While the babies were growing up, Helena studied languages. She was interested in Russian because she longed to know more about the history of her country when it was part of the Russian Empire. She also studied French and German, as it prepared her for the traveling she intended to do with Jan after the children were all in school. She attended the university two nights a week for five years until she and Jan learned they would be parents once more. They had all but given up on having more children, thinking it was just not meant to be.

On July 22nd, the seventh wedding anniversary, tiny Jozef was born. It was another New Moon. He was eight weeks premature and weighed only four pounds.

That evening, as Helena rested next to Jozef's cradle, "Jozef the Hero", now thirteen years old, tiptoed in to see his newest nephew. He whispered as he leaned over the baby, "Don't worry, little man, when I was born, I was your size, and look at me now. You'll soon be big and strong and going on adventures with Piotr, Froggie and me! What? Who's Froggie? He's my kitten, but he's really a big cat now. You'll be meeting him soon, probably after you have your dinner. Maybe, we'll see what your Mama says."

Helena pretended not to hear. She kept her eyes closed and hoped that the tears of love that slipped out would go unnoticed. Strangely, she knew both she and her baby believed the older Jozef's words—that this child would grow to be big and strong. Helena and baby Jozef fell fast asleep.

Jozef the Hero, true to his moniker, became invaluable to Helena and Jan. He even traded some of his adventure time to become part-time nanny to little Jozef and to the twins, then seven years old.

He loved what he called his Uncle Nanny time and was very busy between helping with the children, attending school, doing homework and chores and his latest teenage social interests. He'd confided in Jan that he had his eye on pretty little Sophia Kaminski and he made Jan swear not to tell anyone. Of course, Jan told Helena right away and they reminisced about the Spring Social when the two children played in the young musicians' group. They also recalled that day in Acorn Park when Jozef saved the drowning kitten. They sighed. They were such fond memories. All the children grew up so quickly.

Jan and Helena discussed whether she should continue studying at the university. They agreed with help from Jozef, Franz, Helena's Papa and Jan's Mama, that Helena would pick up her studies where she'd left off before baby Jozef was born.

The mill where Jan worked kept him busy. And as expected, he learned the ropes from his Papa and became the Mill Manager. He was well-suited for the job and respected by all his workers.

It was shortly after that when Jan's Papa was commissioned by the Austrian government to manage a textile mill on the outskirts of Vienna. Big Jan and Mary Jasinski agreed it was best if she lived with Jan, Helena and the grandchildren, due to the political unrest in Europe in 1928. His plan was to travel home by rail for Christmas and Easter each year for as long as his assignment in Austria lasted.

Jan's Mama was welcomed with open arms and loving hearts. Big Jan left for Austria in January of 1929 during a blizzard. He would later write that he did not arrive in Vienna for a full week. The train kept stopping and the engineer asked the passengers to disembark and clear the tracks of ice and snow.

Everyone was saddened by the departure of Big Jan, especially Jan's Mama. She did keep busy helping to take care of the children and the cottage, but she missed her husband. She would miss him a little less when Big Stan came by for Sunday dinner. Everyone would reminisce about times when they were all together. After those dinners Jan, Helena, Jozef the Hero and Jan's Mama would entertain by playing their instrument of choice. Those were wonderful times.

Later in January, there was some exciting news for the Jasinski children—by summer's end, they would have another brother or sister. The twins thought this was the very best news, but Julia wanted a sister and Piotr insisted he should have two brothers so they could be "The Three Jasinski Brothers." It was a good-natured disagreement, and Julia would not really mind being the only girl. That would mean she had plenty of time to herself to practice piano and read.

Little Jozef did not care one way or the other. He always had his Uncle Jozef for companionship and fun. That was all he needed.

Henryk Jasinski was born on Tuesday, August 6th, after only twenty minutes of labor. The midwife had warned that the baby was carried so low that he/she would be born "in a flash." It was a New Moon, just as it was when all their children were born. When the Pawlowski and Jasinski children returned from playing at Acorn Park that afternoon, it was to the cries of the newest Jasinski baby boy.

Thankfully, Jan was at home and he corralled all the children after the birth and allowed them to see Helena and Henryk, one at a time, for ten seconds each. It was just enough to satisfy their curiosity.

Jan's Mama soon dismissed the midwife, saying she could take over. She rocked her grandbaby. Looking at that little face, she recalled when her twins, Henryk and Piotr were born and then when sickness took them away twelve years later. She said a silent prayer that this child would always be safe and well. She realized she was rocking her grandchild in the same rocking chair that Helena's Mama had rocked all her children in. She thought she heard someone singing. The children were all in the garden, Jan and little Jozef were napping and Jakob was still at work. She stopped rocking. She could hear the soft breathing of Helena and the baby. She could barely make out the words to a song, it sounded far away. She strained her ears and heard Marta Pawlowski singing Brahms' lullaby.

ENGLISH	POLISH
Lullaby and good night,	Lullaby i good night,
With roses adorned,	Z roz bedight,
With lilies o'er spread	Z lilie o'er rozprzestrzeniania sie
Is baby's wee bed.	Jest baby's wee lozko.
Lay thee down now and rest,	Ustanowienie thee teraz i odpoczynku,
May thy slumber be blessed.	Moze thy slumber bedziecie blogoslawwieni.

She would recognize that angel voice anywhere. She glanced at Helena, wondering if she heard her Mama's song. There was a smile on Helena's sleeping face. There was no doubt. Once again Helena's Mama was true to her word that she would be there for the birth of all of Helena's children.

Helena returned to her studies at the university just after Henryk's first birthday.

By 1930, a great depression gripped the world. It left no country unaffected. There was mass unemployment. Life presented many challenges for young and old, rich and poor.

Big Jan struggled to keep the Austrian mill running at a profit. His son and Helena's Papa had encountered similar struggles at their mills in Cracow. All three of them worked a minimum of fourteen hours a day, seven days a week, to make up for the necessary layoffs.

It became evident that life was changing. That was the year that Austria signed a Treaty of Friendship with Italy. It would prove to be a bad omen for Austrians, as well as for Polish citizens who were working in Austria.

Chapter Eight

JUNE 1939

Each June in Cracow, everyone joyously celebrated the Wianki (wreath) Midsummer Festival. In other parts of Poland, Zielone Swiatki was celebrated, otherwise known as the Whitsunday Feast. Either way, it was a ritual of fire and water honoring St. John the Baptist and the Sun, on the longest day of the year. There would be fireworks, bonfires, and boat parades, musical acts and singing and dancing until midnight.

The highlight of the annual event was when the maidens, dressed all in white with flower wreaths in their hair, launched candle-lit wreaths from the banks of the Vistula River at sunset.

Helena enlisted the help of all the women and girls in her family to prepare the items on the menu. They had a family planning session the week prior. It was decided that Helena would prepare the main course, comprised of kielbasa, bigos (hunter's stew) and golabki. Jan's Mama would prepare all the desserts with her only granddaughter, Julia. She loved all things domestic now that she was eighteen years old and hoped to have her own home and family soon. They decided to bake mazurek, almond pound cake (babka migdalowa), and of course, Jan and Helena's favorite sand cake. The two also baked breads, including crescent-shaped wheat buns (luky buleczki) and rogi, better known as butter horns.

Mary Kaminski was now part of the Jasinski-Pawlowski family since Jozef the Hero married pretty little Sophia

Kaminski who wasn't so little anymore. She was twenty-three years old, and besides playing the bells, she was a nurse working in her Papa's busy medical practice alongside her Mama, also a nurse.

Jozef and Sophia had been married for four years and just one month before, they had welcomed their first child. Mariola Pawlowski was born on May 7, 1939, looking very much like her Mama with blonde hair and sparkling blue eyes. Jan and Helena's twins, Piotr and Julia, celebrated the same birthday and everyone agreed Mariola was extra-special for that reason alone.

For the Wianki meal, Mary Kaminski volunteered to make the traditional pickled beet soup (barszcz kwaszony z burakow), borscht with mushroom dumplings and kutia. Kutia was one of her specialties and she wanted to make it this year in honor of the birth of her granddaughter—a symbol of good luck.

Jozef had transformed his adventures into hunting. Just days before he'd brought home a bear from his hunt. Bigos was best prepared with the rich fine grain of bear meat. That was his contribution to the meal. It took Helena six days to slowly cook the bigos. She added herbs and vegetables from her garden. Their cottage smelled divine.

Of course, no meal was complete without pierogi. All the women cooked their best pierogi recipes at the last minute, so they'd be hot and fresh. The pouches were filled with beef, cottage cheese, mushrooms, potato, cheese or even bilberries topped with sugar and cinnamon for dessert, as if there was not enough to eat already.

Jan's Uncle Stan could be counted on to toast before every meal, but only after grace had been said. "Jedzcie, pijcie i popuszczajcie pasa" meant "Eat, drink and loosen your belt".

Jan and Helena's cottage housed almost the same kin in 1939 as it did in 1930 except Jan's Mama was back in her own home with Big Jan since he'd retired from the mill in Austria, leaving the room she'd slept in to be used as a den or a guest room once again. Jozef and Sophia had moved into her parents' home after they married.

Franz now had the entire loft area of the cottage to himself. He used the loft room that Jozef had slept in as his private office. No one was surprised when he decided to become an architect, specializing in historical buildings. He contracted with cities and towns throughout Poland and other European countries, so he traveled a good deal of the time. As it happened, he was home for that year's Wianki Festival.

Helena's best friend, Julia, had written months earlier that she and Kazi would be in Cracow for the entire month of June. They had gotten married in 1921, soon after Kazi and his family arrived in America. Sadly, they were unable to have children, so they made themselves happy by leading their church youth group. They enjoyed celebrating holidays, doing fun projects and going on field trips with the children.

Julia had taken a cue from Helena by studying languages. That enabled her to get a job as an interpreter for an import-export company in Yonkers. Kazi worked as a carpenter/painter and stayed very busy. Buttons lived a long and happy life as their "only child" and died in his sleep, of natural causes, at the ripe old age of fifteen, which is one hundred and five in dog years.

When Julia and Kazi arrived in Cracow on June 5th, Helena met them at the train depot. Franz offered to drive as Helena did not have a car, nor did she know how to drive. There was no need for a car as her life was based at home and she walked wherever she needed to go.

In nearly twenty years since Julia and Kazi had moved to America, they had come back home only once. That was ten years earlier when Julia's beloved Babka died of pneumonia. Julia had traveled home by steamship and rail with her Mama. During that visit, Helena and Julia had very little time together because Helena had the twins and two-year-old Jozef to care for. Besides, Julia and her Mama could stay only for the three-day funeral.

At the cemetery, as Helena and Julia said goodbye, Julia pushed up the sleeve of her heavy winter coat and showed Helena the bracelet that her Babka had given her before she left Cracow in 1920. The black onyx absorbed light while the sterling silver reflected it. It was a beautiful harmony between light and dark, life and death.

Julia and her Mama left immediately after the burial. There was now another sad tombstone in their church cemetery. The light of another beloved family member had been snuffed out, leaving a hole in the fabric of their community and their hearts.

Since then, Julia and Helena had kept up with each other's lives by letter. They were excellent letter writers and were always delighted to receive news of each other's changing lives.

***

Helena spotted Julia the moment she emerged from the train. She greeted her with a great hug even before Julia's feet hit the ground. They laughed and cried at the same time. So much time had passed, and they'd missed each other desperately.

Kazi waited patiently on the train steps behind Julia until Helena realized that the poor man was carrying all their suitcases. He could not get off the train until they moved out of the way.

Franz stood by watching the exchange between his sister and her friend. He had to try hard not to let his tears show. He put his emotions into greeting and helping Kazi with the suitcases. It was good to see Kazi and Julia; Franz remembered them from when he was just four years old. They were family to him and to the rest of his family.

The four of them talked nonstop and all at once on the short ride home. Julia and Kazi's arrival was an exciting event.

Helena had insisted that Julia and Kazi stay in their now vacant guest room, small as it was. She wanted to spend every minute possible with Julia. And Jan would be more than happy to have another man his own age in their cottage.

While Jan was at work, Kazi and Franz enjoyed long talks about building. Kazi had become a master carpenter working for his Papa in Yonkers. Franz could never get enough of building and architecture. The two became bonded during that visit.

When Jan and Jakob returned from work, the family enjoyed nightly dinners together. Julia and her namesake, Helena's Julia, helped to gather vegetables in the garden and to collect canned fruits and jams from the cellar for their meals.

The threesome had so much fun cooking that it did not seem like work at all. Every dinner was a mini-feast devoured by all. Every bit of food and companionship was savored.

The Wianki Midsummer Festival was just about a week after Julia and Kazi's arrival. All was in readiness, including their family maiden, young Julia. It was tradition for maidens to wear white and to wear a wreath in their hair. Piotr's twin, Julia, was the only maiden in the family. Therefore, she was the Star of the Day. Julia looked very beautiful and precious as her Mama placed the delicate flower wreath on her head for the festival. Helena's best friend stood by and witnessed the simple ritual, knowing that it was a rite of passage. She remembered her Mama placing the Wianki on her head so long ago. It also reminded her that she would never place a Wianki on a daughter of her own. Helena intuitively knew what her friend was thinking and asked her to help pin the wreath in Julia's hair. It was a moment treasured by the three of them.

The stroke of five meant it was time for the Wianki dinner feast. The table was expanded to its full length and there were seventeen places set, enough for the Jasinski's, Pawlowski's, Kaminski's and the Wolowicz couple (Julia and Kazi). Mary Kaminski had given her daughter some beautifully embroidered table linen as a wedding gift and it was the linen for the special feast.

Helena's Papa said grace before dinner. He thanked everyone for joining in and helping with the meal. All eyes turned to Uncle Stan and he did not disappoint. He gleefully gave his toast—his brand of dinner prayer.

With his last word, the dishes that had been set in the center of the massive table began to be passed to the left from north, south, east and west. Within two minutes, there was no more chatter as appetites were sated.

As was the practice in their family, the men repaired to the living room while the women cleaned up the kitchen and the table, then re-set it with a dessert buffet and fresh linen that would rival a royal table.

Uncle Stan's voice could be heard above the others as he told the story of one of his workers in the mine. The young man had not followed directions and gotten lost for an hour in the mine shafts. The lad was shaken up, but promised that he had learned his lesson. The boy had to endure the snickers of his coworkers and his ego was seriously bruised.

Then Kazi took center stage, so to speak, talking about living and working in America. The elder Jozef was especially interested in hearing about field trips Kazi and Julia chaperoned with their youth group. They'd even visited Bear Mountain, north of Yonkers.

In the kitchen the talk was all about baby Mariola Pawlowski. With both Grandmamas present, no one could get a word in edgewise, but no one really minded.

Sophia was sitting at the kitchen table breast-feeding Mariola. All the family members marveled at what a natural mama Sophia was, and that Jozef was a perfect Papa. But then, both had exemplary role models for parents. Jozef was old enough to remember his Mama when she died, and he still felt the piece of her heart she had left to him with her dying breath. It gave him peace, and enough love to pass on to Sophia, Mariola, and any other children they should be fortunate enough to have.

By the time they had devoured dessert and cleaned up the kitchen, it was 7:30—time to go down to the riverbank for the festivities that would begin at sunset.

Piotr said he would escort his maiden sister to the festival, lest any of the young men get the idea she was unprotected from their advances, as he put it.

Just as they were leaving the cottage, Julia's Papa called to her, "Julia, my beautiful girl, come give your Papa a hug."

Piotr and Julia stopped and walked back into the dining area, now vacant. Jan wrapped his arms around his only daughter and said, "Julia, please take care this night. I love you, now go have fun and stay with your brother."

He then turned to Piotr and said, "I am counting on you, my eldest son, to keep your sister safe. Do not let her out of your sight for one moment. Do you understand?"

"Yes, Papa. You can count on me." Piotr began to get an uneasy feeling about the night. It was very unusual for their Papa to voice warnings about their safety.

Jan reluctantly let go of Julia. He added, "Your Mama and I will be waiting up until you return. If you are not back by fifteen minutes past the midnight finale, you will be in a great deal of trouble!" They nodded. With that, Jan hugged Piotr and sent them off to the festival. As they left, Jan noticed Julia had to reset her head wreath, which he'd accidentally pushed sideways when he hugged her.

Helena wondered where Jan was. She found him staring at the back of the closed front door. "Dear, is something wrong?"

Jan did not want to worry Helena unnecessarily. However, he knew her well enough to realize that if he did not tell her of his intuition about Julia, she would figure it out anyway. Jan said, "Lena, I have a very bad feeling that something could happen to Julia tonight. I told Piotr not to let her out of his sight and that they are to be home directly after the finale."

Just then, the rest of their group was approaching the door where they stood. Not wanting to let anyone else know of their concern, they shared a quick kiss. Helena opened the front door and invited everyone to walk together to the banks of the Vistula River, across from Wawel Castle, to watch the evening fun.

Jan, Helena and Piotr were on high alert for reasons they did not completely understand. Julia was caught up in the fact that as a maiden, she would be launching a candle-lit wreath from the riverbank. She loved being the center of attention; dressed in white with a bit of paradise in her hair. She hoped the young and dashing Michal Kinski would notice her. They were in the same church youth group, they went to school together and shared a love of hiking and bird watching.

The Jasinski twins were popular wherever they went. They were often seen together, so tonight was not unusual. But Piotr knew that his responsibility toward Julia would somehow take on new meaning tonight.

They spotted their youth group and walked toward them. It was a pretty sight—all the maidens in a circle holding their candle wreaths waiting to be lit.

All the young men outside of the circle of white were laughing and joking about the school play that was to take place the next week. The play was appropriately timed with this event—A Midsummer Night's Dream. When the boy who was playing the role of Puck saw Michal making goo-goo eyes at Julia from afar, he loudly proclaimed, "Lord, what fools these mortals be!" They all knew that Michal played the role of Lysander in the play and that Julia played his love interest, Hermia.

Laughter, hoots and hollers filled the air. Piotr pretended to be amused along with the other boys, but he was busy watching the crowd for danger.

Julia heard what the sarcastic Puck shouted and blushed in contrast to her dress. She hated that part of being blonde and fair-skinned. It was nearly impossible to hide emotion. She smiled at Michal.

The bell was struck three times, signaling the start of the evening's events. That meant all the maidens should light their candle wreaths. The eldest maiden had the task of lighting the first wreath from which the other wreaths were then lit, one by one, around the circle. When all the wreaths were aglow, the girls walked to the riverbank and prepared to send their wreaths afloat.

By this time, the townspeople gathered around to watch the ritual of the maidens. The young men were allowed to stand just behind the maidens so they could choose the young lady they wanted to watch the fireworks with later.

The riverbank was sloped and offered the onlookers a good view. Helena and Jan stood on the bank together, holding hands. They were feeling a little more comfortable now that they could see Julia was safe and Piotr was right behind her. The bell was struck again, only once. Each maiden launched her candle-lit wreath. It was a magical moment. The crowd oohed and aahed and cheers erupted. The maidens then turned toward the group of young men, hoping to be picked by the boy of their choice.

Piotr, still behind Julia, was now in front of her as she turned. Michal took a giant step toward Julia just as she saw him; they smiled at each other in acknowledgment. Piotr, seeing Michal's approach, turned to his right to greet him.

Suddenly, a boy ran up from Piotr's left side and in that instant had enough time to get to Julia and knock her backwards into the river. Julia never saw him coming, her eyes were on Michal. Piotr and Michal lunged toward Julia to save her, allowing the boy to escape capture. Julia jumped up and out of the river. She was unhurt but very angry that her night was ruined. She stomped up the riverbank. Piotr ran behind, trying to keep up with her. She was mad at everyone, most especially Piotr, who was supposed to keep her safe.

Back at the riverbank, the crowd was atwitter. Those who'd seen the boy push Julia into the river agreed they'd never seen him before. Then he disappeared so quickly that no one knew where to begin to look for him. The big question on everyone's mind was: Why would anyone be so unkind to Julia Jasinski?

Julia's family tried to press forward through the crowd to get to her. From their position on the slope, they'd viewed the entire episode. It happened so fast that they were in shock. It seemed surreal.

Their group got separated in the confusion. As Helena tried desperately to get to the river, she was forcefully grabbed around her waist and dragged kicking and screaming in the opposite direction. Her screams could not be heard, and no one even noticed. Before she knew it, she was unceremoniously dropped on the front steps of her cottage.

Panic blurred her vision and her recognition of the man who had stolen her away from her family. He was a very large man. That accounted for the ease with which he'd carried her off.

Helena realized the man was speaking to her in a language not her own. She tried to focus her thinking and to slow her breathing. As she became slightly calmer, she first recognized his voice, and then she tried to place where she'd heard it before. It had a kind, refined tone to it. In the next instant, she knew — it was Professor Georg Stein, her language instructor, and he was speaking German to her!

Recognizing this man did not make Helena feel much easier. She tried to catch her breath to speak, to get answers, to understand.

What neither Helena nor the Professor knew was that Franz had stayed behind while the others went to the festival. He was in his loft working when he heard strange sounds coming from the front steps. He peeked out of the upstairs windows just above the steps. He did not understand why Helena seemed to be upset and why she was with this strange man. Intuitively, he felt he should listen and not take action yet. It took him a moment to attune his ear to the fact that the man was speaking German. The man looked like Professor Stein, the well-liked language professor at the university. While that did not make any sense to Franz, he trained all his senses on the words he would hear next.

The Professor had to speak louder than normal because he wanted to be doubly sure that Helena comprehended his message completely. There was no time to repeat his words.

Helena was sitting on the steps and the Professor was bent over her. He put his hands on her shoulders and said, "Helena, I apologize for carrying you off but there is something of great importance that you and your family must know. First, Julia is perfectly safe. To get you alone, I used her as a diversion. The boy who pushed her into the river is my nephew, who is visiting from Lodz. No one would have recognized him. Now, what I need to tell you is that a conversation was overheard between some foreign students in our town square just last week. They assumed, because they were speaking German, that no one would know what they were talking about. However, my German class had just ended and some of the students came across the foreigners who seemed to be surveying the buildings for some reason. Two of my students sat near them, speaking Polish, but of course, they understood most of what the other students said in German. What they were able to make out is that there is a plot involving a Nazi takeover of Poland, with Cracow being a central government staging post for their operations.

"When my students came to me with this information, I immediately went to our local government. I have been asked to gather my best foreign language students to begin forming our underground security effort. Helena, *you* are my best student. Will you help with the underground formation? Helena! Do you hear? Do you understand?" He released her shoulders and stood.

When the Professor took his hands off her shoulders, Helena's mind suddenly cleared. She'd heard and understood every word and she was completely prepared to do anything and everything in her power to protect her family and their town from the Nazis.

She stood in front of the messenger of doom and calmly said, "Yes, Professor Stein, I will help with the underground formation. There have been rumblings for the past two years that the Nazis plan to control all or part of Poland. I will do what I can to help and I know my family members will do the same. My brother, Franz, is an architect and can travel throughout Europe on business without raising suspicions. My other brother, Jozef, is an investigative journalist and will be an asset to the effort too."

Helena saw that the wet Julia, with Piotr trailing behind, was getting close to home. She said, "Go quickly now before you are discovered. Thank you for taking the risk of bringing me this information, although I truly wish that my Julia did not have to be the diversion."

The Professor said, "Yes, I am sorry for Julia too. I will go now and when you come to class on Monday, I will find a way to let you know the time and place of our first meeting."

Franz backed away from the upper window and sat heavily on his bed, alone in the dark. Although he was not surprised at the news of the Nazi plot, he did not expect to be so immediately and directly affected. He had a feeling of deepening dread that spread from his gut to his heart and back again. He then began compiling a mental list of contacts that would surely help with the monumental tasks they would all soon face. He had met quite a few influential people in his travels; people who had the power to be very helpful indeed.

The Professor disappeared into the night before Julia ran to her Mama and threw her arms around her, sobbing. Piotr stood looking helpless and Helena softly said, "Piotr, go ahead and wash your face. We will be in shortly." Gratefully, Piotr obeyed.

Julia was incapable of intelligible speech, so Helena calmed her by saying, "Julia, let us put this night behind us. I am sorry this happened to you, but it cannot be undone. One day, you will tell your children all about this, and it will not seem so bad. You will see, my darling girl."

It was not so much the words that Julia's Mama spoke, but her soothing tone. She felt so much better after being in her Mama's presence. It was like when her Mama had told her she had felt about her own Mama…secure and well-loved.

Julia went into the cottage, dried off and changed into her nightgown. She got into her nice soft bed and was asleep as her head touched the pillow.

Piotr changed into his night clothes. He knew Franz was in his loft. Piotr climbed the ladder, hoping Franz was still awake. He was surprised to find him sitting in the dark. "Franz, is everything alright?"

There was a long pause in the darkness. Franz finally answered. "No, Piotr. I'm afraid everything is not alright."

Knowing that Piotr would soon find out what was about to befall them, Franz told Piotr all he had overheard moments before. When he heard all there was to hear, Piotr asked Franz if he could sleep on the floor in the loft that night. Franz said, "Of course, I will be happy not to be alone tonight."

Both young men were lost in their own thoughts and fell off to sleep before the rest of their family arrived back at the cottage after having cut short the night's activities.

Jan and Helena went into their bedroom to talk privately. She told him why she disappeared when Julia was pushed into the river, and what Professor Stein told her.

Before Jan responded to the news, he told Helena that Michal and Kazi tried to catch the boy who did the pushing, but they lost sight of him. Michal wanted Julia to know that he ran after the boy.

Jan was glad to hear who the boy was and the reason Julia was targeted, although he felt bad that she had to endure the embarrassment in front of the whole town. So now he knew why he had such a feeling of foreboding for Julia before she left home that night.

He wrapped his arms around his wife and said, "Lena, are you hurt? You must have been terrified to be carried away with no one to help you. Please, tell me you are unharmed, my sweet."

Helena smiled, feeling safe in the arms of her husband. She said, "Yes, Jan, I am physically unhurt, but mentally I am working very hard to maintain my equilibrium."

Jan nodded. He realized that Helena's news was just the beginning of some very bad times for all of them.

Chapter Nine

FIRST MEETING

After dinner the following Monday when Helena was alone cleaning up the kitchen, Julia and Kazi interrupted her thoughts.

They wanted to speak with her before she left for her class. Kazi spoke first. "Helena, Julia and I discussed our travel plans after hearing what happened on the night of the festival. We have decided we want to help and the best way to do that is to use our connections in America." Kazi looked at his wife.

Julia continued. "Yes, Helena, we want to stay for the first meeting of the underground before returning to Yonkers. Kazi has trade associations. I have connections through my job with the import-export company. We both have friends in our church, and of course, we belong to the Polish American Society. Do you agree with us?"

Helena had been washing the counter while listening. She folded the dish towel. "Julia, I wish I could be excited that you and Kazi want to stay with us a bit longer, but under the circumstances, I just feel sad. I do agree that your connection to America could be a big advantage to us here in Cracow. But you will be endangering yourselves and perhaps others in America. None of us are equipped to deal with the Nazis, but we will be doing just that. You would be so much better off safe in Yonkers."

Julia shook her head in disagreement. Tearfully, she said, "This will always be our home and you will always be our family, Helena, along with all who are family to you."

"Oh, Julia, I know, I know. Please don't cry. You will make me cry and I don't have time to cry right now. Let's just take one step at a time and we will figure it out together. Of course, you two can stay as long as you want. We can use your help, I'm sure."

She turned to Kazi and said, "I appreciate you both more than words can say. Thank you for being here, and for your support. We don't know what tomorrow will bring, but we will somehow bear it together.

Now I must go or I'll be late for class. Would you mind making sure that Henryk and little Jozef go to bed by nine? As you know, Papa has left for his Monday evening meeting. I will be back by 10:30."

Kazi replied, "Of course, your two little ones will be looking for me to read the next chapter of that adventure book their Uncle Jozef gave them. I think I enjoy reading it to them even more than they enjoy hearing it. It will be *to bed* by nine, though. Have a nice evening, Helena."

She kissed them both on the cheek, grabbed her favorite green sweater and off she went, not knowing just what to expect of tonight's class.

Walking was therapeutic for Helena. She found she could sort her thoughts when her body was in motion. If she walked briskly, it would take twenty minutes to reach the university, then another five to go across the campus to room 312 at Chopin Hall.

It was a pleasant evening, a typical summer night with a light breeze. The street was lit by a full moon, giving the leaves a silvery glow. She was lost in thought and found herself wondering if her Mama was aware of their circumstances and what was about to befall them. Then her imagination took over. She felt as if her Mama was walking beside her. Her Mama said, "Yes, my dear, I know what has happened and what will be asked of you in particular. There are many of us here on the other side who have been and continue to be instrumental in assisting the efforts of all of you. I am honored to be able to help in such important life matters. It will not be an easy path that you will walk, my daughter, but I assure you that I will remain at your side. As always, speak to me as if I am with you, because I am. I will help you. I sent Professor Stein to you and I will send others who will assist in the underground organization that will soon be in place. You will always know what to do...it's one step at a time. Remember that Spanish saying, 'Poco a poco se anda lejos' which means 'Little by little we go far.'"

Helena was so immersed in her Mama's words that she did not realize she had arrived outside of her classroom. She often engaged in mental conversation with her Mama, since she died nineteen years before. But this exchange was so real, so present.

She recognized his touch on her shoulder before she saw him. Professor Stein arrived just after she did, and he was talking to a pretty young woman. They seemed to know each other quite well. In perfect Polish with a German accent, the Professor said, "Helena, I would like to introduce you to Professor Rebekka Stein. She is a physics instructor here. Rebekka, I am pleased to introduce to you Helena Jasinski."

The two women shook hands and as they did, Rebekka kept hold of Helena's hand and said, "It is an honor to meet you, Helena. My brother has told me so much about you."

The surprised look on Helena's face made Rebekka giggle. "Yes, Georg is my brother. Do you not think we look alike?" They all laughed. Georg was tall, dark-haired with deep brown eyes, while Rebekka was fair-haired with blue eyes. He was about forty-five and she appeared to be in her late twenties.

Helena felt relieved that Rebekka was not the professor's wife for some odd reason, but she did not have the luxury of giving it any further thought at that moment.

Before releasing the handshake, Rebekka pressed a folded piece of paper into Helena's palm. So, this was the way that Professor Stein found to let her know where and when the first meeting of the underground would be—clever. Helena discreetly closed her palm as Rebekka released her hand.

The elder Stein said, "Well, ladies, it is time for class to begin, so let us go. Rebekka, I shall see you later."

Helena laughed and said, "Oh, yes, I knew there was a reason I came here this evening!"

Professor Stein smiled broadly, thinking how much he enjoyed the company of this woman.

Helena said, "Rebekka, it was a pleasure to meet you. I hope to see you again."

As Rebekka walked away, she turned and with a glint in her eye said, "I'm sure we will meet again, Helena. Good night to you both."

The other twenty-five students were at their desks waiting for class to begin. The professor took his place at the podium and arranged his lecture papers.

Helena took her usual place in the front. Georg Stein was a genius teacher and she did not want to miss anything he said. Besides, he was very easy to look at and she often fantasized that he was speaking only to her. Then she would mentally reprimand herself for such thoughts.

Helena could not bear the suspense any longer. She opened the small white note Rebekka had pressed into her palm and read:

IN TWO DAYS, WEDNESDAY 9 P.M. - CHURCH BASEMENT. YOU KNOW WHO TO BRING. SPREAD THE WORD BY MOUTH. BURN THIS NOTE TONIGHT.

She felt herself becoming very nervous. Class began and Helena's attention immediately went to Professor Stein. He seemed to be able to communicate with her even while he was lecturing. She felt like he knew she was becoming anxious about the underground meeting and he was telling her *without words* that they would all stick together. She relaxed and focused only on his spoken words…the German ones. After all, it was a German language class.

At the end of class, Professor Stein wrote a research assignment on the blackboard. He said, "You may leave after copying your assignment. Guten nacht."

***

As each person arrived at the darkened church on Wednesday night, they found the doors locked except a side entrance that led to the basement. The full moon lit the dark hallway, showing the edge of each step. Once in the lower level, a few lights lit the way. There were no windows in the basement. The church had been built as a refuge, as well as a place of worship.

At precisely 9 P.M., Professor Stein announced the opening of the first meeting of the underground movement of Cracow. There was a deadly silence in the room. Everyone understood the gravity of this gathering. He said, "We will get right to the business at hand. I would ask each of you to stand one by one and tell us who you are and how you will be able to assist our group effort against our enemies. But first, let us begin with Helena Jasinski, as she has agreed to be our organizer. Please, Helena, will you stand and speak to us?"

Helena stood and faced her friends, family and acquaintances. In the two seconds it took her to get up from her chair, she felt as if time stopped and everyone in the room appeared to be frozen. She heard her Mama say, "Helena, step by step and I will be right with you." She heard a faint whoosh and the activity in the room came alive again. She knew she was the only one who heard her Mama's voice.

Helena began, "Thank you, Professor. Yes, I will be happy to organize our group. I have been asked to assist this way largely because I have studied language for many years. I am just now completing a German course of study with Professor Stein, and previously I studied Russian and French. As we don't know exactly how any of our abilities will come to benefit our efforts, I will also tell you that I am a violinist and a writer. I can sew, I grow fruits and vegetables and I have a large canning cellar for winter food supplies.

"I have asked a number of you here tonight, as you are part of our ready-made network of talented family and friends. Next, I will ask my husband, Jan, to speak. Jan, please."

Jan stood looking self-assured but not arrogant. "Good evening. You all know me as the manager of the mill in the north of town. My Papa, whom we call Big Jan, you might know, was the manager before me. He is also here tonight."

Jan motioned toward his Papa, sitting next to his Mama. They looked drawn and tired.

"I have two hundred and fifty employees who can be asked to help out in any number of ways. They all have mechanical ability. I also have musical talent and can play piano, violin, flute and harpsichord. I will end by saying that I have every confidence in my wife's ability to organize this important group."

With that, he briefly took Helena's hand as he sat. The intimate gesture did not go unnoticed by Georg Stein.

Professor Stein suggested that introductions continue around the circle from left to right.

Big Stan stood to his full 6'4" height. Most people found themselves looking up to him even when they were standing beside him. He said, "I am Stan Jasinski, brother to Big Jan here and the uncle to little Jan." Everyone enjoyed the humor at Jan's expense. He did not mind; he stood over 6 feet tall. Helena and Jan smiled at Uncle Stan. They loved him dearly.

He continued, "I have been the crew chief at our salt mine for all my working days. I have a sense of safety and a crew of strong workers. For what it may be worth, I am a sculptor and a wood carver." As he sat, he added, "I, too, believe that our Helena is well-suited to organize us." Everyone clapped in agreement.

It was Big Jan Jasinski's turn to stand. Again, Helena noticed how tired he looked. But it was not reflected in his voice. "As you all know, I am Jan's Papa, and next to me is my wife, Mary. She's a little shy, so I will speak for her. You know her as our music teacher. She passed her talents on to our son. Lord knows he did not get his musical talent from me!" Chuckles were heard. It was a well-known fact that Big Jan could not play a note or sing a tune to save his soul. His friends had even gone so far as to ask him *not* to sing in church. He was happy to oblige.

"In any event, my Mary will be a great domestic support. She is an excellent cook and will make sure we're all fed," he said as he patted his obviously well-fed belly.

"As my son said, I managed the north textile mill before he took over. Then I accepted a management assignment at a mill just outside of Vienna for five years. I have many business associates between here and Austria. I can offer my mechanical ability too." He sat and motioned for Helena's Papa to speak.

Jakob was as strong, good-looking and charming as ever. His snow-white hair complemented his twinkling blue eyes. Many widows had designs on him over the years, but he'd have none of it. Marta was the love of his life, and after her, no woman could interest him.

He said, "I am Jakob Pawlowski and I have worked at the south textile mill since I was knee-high to a grasshopper, as they say." More chuckles were heard. "I've managed the mill for thirty years. All I can offer is hard work and commitment to all of you, and of course, I too have loyal employees who we can call on. This good-looking young man next to me is my son, Jozef."

Jozef stood and said, "Thank you, Papa. I am Jozef Pawlowski. Some of you will remember me as a crazy little adventurer as I was growing up, and some of you will say that I've not yet grown up. Maybe that's true too. Helena and I share a love of violin and of writing. I am an investigative journalist and I freelance throughout Europe. I also love to hunt, and I can find my way through all kinds of terrain without a compass, not to mention being able to provide meat and fowl for us if needed.

"My wife, Sophia, is not here tonight because she is with our newborn daughter, Mariola. Sophia is a nurse and works with her Papa, Doc Kaminski." He nodded toward Sophia's Papa; they were great friends and were bonded the moment the Doc had delivered him a quarter century earlier.

"Now you will hear from my brilliant brother, Franz." He handed an imaginary microphone to Franz, saying, "It's over to you, genius!"

Franz was accustomed to the kidding of his older brother, and so he stood, pushing away the offer of Jozef's microphone. They both laughed. For just a moment, all the participants forgot the dire task at hand and enjoyed the comedy of the Pawlowski brothers.

Looking at Jozef, he said, "Thank you for that introduction, Jozef." Then, looking around the circle, he said, "It's hard to believe this boy was once called Jozef the Hero, wouldn't you all agree?" Murmurs and snickers were heard. Franz continued, "As most of you know, I am an architect. I travel frequently throughout Europe and my friend Kazi Wolowicz will be connecting me to the architectural communities in America very soon. I specialize in historical architecture and my second language is German. I might add that you should not expect me to entertain with any musical instruments. I have no talent in that area!"

Jozef chimed in with "You can say *that* again!" They fake-punched each other and Franz took his seat.

Doc Kaminski popped up next. He was still spry for his years. "I am honored to be part of this venerable group. You've known me as Doc. My full name is Stanislaw Kaminski. I am a General Practitioner like my Papa before me and his Papa before him. With the assistance of my wife, Mary, who is also my office nurse, I have been able to help our community with every kind of injury from scraped knees to battle wounds. My wife and I, and now my daughter Sophia, will serve as medical support throughout the coming months, that is, as long as we can count on Mary Jasinski to cook her famous meals for us!" Heads bobbed in agreement.

He looked at Julia, who was next to him as he sat. "Julia, tell 'em what you got."

Julia's head was full of travel details, her friends and family back in America, and now her homeland's crisis. She was accustomed to speaking in front of groups, but she was nervous about all that was happening. She began with an apology to break through her own barrier. "I am sorry, I am having trouble grasping the reality of what is about to happen to us. My fears are getting the better of me and preventing me from being able to speak very well."

Jakob stood and said, "Julia, dear, if I may interrupt, I have something to say." Julia nodded her consent.

"Thank you for being brave enough to speak of your fears. You have given voice to what all of us are feeling, but no one else has been as courageous as you. It is wise to air these feelings so we can help each other through the times that approach. Each of us will have good days and bad days, but hopefully, we will not experience the bad at the same time." He smiled sweetly at his daughter's best friend, whom he loved as his own, and said, "Please, Julia, go on and tell us about yourself."

Julia took a deep breath before she spoke again. "As you all know, I grew up here. Helena and I were inseparable as girls. Then in 1920, I moved to America with my family, to Yonkers outside of New York City. I studied languages just like Helena, at the university where my Papa taught math and science. Because of that, I was able to get a job as an interpreter working for an import-export company. That gives me some international connections. I am also still in contact with my tutor, Miss Anna Milewski, who traveled with us to America. She worked at an orphanage in New York to earn her keep until she got a teaching degree. Now she's teaching grammar school in the borough of Queens. She is also a child advocate and will surely benefit our efforts. Now I will let my husband speak. Thank you."

Kazi patted Julia's hand before he stood. "Good evening. I am Kazi Wolowicz. Many of you will have been fortunate enough to have witnessed me and my brothers being yanked into a great puddle of mud at our Spring Social some years ago." Kazi stared at Jan, who gleefully stood and pulled his Uncle Stan up with him; both proudly flexing their muscles. All eyes went to the pair and then back to Kazi. There were obviously no ill feelings. Everyone shared their laughter and then it became a moment of remembering that Spring Social so long ago.

Attention was then back to the church basement in 1939. Kazi continued, "Julia and I were childhood sweethearts and I moved to America with my family only a few months after Julia moved there. We settled in Yonkers, too, because many from our country found work there. I learned carpentry from my Papa and his brothers. That is what I bring to the table, along with trade associations created over the years.

"Oh, and one last thing, many of us who moved to America were sponsored by Father Michalowicz. He is originally from Warsaw and will surely be willing to help us."

Kazi signaled to the pretty young woman sitting next to him to speak next. Franz had taken a special interest in whoever she was, and his interest seemed to be reciprocated.

Rebekka stood and Franz noted how petite she was. Jozef poked his brother as if to say, *Hey! I see you checking her out!*

She began, "Hello, everyone. I am Rebekka Stein, the sister of Professor Georg Stein. I am also a professor at your university. My specialty is physics. Before coming here to work, I taught at a university in Berlin. I have academic associates in Germany, Austria, and Russia as well. I speak German and Russian. As you can tell, my Polish is rough, but maybe someone will give me lessons."

She glanced at Franz, who flushed slightly. Jozef elbowed Franz again, which only added to his embarrassment.

Franz was nothing if not a gentleman. He stood and offered Polish lessons to Rebekka. She thanked him and they both took their seats.

There was one last person to address the group. He was sitting next to Rebekka, looking a bit uncomfortable and somewhat out of place in his tweed sports jacket in the middle of summer. As he stood, it became apparent that he was surprisingly fit. He spoke haltingly in a strange British-Polish accent. "Good Evening. I am Nigel Blake. Professor Stein has asked me to join you because he thinks I may be able to help your underground effort. Currently, I teach literature at your university. I am Oxford educated, and I taught in Montreal for a few years during World War I. I have an avid interest in international history, and I speak Polish, albeit with a British accent, as you may have taken note. My father and brother are both intelligence officers with the British Navy and are willing to do what they can, when they can, to combat the Nazi devils."

In typical dry British humor, he added, "If you wonder how I keep my girlish figure, I am a competitive bike racer." Jan wondered if this Brit could keep up with him in a bike race. They might just see about that sometime later.

"To finish, I believe my Canadian and British associations will prove to be invaluable to us." He began to sit, but remembered he wanted to say something else. He stood again and glanced to his left with a bit of a smirk. "If anyone is interested, I am not married." His meaning was lost on no one, especially not on Rebekka or Franz.

The introductions ended with laughter, complete with a bit of competitive spirit.

Georg Stein stood again. "Thank you all for coming. We will meet here one week from tonight at the same time. At our next meeting, Helena will present organizational charts that will illustrate how we will work together to the best advantage.

"For the time being, I believe we are safe from enemies, but please leave in twosomes or threesomes rather than in a group so we do not attract attention. Good night."

Chapter Ten

THE ORGANIZATION

Helena had slept surprisingly well after the first meeting of the underground. She rose before her children did, but after Jan and her Papa had left for work. She followed the aroma of fresh coffee to the kitchen and found Julia enjoying a cup and gazing into the garden, seemingly in a world of her own.

"Good Morning, Julia. How are you this morning?"

Julia emerged from her daydream, "Good morning to you, Lena. I'm fine. You look bright-eyed and bushy-tailed today. You must have slept well."

Helena stretched out the kinks in her neck and shoulders. "Yes, I did sleep very well. It's a good thing, too. I will need all my mental resources to accomplish what I plan to do today. What will you and Kazi be doing?"

Julia got up and rinsed her cup in the sink. "As soon as Kazi gets up and has breakfast, we will go visit his aunt and uncle. We promised his Papa that we would visit them while we were here. Then we will go to the train station to change our travel arrangements. After that, we'll go to the office of the steamship company and change our passage date. We thought we would plan to leave one week from today. That will allow us to be at the next underground meeting. We also decided to oversee family dinner preparations every night until we leave, to give you the planning time you need. What do you think?"

Helena said, "Wonderful! That all makes perfect sense to me, especially the part where you two take care of our dinners for the whole week!"

Helena poured herself a steaming cup of rich, dark coffee and began multitasking. First, prepared breakfast for everyone, and then she packed lunches for the children. Henryk and Jozef were spending summer weekdays at the church camp. Now that they were ten and twelve years old, they thought they were too old to go to baby camp, as they called it. But in truth, they enjoyed the activities that held their attention. Piotr and Julia were starting their jobs as church camp counselors, now that they were eighteen years old. They were anxious to have summer jobs for the first time, to earn a little bit of money. They spent some time each evening planning the next day's camp fun. The previous night, they had put together a treasure hunt for the children. They'd even drawn maps for three different age groups. They had scoured the neighborhood, going door-to-door asking for donations of little items the children would search for. The night before, they could be heard giggling in Franz's loft as they sorted through the donated items. Helena was relieved that life was happy and normal for her children, at least for now.

The flurry of activity officially began in the Jasinski household when Henryk and Jozef came bounding into the kitchen for breakfast. There was chatter, whistling, cajoling, playful pushing, singing, and scraping of chairs across the kitchen floor.

The aroma of maple-flavored bacon filled the humid summer air. The eggs were fresh that morning. It was egg delivery day—5 A.M. every Tuesday—you could set your watch by the egg man. Helena always asked for medium instead of large eggs as they were more flavorful.

The milkman delivered on Mondays, Wednesdays and Fridays from the Pulaski farm. This time of year, the milk was delivered icy cold, so it would stay fresh in the icebox longer.

"Henryk, will you please fetch a bottle of milk for Mama and put it on the table?"

"Sure thing, Mama! When's breakfast ready? We wanna go soon, ya know!"

Jozef ran to the icebox before Henryk could get there and grabbed a bottle of milk, not realizing it had already been opened. Just as he did, Henryk tried to snatch it from him. Julia and Helena watched the transaction as the bottle sailed through the air, splattering milk on everything and everyone in the kitchen before meeting the linoleum floor. Thankfully, the bottle did not break.

Julia gasped and Helena simply laughed as she was accustomed to the antics of the boys. Helena announced, "Okay, boys, time's wasting. Start cleaning it up!"

Dutifully, the boys mopped up the milk, being careful to wipe off the faces of Auntie Julia and their Mama before they wiped the floor and the counter.

They knew the drill. After they finished cleaning up, they rinsed their cloths in the sink, hung them to dry on the clothesline outside and ran back to the breakfast table. They did not dare to complain that their eggs were no longer hot.

Piotr and Julia came into the kitchen at the tail-end of the milk fiasco. Taking it all in stride, they set their plates on the table and dished up cold eggs and bacon. Piotr got up to get a fresh quart of milk. He passed the little monsters and gave them a disgusted look, which Henryk and Jozef ignored. They did not want to make their camp counselor mad before the day even began.

Ten minutes later, all four children had gone to camp, leaving a deafening yet welcome silence in their wake.

Kazi appeared at the garden door. Julia said, "Kazi! I thought you were still asleep. Where have you been?"

He smiled a sad sort of smile and said, "I could not sleep last night and went out for an early morning walk. You seemed to be sleeping peacefully and I did not want to disturb you. Before I knew it, I'd walked to the Pulaski farm. It's a peaceful place. I sat on a rock listening to the birds. They seem so carefree singing their songs. I was reflecting on growing up here in Cracow and comparing how our lives are in Yonkers. I realize that while we appreciate all that we've been given, we haven't appreciated it all as much as we do now in the face of war coming to our doorstep."

Heavily, he sat on a stool at the kitchen table. Julia decided to change his gloomy mood and she did the unexpected—she jumped onto his lap. Kazi was indeed surprised and thrilled at the same time. Julia accomplished her objective—his mood lightened immediately. He laughed and hugged her.

Helena giggled at her friend's spontaneity, thinking how wonderful it was that they were still so in love and fun-loving.

Julia leaped off her husband's lap and said, "Lena, you have work to do. We will clean up the breakfast dishes for you and then we will leave and be back in time to prepare a tasty dinner. So, go to your worktable and we will be as quiet as church mice."

She gently pushed Helena out of the kitchen.

Helena laughed. "Okay, I'm going. I'll see you two later. Have a nice day."

Helena was still thinking about how wonderful her friend Julia was, as she laid out her work papers on the dining room table.

Since the meeting, she'd decided what organization sections would be needed, which people would fit where and who would best work together.

Julia and Kazi went on their way. All was peaceful and quiet in the cottage. Helena had a premonition that she would have a visitor. One second later, there was a light knock on the front door.

She peeked out of the living room window. There on the steps was Professor Stein. She opened the door with a mixture of delight and trepidation. She was glad to see him, but he'd never come to her home. Except for the night he bodily carried her to the front steps, dropped her, and told her about the Nazis coming.

"Professor Stein, what a surprise. Won't you please come in?"

"Thank you, Helena. I apologize for not making an appointment before simply showing up. I hope you do not think I am terribly rude."

"Of course not, Professor, you are always welcome in our home. Come, let's sit at the dining room table and you can tell me what brings you here." She noticed the smell of apple pipe tobacco as he brushed past. She visualized him in his cottage, living happily and comfortably.

He sat in the chair next to the one Helena had obviously been sitting in. "Please, Helena, call me Georg when it is just the two of us, will you?"

She replied with a grin. "Yes, Georg, and please *do* call me Helena."

There was that delightful humor Georg so loved. They shared a laugh. He reached for a friendly handshake. "Okay, it's a deal, Helena. I came by because I knew you were developing the organization for the underground and I thought perhaps we could brainstorm together. What do you think?"

"I think that's a wonderful idea. Two heads are always better than one, as they say. We think similarly, but you will have some ideas that I do not have and vice versa. We'll make a good team, Professor. I mean, Georg!"

They spent the next three hours bouncing ideas around. First, they determined the mission for their group. They would not be a military organization, but they would appoint a few people to operate a safety section to plan whatever would be needed in the event of an attack. They would try to keep everyone safe, but their primary goal was to keep all the children out of harm's way. They would have to be very clever to outsmart the Nazis.

Helena and Georg agreed the best way to protect the younger generation was going to have to be to send them away before they were kidnapped, or worse.

They tossed around possible code names and thought Acorn Park was an apt title. As they talked, Helena drew charts which included fourteen sections with fourteen interlocking, or overlapping pyramids showing who would cover each section, working in threesomes. She also made a list of resources ordinarily available that could be utilized by the threesomes. Groups could work from the list to come up with strategies. They would have to use diversion, subterfuge, disguises, and the like, to accomplish their goals.

They talked about tactics that had been used to trick enemies during war. For instance, Virgil's epic poem "Aeneid" referred to the use of a wooden horse, which came to be known as the Trojan Horse, in a story about the Trojan War. It was thought to be a peace offering to the Trojans, but it was a hiding place enabling Greek soldiers to gain entrance to Troy so they could destroy the city. It was a clever example of how they might outsmart the Nazis. They'd have to start thinking like that in order to survive.

Presently, their group included sixteen people who made up a superior brain trust. They would surely rise to the task at hand or die trying.

***

The following Monday, Helena dragged herself out of bed before sunrise. It was to be another busy day for her. Along with her normal responsibilities, she would be taking the final exam for her German class, then going on to the meeting of the underground.

She was well-prepared for both. She'd studied for the final on Saturday and firmed up the organizational details of the underground on Sunday.

Being tired made the day seem longer than it actually was, but finally, she was sitting in class waiting for exam booklets to be handed out.

She did very well on the exam and in fact she finished early. She had time to stop by the village coffee shop before going to the 9:00 meeting.

There were several university students sitting at the bistro-style tables. Brightly colored tablecloths covered the small round tables. They were red on white, the colors of their national flag. It was a self-serve shop, so Helena stepped up to the counter and ordered a large café au lait. She heard conversations behind her and beside her. Of particular interest was what was being said by three young men seated to her right. They were speaking German and she suspected they were the same foreign students who had been overheard in the town square the week before. Her ear was keenly trained on the young man who said, "It will be a great relief when the day comes that only Germans walk amongst us in this beautiful town. Wouldn't you say, Dietter?"

"Yes! I agree completely, Hans. I heard this morning from Berlin that it will be a matter of just a few more weeks before we will be free of the Polish _____." Helena did not know what the last word was. But judging from the context, it was not complimentary. She realized these young Germans were not foreign students, but rather, members of the Hitler Youth Squad sent ahead of the SS to scout out the main areas of Cracow. That would explain their apparent interest in Cracow's buildings the week before.

As difficult as it was, she sat at the table next to the despicable three. She was totally revolted by their very presence, but she knew she should get all the details she could. She still had twenty minutes before she had to leave for the meeting. She appeared to be interested only in the book she was reading. She discreetly covered her German book and pretended not to listen to the youth squad.

She was facing the door when a group of students from her class entered the coffee shop, joking and laughing. It was her cue to let them know not to mention German class within earshot of the German youth.

Thinking quickly, she got to her feet, grabbed her books and met the last student coming through the door and whispered, "Hitler's Youth sitting nearest the counter in a trio. Tell everyone not to mention class and to pretend not to understand them. Hurry now!"

She left for the meeting. Thinking she'd be the first to arrive, she was surprised to see the Professor sitting alone. He got up the moment he saw her. "Hello, Helena. I saw you sitting in the coffee shop as I passed by and I would have joined you, but I decided I wanted to be alone here to think about tonight's meeting."

Helena smiled. "I understand. It is a good thing that you did not stop in as I discovered three members of Hitler's youth squad talking about a Nazi takeover of Cracow in a few weeks. I left when six or eight of your students came in after the exam. I whispered to one of them that the Germans were there and to pretend not to understand them. I'm sure you will hear about it tomorrow when you go to the university."

He looked concerned, and before he could respond, voices were heard in the stairwell. It was nearly time to begin the meeting.

Everyone arrived, and the meeting commenced at 9:00. Professor Stein announced that Helena was prepared to outline the organizational plan and he gave her the floor.

The chairs were arranged in a horseshoe formation so everyone could see Helena's flip chart. She stepped in front of the easel. "Good evening to all of you." She looked at Julia and gave her friend a wink. Everyone replied, "Good evening, Helena." As usual Uncle Stan's voice could be heard above the rest. Helena grinned. There would be plenty of time and reason in the coming weeks to become grim and intense. For now, they could all just enjoy each other while they learned how they would be working together.

"Now let's begin with a few ground rules. The only notes will be these charts, and after we get organized in working groups, they will be burned. So please do *not* take notes, but *do* plan to commit your own role to memory. It would also be helpful if you would save your questions until after my presentation."

Helena told the group what she and Professor Stein had decided in a planning session. They would not operate as a military unit, but they would appoint a safety group in the event of an attack on any member or members. Their primary mission would be to keep the children out of harm's way.

She paused and took a deep breath before saying, "The best way to assure that our children remain safe will be to secretly send them to other countries before the Nazis kidnap them or cause them harm in any way."

She looked back at her charts so she would not see the looks of shock. They were all bright enough to know that this would have to happen.

Helena went on, "Our code name is Acorn Park, also known as A.P. We will use this code in all our communications in the future.

"So then, this first chart lists the fourteen sections or groups, illustrating our operations organization. In no particular order, we have: Communications; Transportation; Safe Housing; Food; Workers/Employment; Travel; Foreign Liaisons; Youth Group; Medical; Main Coordination; Liaison with Polish Government, in case they have to operate in exile; Children's Safety; Domestic Liaisons; and Local & Foreign Universities. We will cover these sections in groups of three, multiplied times fourteen sections, which means forty-two slots to fill."

Helena flipped to the next chart. "Here are our fourteen sections set up in overlapping pyramids. I will give you an example of what I mean by overlapping pyramids. Our Communications pyramid will be run by Franz, Jozef, and Sophia. Franz will also be part of Safe Housing; Jozef will be part of Workers/Employment; and Sophia will also serve with our Medical section.

"Each member of Acorn Park has two or more pyramid positions. If you can fill your own positions and assist in other sections, then by all means, do so. However, the original three pyramid members remain responsible unless replaced for some reason.

"I will take the Main Coordination section along with Julia Wolowicz and Professor Stein. I am also part of the Food section with Big Jan and Big Stan, as well as serving on the Safe Housing group with Franz and Professor Stein.

"I will be in a fourth trio operating the Children's Safety section with Kazi, Jan's Mama and Mary Kaminski." She pointed to the chart and said, "You can see all of the pyramids illustrated on this chart. I will explain a couple of others: Local & Foreign Universities will be operated by Rebekka Stein, Nigel Blake and Big Jan. And we are allowing our eighteen-year-old twins, Piotr and Julia, to be part of the Youth section. Their Papa, Jan, will direct them, along with Doc Kaminski's wife, Mary.

"All of these pyramid sections are important, and they will work in tandem. Each section will report directly to the Main Coordination section.

"You all introduced yourselves and your skills at our first meeting. I used that information to determine what I thought would be the most advantageous pyramid sets. In some cases, I combined those of you who have similar connections and in other cases, I grouped you with people who have complementary skills.

"Before entertaining your questions, I want to tell you about a member of A.P. who will *not* be attending meetings. Some of you will remember Miss Anna Milewski. She lived in Cracow and worked as a private tutor some years ago. She moved to America with the Wolowicz family in 1920. She then worked in an orphanage in New York City and earned her teaching degree. She teaches grammar school in a borough of New York City. Miss Milewski will be part of the Travel section along with Big Stan and Mary Jasinski. Her connections with Julia Wolowicz, plus Julia's connections within our group, will be invaluable in getting some of our children to safety in America.

"Oh, and there is one other person we might *possibly* be able to call on for help. Father Michalowicz in New York has sponsored some immigrants from Cracow. He sponsored Julia's family and also Kazi's. He must work within the immigration regulations. Therefore, anyone he sponsors must present proper documentation. Identification will come under the purview of either our Foreign or Domestic Liaison section. We'll keep Father's assistance on the back burner, so to speak. Kazi will speak to him in person, after he and Julia return to America. They plan to leave tomorrow.

"One of the many tasks our Communications section will be charged with is to figure out ways to pass messages and information between us here in Cracow and our group in America, after the German occupation.

"I would also like to say that all fourteen sections will have the task of raising funds to finance A.P. operations. Each of us will have to pull out all the stops by selling personal property such as jewelry, artwork and antiques. We will be saving our children. Their lives are more precious than any material goods.

"Alright then, after looking at our A.P. organizational structure, what questions do any of you have?"

Professor Stein stood and said, "Helena, I would like to add to your remarks that we all must remain vigilant in keeping A.P. secret. It may sound cynical, but trust no one outside of our group. Helena and I, along with Julia in America, will field all questions and concerns, so please keep us informed of any development, no matter how trivial it may seem to you. We will have the bigger picture and determine the import."

All heads nodded in agreement.

Piotr stood next and said, "I have a question, or rather a request. We go to school and to the youth group with Michal Kinski. My sister, Julia, and I think he would be an excellent addition to our Domestic Liaison section because he is going into law enforcement, following in his Papa's footsteps. So, we were wondering if Michal could be asked to join Acorn Park."

Jozef answered his nephew's query. He said, "Good call, Piotr. I have met young Mr. Kinski and I believe him to be trustworthy. He would be an asset to us. I am an investigative journalist, so I should be in the Domestic Liaison section with him. I would be replacing Jan in that section of our organization."

Everyone turned to Helena. She stood and said, "I agree with Piotr and Jozef regarding Michal Kinski. If no one objects, I suggest that Piotr speak with Michal and let me know his response."

No one voiced an objection. Helena continued, "It seems we are all in agreement. If there are no more questions, we will end for tonight. Before you leave, please take note of which sections you will be involved in. Our next meeting will take place this Thursday here at eight P.M. The change in day and time was suggested by Jozef so that we do not become too predictable to outsiders who might wonder what we are up to. At Thursday's meeting, all our sections will be discussing their plans to be implemented after the Nazis invade. Thank you, and good night."

The members of Acorn Park left in small groups. There were some who were talking, but most were grim and pensive.

Helena and Georg were the last to leave. Jan was walking home with the twins.

Georg said, "Helena, you did a wonderful job presenting our organization's plans. You made it crystal clear. Now everyone will have to digest the enormity of this reality."

"Thank you very much. Good evening, Georg."

Helena collected her flip chart and easel and left him to close the church basement.

"Good evening to you too, Lena."

Georg watched as she walked away. He sighed deeply, shut off the lights, and trudged up the stairs to the outside world.

He forced himself to shift gears mentally. There were exams to be corrected and final grades to be calculated when he got back to his lonely cottage.

The Organization

The Underground; Code Name: Acorn Park

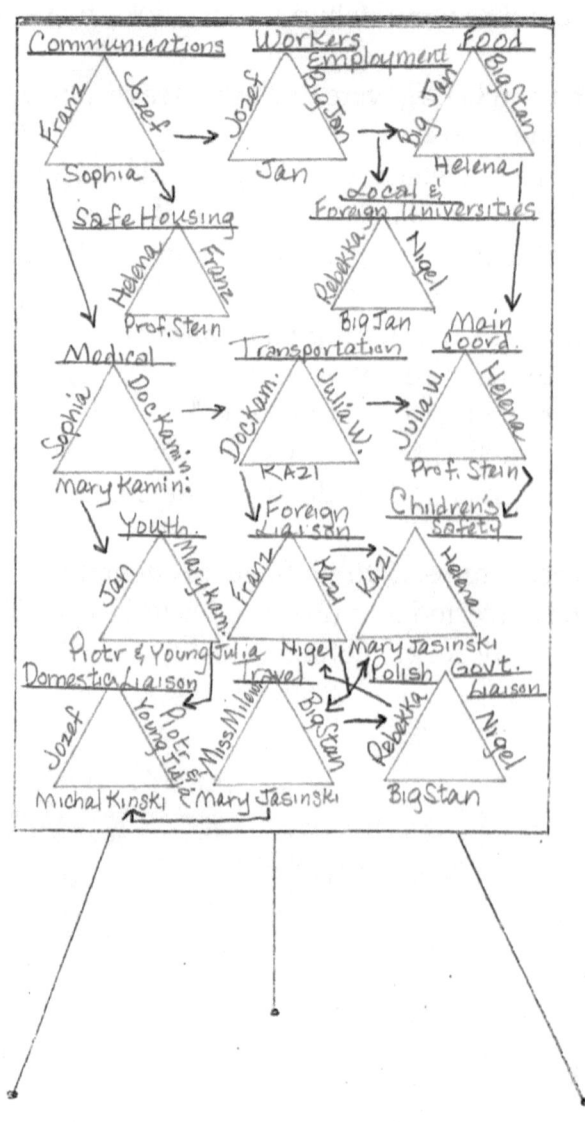

Chapter Eleven

*A*CORN *P*ARK *P*REPARATIONS

The cuckoo clock sounded at the half-hour at nine-thirty A.M. Helena was still reeling emotionally from letting go of Julia and Kazi at the train station before daybreak. The morning mist had cleared from the air, but not the heaviness of her heart.

She had to reach deep within to muster her pretend smile. This time, no one had been fooled.

Kazi had stepped forward and hugged Franz, then Helena. No one spoke. Kazi shouldered the luggage and shared a look with his wife as if to say, "I will see you on the train."

Julia and Helena stared at each other, frozen in place, staring at each other. Neither could leave. Franz broke the ice by grabbing Julia and hugging her with all his might before swiftly walking back to the car.

Somehow, Julia found the courage to rise above her heartache. She said, "Lena! Don't be so sad. Look to the bright future when we will be together again, sharing life's joys!"

Helena could not hold back tears any longer. She clung to her friend, her soul sister. "Julia, you give me the strength to endure and go onward. Thank you. Safe journey and remember that I love you."

"I love you too, Lena!" As she moved away, Helena saw the sparkle of the bracelet Julia's Babka had given her. It reminded her of something.

As Julia waved and backed away, Helena shouted, "Julia, wait! I have something for you!"

Julia looked behind her at the train. The whistle blew to signal its imminent departure. She was not sure she had time to spare.

Helena ran forward, bridging the gap between them. She thrust something small and hard, wrapped in paper, into Julia's hand. "Take this, there is a note to explain. Go now and open it on the train!"

There was no time for Julia to do anything other than to clutch the gift and run for the train, which was already slowly creeping forward. She easily jumped from the platform up the two steps, then turned to wave to Helena.

But Helena had disappeared in those few seconds. Julia understood. To her right, Kazi was holding the heavy train car door open. She made it to her seat before bursting into tears. She hated leaving Helena and Poland. She forced herself to see through tears to take one last look at where she had grown up. She knew this country would soon never be the same.

Julia's hand began to hurt. She realized she was holding the gift from Helena so tightly that it was poking into her palm. With tears streaming down her face, she read the note:

Dearest Julia, these earrings are most special. Papa gave them to me for my 30th birthday. He had given them to Mama as a wedding gift. He told me they were a Pawlowski family heirloom handcrafted by a jeweler in London in approximately 1865. A jeweler in Cracow deciphered the markings and gave us this information. One of the clues was that they are 18K gold. As you see, the delicate, gloved hand of the earring has a tiny pearl at the wrist and is holding a petite flower wreath with a wee pearl at the center of each of the three flowers. I know you are looking for the other earring—I have it. Both of these precious earrings will give us hope when days are dark. The wreath will remind us of the Wianki Festivals in our beloved Cracow and the three flowers are like the sides of our Acorn Park pyramids, all existing at once—past, present and future. The hand is the hand of fate that will give us strength and love and guide us back together one day. Always Love, Lena

Julia looked at the earring. It was barely an inch and a half long and one-half inch wide at the wreath. It was amazing, and Helena's written words went directly to Julia's body, mind and spirit. She thought of Helena having the other half of the pair and imagined their meeting somewhere, sometime in the future. Yes, she believed the little golden hand had special powers. She reached into the top of her undergarment and securely tucked it into the secret pocket she'd sewn there only the day before.

Kazi read the note along with Julia, and he saw the gift. With tears in his eyes, he pulled his wife into his side and she laid her head on his shoulder. She fell asleep, leaving him alone with his thoughts.

***

Jan sat at his cluttered desk. For the moment, all was going smoothly in the shop. It had been a busy morning, and he was relieved to have time for a cup of coffee. As he sipped the acrid brew, he wished he had some cream and sugar. He decided he would have to do without. He unwrapped the muffin Helena had baked for him. It was made from his favorite sand cake batter. Oh, but this muffin was laden with fresh blueberries and topped with butter cream frosting and walnut meats. He savored each bite, thinking of his Lena.

Like a bolt of lightning, he was struck with the verse that he had composed in his sleep the night before. After clearing his desk with his forearm, he grabbed a scrap of paper and wrote.

He re-read his words and marveled at what he must have done to deserve such a woman. Well, he thought, best not to look a gift horse in the mouth as the saying goes. He neatly folded the scrap of paper and put it into his lunchbox. He went back to work feeling self-satisfied. He made up his mind to go home promptly at five.

The rest of his day passed uneventfully. The quitting whistle was a welcome sound to Jan. Aloud, he thought, "It's *to home* for me right now!" As he passed Old Clem, he asked him to wait for everyone to leave, then shut off the machinery, turn off the lights and lock up.

With a wide grin, Old Clem replied, "Yes, Sir, Mr. Jasinski! I'll be happy to do that. Leave it to me. Looks like you have big plans this evening. Care to share with an old man?"

With a laugh, Jan said, "Right you are. Big plans with someone special tonight and I'll not be sharing them with you, no matter what your age! Thank you and I wish you a good evening, Clem."

Jan went off whistling a happy tune. Outside, he hopped on his trusty bike, tossed his lunch box into the wire basket and pedaled home.

His thoughts turned to dinner. It was Tuesday and that meant it was golabki night and a great start to this evening!

Jan parked his bike inside the garden gate and entered the kitchen. He was greeted by the sumptuous smells of dinner, but not by Lena.

Leaving his lunchbox on the counter, he went in search of her. She was not in any of her usual places. She was in the last place he looked — in their bed.

He realized this was not such a surprise. After all, she was up before dawn to see Julia and Kazi off that morning.

As she slept, he stood admiring her. How he loved her. The past weeks of activity and turmoil had served to bind them closer, if that was possible.

She stirred and became aware of his presence. At once, they were in each other's arms, without words, only feelings — the very best kind.

Afterwards, Jan said, "That was quite a greeting, my love!"

"You bring out such passion in me. How could I resist you?" Nuzzling his neck, she said, "I will always love you, Jan."

Together, they lay content and happy. They dozed briefly until they heard, "Mama! Papa! Dinner is almost burnt! Where are you?"

Giggling like teenagers, they jumped from bed, dressed, and prepared for an evening with their family.

Dinner was wonderful as always and was topped off with the family favorite — sand cake. It was Piotr and Julia's turn for KP duty. While they got on with cleaning up, Helena opened Jan's lunchbox to repack it for the following day. There was a folded note inside. She wondered if she should read it. She decided they had nothing to hide from each other. She unfolded it and deciphered his chicken scratching:

Always

The journey of my life has been richly rewarded with you by my side, Lena.

You are always in my heart and in my thoughts, whether in my arms or out of sight.

We've weathered many a storm, you and I, always as One.

You keep me young, you keep me inspired and you keep me interested

in everyone and everything about our world.

I should ask for no more and yet, I do.

I ask that you are with me...Always.

Helena was struck as if by lightning. Her heart skipped a beat. Of late, they'd had little time together and she worried that Jan no longer felt romantic love for her. Here was proof she had nothing to worry about.

She did an about-face and marched right into Jan's arms. He had been standing at the hearth talking to her Papa.

Jakob smiled and left the two alone. As he passed the old rocking chair, it momentarily came to life, confirming that his Marta was with him in spirit. He knew she was happy for their Lena and Jan.

He acknowledged to himself how much he missed his wife. However, he was very glad that she would not have to endure the terror soon to come.

***

Thursday night, Jan and Helena walked into the meeting of Acorn Park hand-in-hand. Most everyone was already in attendance, talking in small groups.

Georg was talking to Rebekka and Nigel Blake. Franz joined the threesome and stood between Rebekka and Nigel, who scowled at the appearance of Franz.

Ignoring Nigel's unspoken complaint, Franz greeted them in German, "Guten abend!" Inwardly, Franz smirked, acknowledging that Nigel did not speak German.

Georg and Rebekka appreciated the greeting in their native tongue but replied in Polish in deference to Nigel. "Good evening, Franz. How are you tonight?"

"I am well, thank you." Franz zeroed in on Rebekka. Just then, Jan approached Nigel and asked if he'd like to discuss bike racing. Nigel immediately forgot his romantic competition in favor of a potential bike race, and the two walked away for a little talk.

Helena came by to ask Georg if she might have a word with him before the meeting, leaving Franz and Rebekka to themselves.

Franz seized the moment and leaned close to her. "Rebekka, would you join me for dinner tomorrow evening?"

She was surprised by his confidence. After all, they'd only just met. However, she confessed to herself that she thought he was dashing, handsome and very interesting. "Yes, I would be delighted, Franz."

Before she could say more, Franz said, "Very good! I have made a reservation for two at eight P.M. at the Cracovia Seafood Grille. I hope you like seafood, Rebekka."

She could not get a word in. "We will be seated at the best table overlooking the Vistula!"

Georg announced the meeting would begin shortly. Rebekka said, "I will see you at 8:00 tomorrow evening then." She smiled and took her seat next to Nigel, who looked at her quizzically.

Franz fairly skipped to his seat and sat next to his brother. Jozef had watched the body language of his bachelor brother as he stood with Rebekka. As he sat, Jozef gave him a "thumbs up" along with a nod. Franz grinned.

Georg was waiting to hear what Helena wanted to talk to him about. She only wanted to remind him that he had not given her the score of her final exam or her grade for German class. He was pleased to inform her that she aced the final and earned a 4.0 for the course.

Helena said, "Thank you, Professor. You have been a wonderful teacher, and I promise you that what I have learned will be very useful!" She touched his arm, and he had to concentrate his willpower not to visibly react.

She took her seat next to her husband. She looked very happy, and Georg supposed it was not only due to the scores he'd just given her.

Georg glanced at the clock—time to begin. He clapped once to get everyone's attention and announced that the groups should gather independently to strategize and plan. He suggested that they spend approximately thirty minutes in a group, then move on to their next group.

Most members had two different pyramid positions. There was some downtime while one or more of their next threesome was still with another group.

Georg and Helena were responsible for the Main Coordination section, along with Julia, who was now in America. They decided it was a good opportunity to begin their coordination efforts and to split their time between the other thirteen groups. Whichever one of them finished with six groups first would take the seventh. They agreed to ask one person in each section to keep in touch with the Main Coordination section.

Georg moved to the Communications section. Sophia, Jozef and Franz were already deep in discussion. Jozef said he'd been working on a code that would be very difficult for outsiders to decipher and that it was nearly complete. He went on to say he was using a combination of letters, numbers and pictograms to encode messages. Once he figured out the sequence to be used, he would teach the others the code he dubbed "Oak."

They were all aware of the significance of the oak in their culture, but Jozef reminded them anyway. He said, "Our Cracow was founded by Krakus. 'Krak' is a Slavic word meaning oak, once a sacred tree. The sacred tree relates to family lineage and thus represents our family trees. The code name is also significant because our underground organization is named Acorn Park."

Franz elbowed Sophia and said, "Watch this." He said, "So, Jozef, you are suggesting that acorns come from the oak tree?" That got a big laugh from everyone within earshot.

Jozef enjoyed the joke and said, "Very funny, brother—your jealousy is showing!"

Before going on to the Local & Foreign University section, Georg said, "Jozef, I am very impressed with your code. It will enable your section to keep our entire outfit informed on a timely basis." Franz and Sophia wholeheartedly agreed, clapping Jozef on the back.

Rebekka, Nigel and Big Jan were busy talking about universities. Big Jan's experience in Austria was proving to be an invaluable connection to Nigel's Oxford network and to Rebekka's Assistant Professorship time in Berlin. Even though Big Jan did not attend the university while he worked at the mill outside of Vienna, he became acquainted with many who were alumni of the University of Vienna—the oldest German-speaking university in the world. Rebekka said, "This is a most wonderful connection for us!"

Georg was taken by his sister's enthusiasm, "Yes indeed, Rebekka! It's truly amazing how connections seem to mesh almost magically. Wouldn't you agree, Nigel?"

"Why yes, Professor. We'll be ship-shape and Bristol fashion—ready to take on the enemy!" By the looks of confusion, Nigel realized he'd used a British expression they did not understand. "Oh, sorry, that means that we'll be in first-class order. I was brought up in a naval family, you understand."

They laughed. Nigel was sort of growing on them, despite his overinflated ego.

On the opposite side of the room, Helena stopped by the Travel section. Jan's Mama was grouped with Jan's Uncle Stan, aka Big Stan and Anna Milewski. Helena stood in for Anna, who would not be attending meetings, since she was in America. They acknowledged that their section would work closely with the Communications section so that undercover travel plans would remain secret from the Germans. Helena informed them that Jozef would teach his secret code over the next few weeks.

Big Stan and Mary Jasinski worked well together. The two had a tight bond, steeped in family tradition and common history. Big Stan was a compassionate and physically protective man, while Mary was emotionally understanding and extremely maternal.

Helena left them to continue planning and turned toward her husband with the Youth Group section. He was sitting with Mary Kaminski and the twins. Helena congratulated herself for putting this group together. Jan was loved by children, Mary had years of experience in the medical field and of course, Piotr and Julia were just teenagers themselves. The group had already progressed to the point of discussing the organizational flow from Youth to Medical and then to the Domestic Liaison section.

Helena rose to approach the Polish Government Liaison group and bumped smack into Georg, who apparently had the same idea. They startled each other.

Putting his hand on her arm, Georg said, "Oh, excuse me, young lady, I did not see you there. It looks as if you are headed for Rebekka's group too. Why don't we both sit with them?"

Helena said, "That's a wonderful idea, Professor."

Georg pulled up two chairs and placed them between Rebekka and Nigel. Big Stan chimed in with, "Yes, join our little troupe. We can use your help!"

As Helena and Georg got comfortable, they were unaware that Jan was watching them. Jan did not like how Georg Stein related to his wife, and he hoped he would not have to confront the Professor on the topic of Helena. However, he was prepared to do so if it became necessary.

After another ten minutes had passed, Helena stood and asked for everyone's attention. "Please finish up with the group you are with and move on to any group you have not met with yet. Then spend fifteen to twenty minutes there, after which we will come back together for closing."

For a moment, the volume of the voices rose, and everyone was walking around figuring out where their last stop was. Soon, all were seated again to finish the night's important work.

Georg and Helena met in front of the room. He said, "Helena, this meeting has been extremely productive, thanks in large part to your efforts."

She touched his hand and warmly responded, "You give me too much credit, Georg. I am also very pleased with how Acorn Park is coming together. While we are on the subject, I know you asked Nigel to join our group. How do you think he's fitting in?"

Georg looked confused and said, "I don't understand exactly what you mean, Helena. I know he's a bit of an odd duck, but I assure you that he is 100% loyal to our cause. Did he say something to cause you concern?"

"I apologize if I have offended you, Georg. But I cannot ignore my feeling that there is something important about Nigel that we do not know."

Georg said, "I understand intuitive clues. I will keep alert to anything we need to know about Nigel. Will you leave it with me, Helena? I will have a heart-to-heart with Nigel and report back to you directly, Admiral!" He saluted her in fun.

Helena's concern dissolved, and she laughed as Jan appeared. "What's amusing?"

Not wanting to worry Jan needlessly, Helena said, "Professor Stein was just telling me a funny story about what happened in the university bookstore today."

Jan did not believe that for one minute. Nor did he appreciate not being let in on what was going on between Helena and Georg. He changed the subject by saying, "Helena, it looks as if everyone is ready for the wrap-up."

Since Jan called her Helena instead of Lena, she simply replied, "Okay, Jan." She turned to Georg and said, "Your voice is stronger than mine. Will you please ask everyone to arrange the chairs in a horseshoe?"

Georg gave her a wink and a smile. "Certainly." Jan missed the gesture.

With the semi-circle back in place, Helena said, "We are now on our way to creating the best possible scenario to protect our families from the Nazis. Over the coming weeks, you will work with your sections independently and jointly. On a related topic, we talked about selling our valuables to finance our operation. I've made a connection with a fine jewelry shop in the Jewish quarter of Cracow. The owner, Hanna Bjorn, has agreed to accept our items on consignment for a generous 75/25 split in our favor. She will accept jewelry, watches, clocks, and all types of antiques and artwork.

"Hanna told me that her Papa is a Swedish physicist and her Mama is a banker here in Cracow.

"The shop is 'Time and Again' at 722 Main Street in our Kazimierz section. When you take your goods there, just mention my name and she will know what to do. Her establishment is a franchise with shops throughout Europe. Hanna expects our items to be sold quickly and will pay us in cash on a weekly basis. I plan to open an account with the bank that Hanna's Mama, Elena Bjorn, works. I will make the weekly deposits there.

"We should not be too obvious when taking our possessions to Hanna. I will leave it to your good judgment.

"Alright then, it's been a long night and we've accomplished a great deal. We will not need to meet again as a group. But you will be meeting in sections as needed, and of course, you all will stay in touch with Professor Stein or me all along the way. Thank you and good night."

Piotr and Julia said they wanted to stop by the village coffee shop, and they would be home within the hour. Jan looked at Helena and she nodded her consent. Michal Kinski said he'd like to join them and they left in a happy group.

Out in the street, Jan and Helena turned left, while the teenagers took a right toward the coffee shop. It was a lovely summer evening and it felt good to be out in the fresh air after spending a few hours in the church basement.

Jan tried to sound nonchalant. "Lena, what were you and the Professor talking about this evening when you were laughing?"

Helena hesitated. She did not mean to cause Jan to think there was anything unseemly going on between her and Georg. Thinking she had better clear it up before it went any further, she said, "I was asking Professor Stein about Nigel Blake. I have an unsettling feeling that there is something he is hiding from us. Since Georg asked Nigel to join our group, I thought he might try to find out more about him. I was laughing when Georg gave me a mock salute. That's when you walked up." She grabbed Jan's hand. "That's all it was, my dear."

Jan knew the truth when he heard it. He realized he had no worries about his wife, but he still intended to keep an eye on the professor. "I understand, Lena. Thank you for telling me. If there is anything we need to know about Mr. Blake, we shall soon find out, I'm sure. Let's go home and check on our family."

Chapter Twelve

SUMMER'S END 1939

The Acorn Park members were extremely busy during the dog days of August. Within days of their last group meeting, "Time and Again" had taken in more valuables to be sold than could be catalogued in a week. Everyone seemed to be of the same mind—that Acorn Park should have the money rather than waiting for the Nazis to steal their precious family heirlooms.

When Helena stopped by Hanna's shop, she was greeted enthusiastically. "Helena, it's good to see you. I am so glad you chose today to come by!"

From the time they first met, Helena sensed something special about Hanna, and she knew intuitively that they would become close friends.

"Thank you, Hanna, it's good to see you too. Why are you glad I chose today to stop by?"

Excitedly, Hanna said, "Well, I've only just now received a large payment for items consigned by your group! The jewelry was purchased by a fine jewelry shop in Stockholm. However, most of the other valuables were purchased by an artist in Lisbon. Oh, and I should tell you that the special clocks were bought by a clockmaker in Bavaria."

Helena felt a pang of regret. Her precious cuckoo clock must now be in Bavaria, where it was originally crafted. She quickly dismissed the thought and reminded herself of why they were giving up their worldly goods.

Before she could respond, Hanna said, "As we discussed, normally items are purchased individually, so to have sold your valuables in large lots is unexpected. It's as if your guardian angel interceded on your behalf!"

Helena thought of her Mama and smiled. "Yes, Hanna, my Mama is my angel. I am not surprised that so many precious pieces were sold. I kept a mental tally of how many local families visited your shop over the past weeks. By my count, it was forty-seven different families, including our own small group. They all wanted to help Acorn Park. Once again, Helena thought how perfect the name of the underground was. It would appear to outsiders that they were raising money for the physical Acorn Park in town.

She hesitated and thoughtfully continued. "Giving up our material items is very difficult. But of course, the monetary gain will sustain many lives and families through the coming months.

"Those who consigned with your shop, visited me first, to let me know what they were contributing to our cause. Among the items was lead crystal, sets of Limoges china, porcelain from China, sterling silver serving pieces, beautifully carved music boxes, scores of Swiss-made clocks and watches, oil paintings by Monet, Gauguin, Van Gogh and even some of Chopin's original sheet music. I am certain that among the most valuable items was the 18K gold jewelry from the Victorian era, crafted in Eastern Europe.

"I know that some of our professors gave up their prized textbooks along with research materials, in the hope that those items would find their way to universities that would value them and keep them safe.

"Hanna, I feel so lucky that we are connected and that we can help each other!"

She replied, "I could not agree more, Lena! Now, I must leave for an appointment. So, I will turn the payment over to you. I must warn you; it's a substantial sum."

Hanna knew exactly how much cash she had for Helena. However, she enjoyed the drama of counting it out for her. "Hold out your hand, Lena." She began placing the large denomination bills in Helena's hand one by one. As the stack grew, Helena held her breath, her eyes got bigger and bigger. Just as the stack threatened to topple over, Hanna said, "There! Now, what do you think, my dear friend?"

Helena gasped, and the bills fell onto the counter. Both women tried to catch them. It was an emotional moment. They stared at each other and giggled.

"What do I think? I think we have created a miracle together, Hanna! But you must go, and I must get to the bank to deposit these delicious profits. I will never be able to thank you enough, Hanna!"

Helena shoved the bills into her satchel. They hugged and went their separate ways.

Thankfully, the bank was only a few doors from "Time and Again." Helena was relieved to see that Hanna's mama was seated at her desk and not with a customer. As nonchalantly as she could, she walked to Elena Bjorn's desk. "Excuse me, Mrs. Bjorn. I am Helena, a friend of Hanna's. I have some cash to deposit. Can you help me, please?"

Elena looked around the bank lobby. When she was satisfied that no one was paying attention to them, she quietly said, "Yes, Helena, my daughter asked me to look out for you. Please sit, I will be more than happy to assist you, dear."

Helena breathed another sigh of relief. She had so much cash, it seemed she'd robbed a bank. She felt safe sitting across from Mrs. Bjorn. Helena thought she had a very special connection to this woman for some inexplicable reason.

Elena interrupted her thoughts. "Helena, I commend you for what you are doing. I promise you that I will do everything in my power to help you."

Elena paused and considered her next words. "I knew your Mama, Helena. We met when we took voice lessons at the Music Conservatory, we were just young girls. We became very close. Actually, we were inseparable. Helena, do you have a friendship like your Mama and I had?"

Helena responded immediately, "I do. My friend Julia and I are just like that. What happened to separate you two?"

A sad look came over Elena's face, "The First World War happened when we were about the age you are now, Lena. My husband and I took Hanna and moved to Venezuela. That's where Hanna became interested in antiques."

Helena had been listening intently. When Elena called her 'Lena', a distant memory was sparked. She said, "Elena Bjorn...of course! Mama told me about you two growing up together and that she named me in your honor...we are both called Lena! It is no wonder I am so comfortable with you, and with Hanna too!"

She looked behind Helena. Standing there was sour old Mrs. Kunitski, waiting to speak with Elena.

Elena was forced to change the subject. Quietly, she said, "Lena, we will find time to talk later. Please tell me the amount of your deposit, and I will take it to the teller and bring you the receipt."

Helena whispered the amount to Elena, and she said, "I will be back in a minute." As she passed Mrs. Kunitski, she told her she would be with her momentarily.

Mrs. Kunitski sniffed. "I should certainly hope so, I have waited here long enough!"

Elena was back in less than two minutes. She handed Helena the receipt and grasped her hand. For a moment, Elena's face was Helena's mama. And just as suddenly,

Elena's face reappeared. Yes, Helena's mama was her guardian angel and still at her side as promised.

Helena said, "Thank you so much, Mrs. Bjorn. Have a nice day."

Elena smiled warmly, "You do the same, Lena."

***

Out in the street, Helena jammed the bank receipt deep into her skirt pocket, so it was sure to stay there safely. The village coffee shop was around the next corner on her way home. She decided to stop in and enjoy a steaming cup of her favorite French roast café au lait.

Just about everyone knew everyone in Cracow. So, you could usually expect to share company with someone you knew at the coffee shop. This morning was no different. Sitting alone at a table for two in the far corner was Professor Georg Stein. He seemed to sense her presence. He looked up from the book he was reading before the door closed behind her.

Georg smiled and waved to her. Helena signaled that she would sit with him after ordering.

When Helena got to his table, he rose and pulled her chair out. "Madame, I am happy to have you join me."

"Thank you, Professor." She leaned closer to him and checked that no one else was close enough to overhear what she was dying to tell him. Once she was sure they were safe from prying ears, she said, "Georg, I've just come from 'Time and Again' where I collected a great deal of profit for Acorn Park. It should be enough to operate for a full six months! Isn't that wonderful?"

Georg was thunderstruck. He struggled to maintain decorum lest someone take notice and wonder at the cause of their excitement. "Helena! You have exceeded my expectations once again; I am very pleased! You deposited the cash, I presume."

"Of course, I have the deposit receipt right here," she said, patting her pocket.

Helena stopped talking as she noticed that Georg appeared to be in a trance. She said, "Georg? Are you alright?"

He snapped out of it and assumed a most serious demeanor. "I suddenly realize that within a fairly short period of time, we will not be seeing each other anymore, Helena."

When she was about to protest, he put up his hand and asked, "Do you mind if I am perfectly honest with you?"

Helena looked puzzled. She hoped he was not about to tell her that he was ill. She nodded. He said, "I have fallen in love with you. I am like a schoolboy. You possess my every waking thought. It is at once the happiest and the saddest I have ever been — happy to be in love with you and sad because we will not be together. I am even sadder knowing that war will completely sever our relationship. I will not know where you are after the Nazis attack."

He was searching Helena's face, waiting for her reaction. With no warning, tears slid down her cheeks. She could not decide which of her thoughts and feelings she should reveal to him.

Not knowing how to interpret her tears, Georg said, "Helena, I am sorry to upset you. Will you forgive me?"

She gained control of her emotions. "Please do not be sorry for being honest with me, Georg. I have been struggling with my feelings for you since the day you dropped by my cottage as we began planning Acorn Park. My tears are made of the same mixture of joy and sorrow that you feel. I know what you say is true — that we will lose contact in the near future."

She took a deep breath and gave him the opportunity to respond, "Thank you, Helena, for your candidness, and for letting me know that I have not been in love alone." He desperately wanted to take her hand, but he knew it would not be enough to satisfy him, and so he folded his hands on the table.

Seeing the gesture, Helena thought the man in front of her deserved much more than apparently was in store for him. That is, if they believed the intuitive thoughts they had. She wanted to reach out to him, to let him know how deeply she cared for him, but she knew she could not. Instead, she said, "We live in uncertain times and we will be called on to make sacrifices in the name of life and love. I so wish it were different for us, Georg. But I am happy we are together now. Please know that I will keep you in my heart, always."

They could say no more. The die had been cast, and they saw where fate had tossed it.

There was a crowd drifting in for lunch, mostly university students who knew both Georg and Helena. They shifted their posture and changed the conversation to intellectual topics.

Helena spotted Franz with Rebekka. They'd become the talk of the town as of late, the beautiful young professor and the handsome, successful architect. Georg saw them too. He leaned forward and said, "Those two — I'm jealous — they are so much in love."

Helena agreed, "Yes, they are a perfect match, aren't they?"

Franz called Rebekka's attention to Georg and Helena. The lovebirds approached their table. Franz was the first to speak. "Hello Lena, and Professor. Lena, I'm glad to find you here. I've invited Rebekka home for dinner tonight. I knew you would not mind. We have something to tell the family. I told her to come at 6:30. Is that alright?"

"Of course, Franz, it will be wonderful to have Rebekka with us. Georg, you'll join us, won't you?"

Georg looked serious. He would have loved to join them, but he did not think he could bear watching Helena and Jan together. After a moment, he said, "I'm sorry to say that I have a previous commitment. I hope you understand."

Helena said, "We do understand. We will give you a rain check." She left it at that, suspecting the true reason Georg declined.

Franz and Rebekka shared a look. They wondered what they had interrupted.

Georg said, "It's getting crowded, and we were just leaving, so please take our table. I'll say goodbye. Have a nice time tonight."

Helena said, "Yes, sit here, you two. Georg, I will walk out with you. Goodbye Rebekka. Franz, I will see you at home, and I will look forward to your news tonight!"

As Helena was leaving, she was stopped by Franz calling to her, "Lena! I forgot to tell you!"

She stopped and laughingly said, "Love will do that to you, little brother. What did you forget to tell me?"

"We just passed by Julia, Piotr and Michal Kinski. I invited Michal to dinner too. Okay with you?"

"You know how I feel about friends and family, Franz — the more the merrier. Besides, it's your night for KP duty, so why would I mind?"

Georg took note of Helena's humor and her impish grin. It was another moment he would not forget. Outside of the coffee shop, Georg and Helena said goodbye and walked in opposite directions.

***

Dinner at the Jasinski-Pawlowski cottage that night was exciting. It seemed everyone had good news. Helena's Papa sat at the head of the banquet table and Jan sat at the foot, although he insisted it was the second head of the table and not the foot.

After dessert was devoured, Franz and Rebekka cleaned up the dishes. When they'd finished, Jakob Pawlowski stood, wearing a devilish grin and said in his best announcer's voice, "Ahem, I believe my second son has something he'd like to tell us. Franz, go ahead and tell us something that will be a complete surprise!" There was a moment of chuckling.

Franz stood at his chair. He looked at Rebekka, took her hand and asked her to stand. With a shy smile, Rebekka stood saying, "Franzie, what are you doing?"

He answered with, "Bekka, you are the light of my life, the stars in my sky. I love you beyond words. Will you marry me?"

No one was the least bit surprised at the proposal—except Rebekka, that is. Confusion reigned until Franz said, "You're probably wondering how Rebekka could be surprised when none of you are. Well, I confess, I told her I was going to announce my plans to move to Paris. She did not even know that I had this. He reached into his vest, where he normally kept his pocket watch and produced a small black velvet box. As he opened it, he knelt on one knee in front of the astonished Rebekka. He repeated, "Rebekka Stein, will you marry me?"

Rebekka was crying, but she managed to squeak out her reply. "Yes, Franzie."

Clapping and cheering ensued while Franz slipped the sparkling one-carat emerald-cut diamond engagement ring onto her finger. It fit her perfectly.

Jakob stood again and said, "Congratulations, Franz, may you two be very happy." He lifted his vodka glass and said, "I propose a toast—to Rebekka and Franz!"

Jozef jumped up and said, "Yes! Congrats, little brother! But what's this about a move to Paris? You just slipped that little detail in!"

Franz was still holding Rebekka's hand. "Yes, I've accepted a temporary architectural assignment with the Paris Historical Society. I will leave in two weeks. Lena, how quickly can you plan our wedding? I intend to take a wife with me!"

Now Helena was surprised and visibly flustered. She blurted out, "I don't know if I can do your wedding justice on such short notice, Franz."

The twins and Michal nodded to each other. Piotr said, "Mama, you can do it. We will do everything you tell us to do — all three of us!"

Everyone at the table offered their help to pull together a smashing wedding celebration for Franz and Rebekka. They all agreed that Helena would organize and direct, and that it would be as simple as pie for her.

Helena gladly consented. They had nine days until the Sunday wedding. She glanced at her husband. Jan was looking at her with admiration. She looked back at him with an equal amount of admiration.

Jozef was standing. He, too, had news to share. He'd completed the Oak Secret Code. "This is the perfect code. No one, and I mean no one, will be able to break this code unless I personally train them." All eyes turned to the flip chart in the corner of the dining room.

OAK SECRET CODE

Abbreviations

C = Communications   W = Workers   F = Food
S = SafeHousing   Me = Medical   TL = Travel
M = Main Coord.   T = Transportation   LFU = Local & For. Univ.
CH = Children   DL = Domestic Liaison   Liaison
Y = Youth   FL = Foreign Liaison   LPG = Polish Govt

Pictographs

Meeting Points

Bird = Pulaski Farm
△ = Crystal Salt Mine East Entrance
~~ ● = Church Cemetery @ Dark
V△ = Bottom of Mtn By the rock

Mode of Travel

Violin = Train
Piano Keys = on foot
Flute = Horseback
Drum = Horsedrawn Cart

Actions

@ = at
8/8 = wait / don't wait
→ = take
← = leave
→← = meet
☆ = deliver
☽ = help/assist
; = then
☆m = deliver message herein

Time ●

= Time (A.M.)
= Time (P.M.)

● Count tree trunks for hour

Jozef was as proud as a peacock. "Here, I'll give you all an example of the code's simple perfection." He held up a pad of paper on which he'd written a message in Oak Code. It read:

Me + F @ bird piano →←— Y; star m

Jozef gave the meaning, "Medical and Food sections go to Pulaski Farm on foot to meet the Youth Group section, then deliver the message herein." He gave a second example that read:

Y star F + Me Ch @ ~~ •

He said, "This one means Youth Group delivers food and medicine to the Children's Safety section at the church cemetery at dark.

"Just as we committed our A.P. sections to memory, we will have to commit this code to memory so it remains secret. I will personally teach the code to each group member. We will be unable to use this code to communicate with Kazi and the others in America. Therefore, Helena will make short telephone calls to Kazi to inform them of the most important instructions."

Jakob stood and said, "Let's give our brilliant investigative journalist a round of applause! Thank you, Jozef!" When the clapping ceased, he said, "Now, who else has news for us this night?"

Julia cleared her throat and nudged Michal. Jakob said, "Don't be shy, Mr. Kinski. We won't bite. What is your news?"

Michal was clearly intimidated by the Jasinski-Pawlowski brood. Julia had told Helena Michal's news, so Helena volunteered to reply. "Michal has just been promoted to Lieutenant by our Cracow Police Department." Helena looked at him and said, "Congratulations, Michal. We are all very proud of you!"

Jan spoke next. "Yes, we are, Michal. Now, I have some news of my own. You are all invited to a bike race around

Acorn Park this Saturday at nine A.M., rain or shine. There will be only two entrants—Mr. Nigel Blake and me! I will tell you that we've made a wager that if he wins, which is very unlikely, I will drive him through the streets of Cracow in the rickshaw he made for himself. If I win, he will post signs throughout the park declaring me the better biker!"

Jan did not wait for a reaction. "Well now, if that's all of the announcements, let's retire to the living room and make some of our famous music, shall we?"

Jan took a seat at the piano bench with Julia at his side. Jozef and Helena prepared to play their violins. Sophia even had the bells she'd played at the Spring Social when she was four years old.

Everyone else found a couch, a chair or a spot on the floor to enjoy the making of another family memory in their precious cottage.

The evening ended on a high note with everyone looking forward to Saturday's event in Acorn Park.

***

On Saturday morning, many of the townspeople turned out for the bike race. Nigel had announced that it was the Good Biker vs. the Better Biker. Jan agreed, but of course with the opposite interpretation.

Georg was on hand to be the starter. At precisely 8:59.9, he shouted, "On your mark, get set, and GO!"

Nigel yelled to Jan above the cheers, "May the best man win, old boy!"

Jan did not waste his breath. He had no intention of losing and driving Nigel around in a rickshaw. He disappeared around the first curve in a flash, ahead of Nigel.

Nigel looked pained. He obviously did not expect Jan to get ahead of him.

The crowd did not care which man won. It was simply a fun event that got everyone together in the park on a beautiful weekend morning.

The course was two times around the park. At 9:08 Nigel came zooming over the halfway point, looking like he was straining to make up for lost time.

The onlookers watched him disappear around the first bend. The clock ticked...9:10, 9:11, 9:12...still no Jan. Finally, at 9:15 a biker rounded the last curve and raced toward the finish line. It was Nigel. He hopped off his bike, dropped it to the ground and plopped down on the grass to recover.

Georg walked to him and said, "Congrats, you won the race."

Nigel looked confused and said, "What do you mean? Jan was ahead of me all the way! Where is he?"

Helena was still looking for Jan. She ran over to Georg and Nigel. Trying to control her anger, she said through clenched teeth, "Nigel, what have you done to Jan? I knew this was a poor idea! Where is my husband?"

Nigel was very upset and could not find words to respond to her accusation. Georg scolded her, "Helena, Nigel has done nothing except challenge Jan to a bike race. How could you think him responsible for Jan's disappearance?"

Helena turned on Georg, "How dare you defend him! I count you responsible for whatever has happened to my husband—you brought this man into our lives!"

Michal, Julia and Piotr ran to Helena. They all screamed at once, "We found him, we need help to carry him. He got a flat tire and careened off into the marsh—hurry, hurry!"

Helena said, "I'll come too. Is he badly hurt?"

Piotr said, "No Mama, stay here. Michal, Georg and I can carry him."

Piotr looked at Georg. "Come with us."

Helena glared at Nigel before walking in the direction the trio had run. Julia stayed with her. No one noticed when Nigel picked up his bike and rode away.

The rest of the crowd anxiously waited to see Jan carried out of the marsh. Fifteen minutes later, they broke into cheers, mixed with laughter. Helena and Julia were very angry. It was no cause for laughter.

What they saw next was an amazing sight. Nigel was riding his bike with the rickshaw attached, with none other than Jan reclining in it! He obviously thought quickly when he heard that Jan was injured. Nigel had gone home to get his rickshaw. Piotr and Georg were following close behind, carrying Jan's bent bike.

Jan's expression was a mix of pain, embarrassment and delight. Nigel stopped in front of Helena. Jan gingerly got out of the rickshaw with Georg's help.

Before Helena could say anything, Jan blurted out, "Next Saturday we'll have a rematch! Darned bike tire anyway! When it blew, I fell off, and I think I sprained my ankle."

Helena spat, "You will be doing no such thing, Jan Jasinski!" She looked from Jan, to Georg, to Nigel. "Thank you for helping Jan. I apologize to you, Nigel, and to you too, Georg."

Nigel shook hands with Jan, "Let's call this a draw, Jan. I'm sorry you are hurt."

"Why thank you, Nigel! You are a jolly good sport," he said with a poor British accent. "Anyway, all's well that ends well, eh?"

Humbly, Nigel responded, "You're welcome, Jan. Can I drive you home?"

Jan said, "No, thank you. Piotr will help me walk from here."

The crowd disbursed, and Jan limped home with his family.

***

The following week flew by. There was so much to do. All the Acorn Park sections were meeting to finalize plans and Helena was especially busy organizing plans for Franz and Rebekka's wedding.

It was not until Wednesday that Helena had a reason to meet with Georg. She'd not seen him since the bike race. She asked him to meet her at the coffee shop to go over some A.P. matters.

Georg was seated at the corner table when Helena arrived. There was no one else in the shop, leaving them a bit of privacy.

He was relieved to be greeted with a smile. "Hello, Helena. How is Jan's ankle?"

She responded with a laugh, "Oh, it's healing; along with his ego, that is! He assures me he will be able to dance at Franz and Rebekka's wedding on Sunday. As you know, it will be a small group of close friends and family, but we must have music and dancing for a wedding!"

Georg pressed a hand to his gut, thinking of seeing Helena dancing with her husband. "Of course, we must have music and dancing, and I'm sure it will be lovely! I could not be happier for Rebekka and Franz."

Helena and Georg spent the next half hour exchanging information they'd been given by the spokespersons of the various Acorn Park sections.

Helena looked at her watch as she scooped up her papers. "If I don't hurry, I will be late for my meeting with Rebekka about the wedding. I will see you on Sunday, Georg. Goodbye."

He rose from his chair, "I must go too. It's been very nice seeing you, Helena." He held the door for her. She thanked him and rushed off.

He watched her leave and muttered, "She's always walking away from me. Maybe one day she will be walking toward me." He sighed at the unlikely prospect.

***

Franz and Rebekka's wedding day was perfect. There was not a cloud in the sky, the temperature was an unseasonably warm 70 degrees and the closest family and dearest friends were in attendance.

Franz had visited the village priest to arrange for a last-minute church wedding. The Monsignor informed him that he would surely accommodate the late date. However, he would not consider marrying a non-Christian to one of his parishioners.

Franz knew it would be an uphill battle to convince him to perform a church wedding to Rebekka, as she was half Jewish. But he was not prepared for a flat-out *no*. It seemed nonsensical to Franz, who was somewhat of a nonconformist.

After that, he went to City Hall and asked for a Magistrate to perform their marriage ceremony.

Franz happily married Rebekka in front of a Magistrate in the cottage garden on a beautiful Sunday in August. After they took their vows, while placing the wedding ring on her finger, he recited the poem he'd written for her:

> As I marry my Princess, she becomes my true Queen.
> All our past lives flow into our here and now.
> Together we shall find what destiny has in mind.

Rebekka put her hand on Franz's heart and responded:

> I have searched for you from then until now
> always hearing your voice guiding me to this one moment.
> Long ago and far away, we shared this promise;
> to allow our hearts to be led by our souls
> from then until now.
> And so, we are here;
> our promise fulfilled, as again we become One.

The couple shared a long kiss while their family and friends marveled at what they heard. There was not a dry eye, it was a beautiful moment.

It was Jakob's task as Papa of the Groom to be the first to congratulate the newlyweds. Loudly, he announced, "Congratulations to Mr. and Mrs. Pawlowski!" His voice cracked with emotion as he recalled his own Papa making the same announcement so many years ago when he married his Marta.

He ended with, "Let's all eat and be merry!"

They moved inside to the dining room, where the wedding feast was waiting. It had been prepared largely by Piotr, Julia and Michal with the help of Jozef and Sophia. And with Helena's numerous "what to do" lists, of course. Bread and salt was between the place settings of the Bride and Groom. It was a traditional offering from Jan and Helena.

The guests knew where to sit. Helena had designed a place card for each. She had been careful to keep the tiny crystal place card holders a secret so that they would be a surprise to Franz and Rebekka. She'd seen the holders the last time she visited 'Time and Again.' She knew immediately she had to buy the lead crystal treasures. There were twenty-four of them—more than enough for the guests at the wedding. As she'd written each name in her flowing calligraphy, she could feel the joy of the upcoming event and the mounting excitement.

The music was provided by Jan on the harpsichord and by his Mama at the piano.

Georg was Rebekka's only family member present, so he danced the first dance with her while Helena danced with Franz. As was tradition, midway through the waltz, they switched partners and the Bride was given to the Groom by Georg. That left Helena to dance with Georg.

She glanced around the room, noticing that everyone was having a wonderful time and involved in their own little groups.

Georg was holding her appropriately at a short arm's length—close enough so they could have a private conversation. He looked into her eyes. Helena thought she might melt into him.

His words stunned and saddened her. "Helena, my dear Helena. It breaks my heart to tell you that I must say goodbye to you. I am sorry to leave you with the coordination of Acorn Park. However, I must go. I do not know when I will see you again."

The dance called for him to twirl her. When they came back face to face, Helena gasped, "Where are you going, and why now?" She surprised herself by saying, "I don't want you to go, Georg." She stopped herself from saying more.

The dance was coming to an end and Georg had only time to say, "I cannot tell you where or why I go, only that it is you, Lena, who is always in my heart."

With that, the dance ended and Helena watched as Georg bid the Bride and Groom good night.

She turned her attention to Jan. She could not bear to watch as Georg walked out into the night and out of her life. Perhaps forever.

Chapter Thirteen

THE LAST WEEK OF AUGUST 1939

It was late on Tuesday night by the time Jan and Helena returned from an emergency meeting of the Acorn Park Underground. At church on the previous Sunday, Helena had received information through Jozef's sources that the Nazis were set to attack Poland sooner than A.P. was prepared for. That prompted a family meeting on Sunday evening. They wanted to be sure that the Jasinski's and Pawlowski's knew their role, should the worst happen. They had decided as a group that another meeting would be called for Tuesday evening, after dark.

***

Walking toward the church felt somewhat like trudging to an execution. The full moon added to the ominous atmosphere. The Nazis would not likely attack under a full moon. Their modus operandi was to attack under the cover of total darkness — like the dark soul of the Nazis.

Helena felt the absence of Franz and Rebekka, Kazi and Julia, and Georg. More than that, every section of their organization was now run by one or two members instead of three, as originally intended.

The meeting began at 9:15 P.M. The first order of business was the reorganization of the sections. Helena had drawn up a new chart showing a more streamlined underground in light of the fact that six of their nineteen members, including Miss Milewski, were elsewhere.

Helena walked to the center of the small half-circle of A.P. members. "You all know that it looks like we will be putting our underground into operation soon. Please look at the chart of our reorganization. It is simplified into three pyramids. After tonight, the Main Coordination section will become unnecessary. It has been replaced by the first combination pyramid, comprised of Communications and Safe Housing. Note that Safe Housing is now known as Temporary Housing because we will not likely be able to stay in Poland after the attack. That first pyramid will be run by me, Jozef and Sophia.

"The second combination pyramid will be comprised of the Food, Medical, Travel, Children's Safety and Transportation sections. Doc and Mary Kaminski, Big Jan, Nigel and Mary Jasinski will keep those sections running.

"The third and last pyramid includes the Domestic Liaison, Local and Foreign Universities, Workers Employment and the Polish Government Liaison sections. Piotr and Julia, Michal, Big Stan and Jan will commandeer that pyramid.

"It should be easy for members of these combined sections to stay in discreet contact with each other. Each of the newly formed sections will now be known simply as #1, #2 and #3.

"Now we'll hear from Jozef, who is the spokesman for #1."

Jozef slowly walked to where Helena had been standing. It was obvious to all that the enormity of the situation weighed heavily on him. He looked around at each member, took a deep breath, straightened his shoulders and began. "First, I'd like to say that it is an honor to be part of this amazing group of people. I've spent quality time with each of you teaching the Oak Code. I am confident you all know the code well."

He pointed to the chart that Helena had placed at the front of the room. "The three-pyramid reorganization simplifies our secret code. Instead of letters denoting fourteen sections, we can now use one of three numbers to signify which section a message refers to.

"That being said, let's talk about Safe Housing, now known as Temporary Housing. We've set up two primary housing sites for any of us who become displaced.

"The first site is actually within the crystal salt mine south of town. During the last few months, Big Stan Jasinski has been operating a midnight crew to open a new entrance to one of the underground chapels. That entrance is well hidden. I will caution anyone using the temporary housing of the crystal salt mine *not* to walk directly to the secret entrance. That way, if you are seen, you will not lead the enemy to our safe haven.

"That also goes for our second temporary housing site. That one is at the Pulaski Farm just to the west of town. It's the abandoned barn attached to and behind the pig barn. If you did not know the second barn was there, you'd never see it. It's secluded in a pine grove. It's sort of unpleasant to walk through the pig barn to get there, but I don't suppose the pigs will mind very much!"

There was a moment of snickering and someone made some pig noises.

"Farmer Pulaski is on board with our plans and if we need to leave Cracow, he and his wife will join us.

"Both of the housing sites can accommodate up to twenty-five people. They've been stocked with food, bedding and medical supplies. If you go to one of these sites, you will have to travel with very few personal belongings. And, it pains me greatly to say that we cannot accommodate family pets."

Someone gasped. It was Sophia. They'd just adopted a puppy. Jozef turned to his wife and said, "Yes, Sophia, I know that leaving Jasper will be devastating. I wish there could be another way, but we must save ourselves. Pets leave a trail, they can be noisy, and they are not equipped to be confined inside."

Sophia sat back in her chair, with tears streaming down her face. Everyone felt the blast of reality. It hit hard.

Jozef said, "To finish up with #1, our temporary housing sites will be manned by the spokesmen for #2 and #3; Big Jan is spokesman for #2 and closest to Pulaski Farm and Big Stan is spokesman for #3 and closest to the crystal salt mine site. Since these sites are temporary, Big Jan and Big Stan will be in charge of moving us completely out of Poland to safety at the proper time. Obviously, this will not be an easy feat, but it's being worked on, in concert with our #1. Thank you. Now Big Jan will tell you about the new #2."

Jozef sat next to Sophia and put a consoling arm around her shoulders.

Big Jan stood. He was among the oldest members of A.P. and determined to keep his family safe. He said, "I have only one thing to say. We are set for the fight of our lives, and we will see our way to safety by the grace of God. We will rely on each other—stay brave!" He emphasized the last two words and it seemed as if his belief inspired hope and belief.

Big Stan rose as tall as his brother, but with far more feistiness. His voice boomed, "We are proud Polish! No one takes that from us! We are planning to outsmart the Nazi devils and that is *precisely* what we will do—with ingenuity and good old-fashioned Polish determination! We will *not* fail if we stick together!"

He looked around the room at his friends and family. He took note that Nigel looked somewhat sheepish and out of place. Since Georg and Rebekka were not there, Nigel was the only foreigner in the group.

Suddenly, all eyes were on Nigel. He felt compelled to say something, although he had no clue what that might be. Slowly, he stood, paused, and in his strange English-Polish accent, said, "I am not sure that you all know this about me, but I am not Polish."

When everyone laughed, he knew what to say next. He continued, "However, I *am proud* to be part of this Polish group!"

With a smirk, he added, "It's appropriate that I am part of #2 involving travel, transportation, and medical because my rickshaw *did* serve as the ambulance for a certain someone we all know and love!"

He waited until the jeers and cheers that were pointed toward Jan died down before he continued. "Professor Georg Stein asked me to join your group, knowing that he may not be able to stay here himself."

That information gave Helena a jolt. She could not figure out how Georg would know such a thing, months in advance. Or for that matter, how Nigel himself fit into all of this.

Nigel continued, "In any event, I *do* have your best interests in mind and I intend to work to keep all of you safe. Thank you for accepting me."

He sat, secure in the knowledge that he'd convinced everyone of his sincerity.

His self-satisfaction met with a stone wall. Helena looked at him with an intensity he'd not seen from her before. He felt his gut tighten. Could she know what his true intention was?

Helena was on high alert. She recalled asking Georg what he knew about this Nigel Blake character. He never did answer to her satisfaction. That led her to have serious concerns about Georg's loyalty to their organization. Was there an internal plot afoot that would compromise all of them?

As Jan and Helena prepared for bed that night, she voiced her concerns.

His response was, "Lena, your mind is working overtime. It is perfectly normal to experience fears in the face of imminent danger. Let's go to sleep. Everything will look better after a good night's sleep."

Jan kissed his wife and turned the light off.

Helena knew by his breathing that Jan was immediately asleep. However, her brain was awake and churning—trying to read between the lines of what Nigel had said at the meeting. Her last waking thought was that if Nigel was a spy, that must mean Georg…

When Helena awoke, it was with a clear head. Everything did *not* look better as Jan suggested. In fact, everything looked considerably worse. With Nigel in their group, he was privy to the secret code *and* to their temporary housing sites. To complicate matters, Helena seemed to be the only one who was aware of Nigel's intentions. And where in God's name was Georg?

She was in a quandary. Then she knew what she had to do. She would take matters into her own hands — and quickly. She hatched a plan that she would implement when the time was exactly right.

She was beginning to feel better, knowing that the problem of Nigel was soon to be solved.

RE-ORGANIZATION

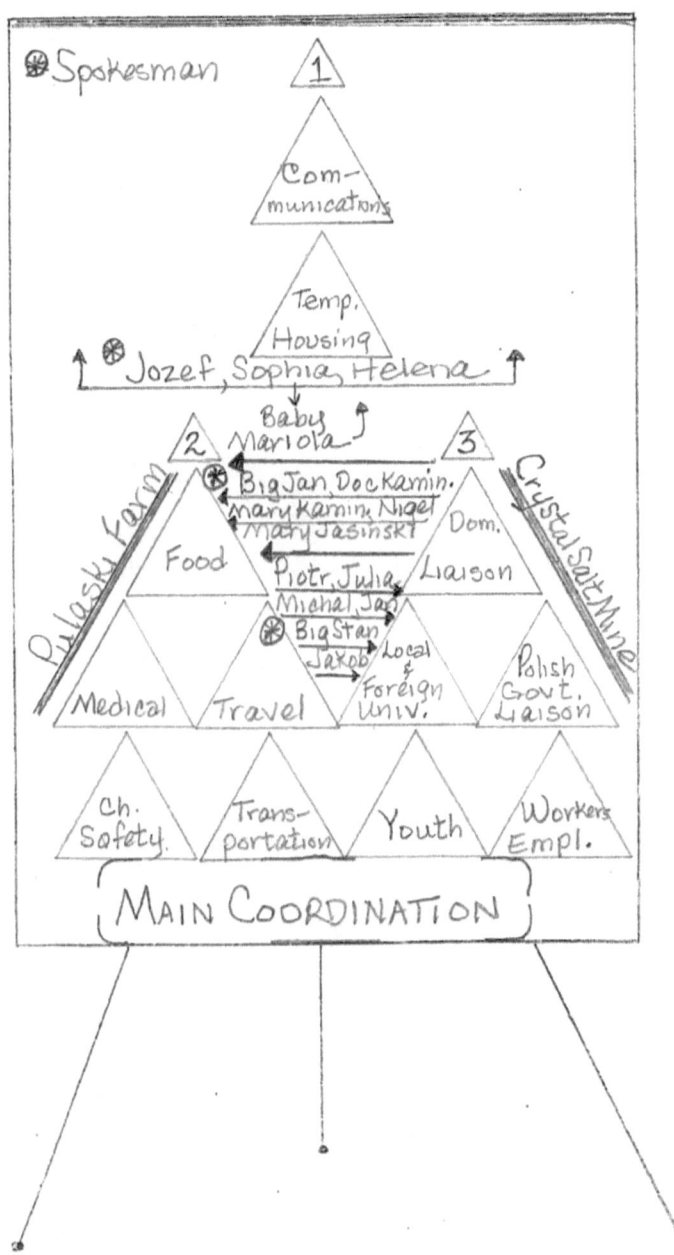

Chapter Fourteen

THE ARRIVAL OF SEPTEMBER 1, 1939

Friday, September the first of 1939...a date **never** to be forgotten. It was the beginning of yet another war for the beautiful towns, cities and countryside of Poland.

It was the war that signaled the onset of war for the entire world. Even though the First World War was referred to as the "war to end all wars," a Second World War was visited upon the earth and it began with the attack upon the brave and proud Polish people.

The next morning, every able-bodied man and boy took up arms against the Nazis. That included Jan, Jozef and Piotr. Michal stayed in Cracow to work with the local police.

A.P. Underground was now reduced to nine local members. Helena watched her husband, her brother and her son go off to fight for all that was sacred to them...no long goodbyes, only *FORWARD, MARCH!*

She took no time to feel sorry for herself. She set about putting her plan into action. She waited until everyone in the cottage was sound asleep. Then, first things first — she had to disguise herself so that she would be taken for a German soldier. She went to her hidden satchel and pulled out the scissors. She took a long look at her beautiful blonde hair, which had been carefully braided, and with two giant snips of the scissors, there was two inches of hair left. She stashed the severed braid in her satchel and after washing her hair in the kitchen sink, she was satisfied that she no longer looked feminine.

On to the next layer. She reached to the bottom of her satchel and pulled out a Nazi uniform complete with insignia, hat and boots.

She recalled how she found the uniform. She had visited Hanna's shop looking for a uniform that would pass for German. Hanna said, "I think I have just what you are looking for, Lena. Come with me."

Helena followed Hanna into the storeroom. There, under an assortment of draperies, was a large wooden trunk. Hanna tossed the drapes aside, threw open the trunk, and pulled out two complete German uniforms. One set dropped to the floor, and Hanna held up the other set. "Here, Lena, this looks like it will fit you — try it."

The adrenaline pumped through Helena's body. She was going to pull off her plot to fool the Nazis into thinking that she was one of them! She reminded herself of the members of Hitler's Youth Squad whom she'd overheard in the coffee shop. When she looked into the old dusty mirror, she realized she looked very much like the one called Dietter!

"Hanna, I don't know where you got these uniforms, but this one is perfect! How much do I owe you?"

Hanna threw her arms around Helena and said, "Please consider this my gift to you, dear Lena. I hope whatever you are planning to do works out!"

Both of them were crying silently. Neither said what they were thinking — that they may never see each other again.

Helena quickly changed back into her own clothes, hugged Hanna, said goodbye, grabbed the uniform, folded it into her satchel and quickly walked home to hide it.

Helena brought her thoughts back to the present. By the time she was outfitted in the Nazi uniform, her freshly cut hair was dry. She did not look at herself in the mirror as she tiptoed to the guest room; she knew what she looked like.

She had told Julia she would be leaving early in the morning for a meeting, so she would not panic when her mama was not at home.

Helena sat in her mama's rocker in the guest room. She would wait until normal business hours to go to the bank. She hoped to get the A.P. money out of the bank before it was looted by the Nazis.

She gently rocked back and forth, remembering her mama sitting in the rocker doing needlework and chatting with her. They'd had some of their best talks beside this rocker.

Helena dozed off, dreaming of the Christmas in their cottage when she was five years old. The sun was just rising to shine on the newly fallen snow; it was not fully light out yet. Little Lena had been told to stay in her bed until daylight. She kept squeezing her eyes shut, hoping each time she opened them that it would finally be time to get up and run to the Christmas tree to see what Santa Claus had left for her.

When it was just about time, she heard a strange whimper, her bedroom door flew open, and a puppy jumped onto her bed and licked her face! Oh, what joy she felt—but how did Santa Claus know her secret wish was for a little brown fluffy puppy? She'd only told her mama.

Helena sighed in her sleep and smiled.

The sunlight on her face broke into her dream and woke her. The contrast between memory of that Christmas and the realization that she was dressed as a Nazi, threatened to knock the breath out of her. As she struggled to cope with her present reality, it seemed as if the old rocker moved by itself.

She heard her mama say, "Lena, calm yourself. I am with you. Just stick to your plan with confidence. I promise that you and your daughter will remain safe." As Helena formulated a question to ask her, the chair stopped rocking. She no longer heard her mama, but she did feel her presence.

That gave her confidence. Quietly, she left her cottage through the garden gate.

She headed for the bank, walking with a purpose, hearing the heels of her boots clicking against the pavement. As she walked, she met eyes with no one.

Downtown was in a state of quiet chaos. German soldiers were milling around as if they had not received their orders yet. That was a good thing for Helena.

Elena Bjorn sat alone at her desk with her head in her hands. Helena knew the presence of a Nazi would scare Elena greatly. She tried to lessen the blow by speaking softly, "Excuse me, Ma'am. I wish to close an account."

Thankfully, Elena recognized Helena's voice right away. "Of course. What is the account number?"

Helena rattled off the account number from memory, and Elena rushed to the teller's cage. Because the account was being liquidated, it took a full six minutes for Elena to return. It was a very long six minutes. Helena controlled her emotions with slow breaths. She heard a commotion at the main entrance and discovered that the Nazis were not allowing residents to enter the bank. She'd gotten there just in time. But getting out of the bank might prove to be difficult.

Elena finally returned. She whispered, "I'm sorry to give you so many small bills, but this is all we have on hand. Go now, and may God be with you, Lena."

Helena was prepared to stash the numerous bills. The uniform jacket was slightly big on her, so filling the pockets made it fit better.

She dared not take any more time inside the bank. Helena locked eyes with her. "I wish I could help you, Elena. Goodbye."

With a huge lump in her throat, Helena purposefully blasted out of the main entrance, surprising the young Nazis who were guarding it.

She glared at them and said in perfect German, "Get back to work, you morons!" They snapped to attention and saluted her.

With no expression and no response, Helena walked down the block to Hanna's shop. The door was locked and the sign read, "Closed. Please Call Again."

Helena looked around and saw that no one was nearby. She pulled her jacket sleeve down around her hand and punched out a small pane of glass in the door. Then she reached in and easily unlocked the door.

She stepped inside, closing the door behind her. If Hanna was there, Helena knew where to find her. She went directly to the storeroom. Looking left and right, she approached the trunk where the uniforms had been found. Very slowly, she opened the lid, and there in that big old musty wooden trunk was Hanna — curled up and sobbing.

Helena reached for her. "Hanna! It's me, Lena. Come, you will be safe with me."

Hanna's sobs turned into nervous laughter. She said, "But Lena, how can I get past the Nazis in the street?"

Helena had a ready reply. "Don't worry, we'll make it appear that I am taking you to their command headquarters for interrogation. You will have to struggle a bit. I will have to scream at you in German, and I'm sorry if I hurt you, but if we don't make this realistic, we'll both be captured. Are you ready?"

Without waiting for Hanna's reply, Helena said, "Mach schnell!" Hanna did not speak German, but she assumed correctly that it meant "Hurry up!"

She grabbed Hanna by her arm, practically dragging her out the door into the street. They got as far as the village coffee shop before gaining the attention of a large group of German soldiers. Hanna was genuinely crying.

Helena chose the soldier who appeared to be in charge and stopped in front of him. She got right in his face and with venom in her voice said, "What is your name, Lieutenant?" Helena knew enough about insignia to know that the soldier was not a Lieutenant.

With a salute, he said, "I am *Captain* Heinz, Sir!"

Ignoring the correction, Helena said, "Well! Lieutenant Heinz, shall I report your negligence to the General, or will you get your useless troops out of my sight?"

With a heel click and another salute, Heinz scurried off with all the soldiers.

The Nazis had set up their General Government at Cracow's beautiful Wawel Castle. Since it was on the way to Helena's cottage, none of the soldiers would think it was odd that this Nazi should be dragging a citizen in that direction.

Helena was careful not to walk past the bank again. She did not want Hanna to see that her mama was in trouble.

As soon as the two were out of sight of the soldiers, they ran the short distance to the cottage, burst through the garden gate and into the kitchen.

Julia was just walking into the kitchen with a small suitcase. When she saw a soldier and a woman she did not know, she backed up and screamed. Helena stopped and said in the most normal voice she could muster, "Julia, it's Mama."

Julia ran to her mama and threw her arms around her, saying, "Mama! I was so scared; I did not know if you were captured, you were gone so long!"

Julia paused and blinked disbelievingly, "Mama! What have you done to your hair?"

Helena said, "I know, I don't like it either, but it had to be done. Julia, this is Hanna Bjorn. I told you about her and that her mama was friends with my mama. Hanna, this is my daughter, Julia."

Hanna put her arms around Helena's only daughter. Words were not necessary; the bond was already there. Julia felt it too.

Helena slipped into the guest room to change into her own clothes. She left the money in the jacket's uniform pockets. She went back into the kitchen wearing gardening clothes and her apron with Katrynka in the pocket. She wore a babushka with her clipped braid attached to the back. The head covering was pushed far enough forward to cover her hairline. She felt a little more like herself, but not completely.

Helena's papa came into the kitchen looking as if he hadn't slept for days. In fact, he had not. Helena poured him a cup of coffee while Julia introduced him to Hanna.

When Jakob heard who the young woman was, tears appeared in his eyes. He said, "It is an honor to meet the daughter of Elena Bjorn." He gauged from her expression that he should not ask how her mama was.

Hanna smiled through her tears and allowed him to give her one of his famous bear hugs. In that moment, she felt safe. Jakob held Hanna at arm's length and said, "Do not worry, Little One. You will be safe with us." He meant it, and she believed it.

For the next hour, a steady stream of A.P. members came through the garden gate into the cottage. Everyone knew that they would have to leave their homes now that the Nazis were taking over. Sophia and Baby Mariola were the first to arrive, laden with personal belongings. Out of the back of the stroller jumped Jasper. Sophia, looking sorrowful, said, "I could not imagine leaving my second baby alone — he's just a puppy!"

Julia stepped forward to help Sophia. She picked Jasper up and said, "Don't you worry, Jasper Boy, we'll take you with us no matter what! But I'm telling you now, you better not bark, okay?"

The puppy's concerned look turned to joy, and he seemed to understand completely. He replied with a silent closed-mouth bark and a lick for Julia. It was a lighthearted moment.

Big Stan was the next to arrive along with Michal. They were out of breath from running. Big Stan said, "Our cave entrance is swarming with Nazis. We'll all have to use the Pulaski Farm!" He did not speculate on how the Nazis would have knowledge of the well-hidden cave entrance, although everyone had the same thought. No one had seen Nigel.

Big Jan and Mary Jasinski came in just behind Doc and Mary Kaminski. Sophia's Mama asked to hold her grandbaby and Doc hugged his precious daughter, Sophia.

The elder Jasinski's were suffering as much as anyone. Their own son and grandson had gone to fight the Nazis, along with Helena's brother, Jozef.

Now the group numbered ten plus Baby Mariola, Hanna, Jasper, plus all the personal belongings that could be carried or pushed.

Still, there was no sign of Nigel. They all thought the worst of him and the worst *for* him.

There was a tiny tap on the kitchen door. Helena peeked out of the window and recognized Michal's mama and papa. She quickly opened the door and invited them in. She said, "Mr. and Mrs. Kinski! I see you have your suitcases. You are welcome to come with us to a safe place."

Michal Kinski, Sr gave Helena a great hug and said, "Bless you, Helena!"

Anna Kinski dropped her bags and rushed to her son. "Michal, I am so happy you are safe. We will be together now, thanks to this wonderful group! Oh, and there is Julia. It's so good to see you, dear."

Julia hugged the woman who would become her mama by marriage, although she and Michal had not shared the news with their families yet. They wanted to wait until everyone was safe.

Jakob called for everyone's attention. He thought Helena had done enough for the moment. He took charge saying, "The next thing for us to do is to get every one of us to the

Pulaski Farm without being seen by the Nazis. It's a ten-minute walk under normal conditions. We will wait until dark. I suggest a brisk pace so the walk is five minutes maximum.

"Michal, I will ask you to begin a discreet lookout for Nazis, just before dark. I will give you my binoculars."

Michal said, "Yes, Sir. I can do that."

Jakob continued, "Between now and then, let's feed everyone. Julia, I will ask you to collect all the fresh vegetables from the garden that you can manage. Vegetables will come in handy. We will be rationing our food as we do not know how long we will be hiding."

Doc Kaminski spoke up, "My wife will help Sophia with the baby and I'll take care of the puppy."

Jakob said, "Helena, if there is anything else you wish to pack, perhaps Jan's Mama will help you."

Helena frowned. "Papa, the only thing I would really like to take is Mama's rocker. But I know it is too big."

Big Stan knew how important the rocker was to Helena. He said, "Nonsense, Child! I will disassemble and pack it for you! Just find me a bag that is at least 24" wide and 12" deep."

Helena was jubilant. "Oh, Uncle Stan! Can you do that?"

Jakob smiled to see Helena happy about something. He said, "Okay, that's it for now. Let's eat!"

The rest of the afternoon passed peacefully into the evening. Just before dark, Michal set out with binoculars to hide in the nearby brush and watch for Nazis. Half an hour later, he came back and reported the last truckload of Nazis passed twenty minutes earlier. The group agreed it was safe to walk to the temporary safe haven at Pulaski Farm.

No one talked. They all gathered suitcases, boxes and packages and began the solemn walk away from the only home they had ever known. Within five minutes, everyone was in the hidden barn in their own little niche.

The baby and the puppy slept peacefully while the adults gathered for a planning session. They needed to come to a consensus regarding when and how to get to a new home, but also *where* to go. These were big questions and everyone had an opinion.

Talking lasted for hours until it was determined there was no agreement. They decided to sleep on it and take up discussions in the morning.

Helena was bone-weary but could not sleep. The core of her family was somewhere fighting the Nazis. She sighed deeply and tried to relax her mind and body. Finally, she drifted off to sleep, hearing Jan's voice telling her he was safe and Piotr and Jozef were safe too. When she woke a few hours later, she wasn't sure if she'd dreamed Jan's voice or if he'd communicated with her telepathically. She decided it was the latter and she felt a little better.

Helena was the last to awaken. When she opened her eyes, she saw Hanna playing with Jasper. "Where is everyone, Hanna?"

Hanna said, "The men went out behind the barn to see what resources might be at our disposal. Michal is on watch with the binoculars, hiding beside the road. He will alert us with a bird call if the Nazis are nearby. The women are entertaining baby Mariola."

Helena looked at Hanna. "You look sad. Are you alright?"

Hanna's eyes welled up with tears. "Yes, Lena. I am as alright as I can be. My heart is broken for my Mama and my Papa. He is in Sweden and does not know what has happened to us."

There was no way to sugarcoat the reality of Elena Bjorn's fate – she was Jewish and now in the clutches of the Nazis. Helena did the only thing she could do. She hugged Hanna and let her cry.

By midmorning, the group had come to two decisions. First, they should leave as soon as possible and second, they would begin life anew in America. The decision as to how they would get to America was impossibly complicated. There was no safe way out of Poland at that point.

Big Stan said, "There is no good way out of Poland. So then, I suggest we stay within Polish territory and make our way north along the Danzig Corridor to the Baltic Sea. From there, we'll pay for a boat to get us to Sweden and hope that it is still a neutral country!"

Helena's Papa responded with skepticism, "Stan, it is a great distance from here to Danzig and we would be traveling along the German border. If the Nazis are in Cracow, they have invaded all along our western border for sure. It does not seem that we have any option for safe travel."

Helena cleared her throat and everyone turned to her. "What I am about to say does not make logical sense. I do not have any idea how I know this, but someone will guide us to safety. I don't know who or when, or how. I simply know it is true."

Everyone agreed it was a nice sentiment, but nothing to hang the proverbial hat on.

Doc Kaminski said, "I wish my son-in-law was here. His investigative skills are near criminal! Jozef would know how to get us out of this mess!"

No sooner was that said than Jozef and Piotr burst through the barn door, completely startling everyone in the barn. Their clothing was torn and they were covered in soot. One looked worse than the other. They both collapsed on the nearest hay bale coughing and choking.

Helena ran to her son, and Sophia ran to her husband. Big Jan ran to get water from the pump behind the barn.

Helena gently hugged her son, "Where is your Papa, Piotr?"

Piotr shook his head and with unimaginable sadness, said, "I don't know, Mama. The Nazis were all around us. They burned down the shed we were in! Papa told us to make a run for it while he ran in the opposite direction as a diversion. We heard shots, but I don't know what happened to him!"

Helena said, "How did you get here safely?"

A voice was heard from the open barn door. "I helped them." It was Nigel, dressed in a Nazi uniform looking none the worse for wear!

Jakob turned to Nigel. "Just who *are* you, anyway?"

He answered first in Polish, then in impeccable German, for Helena's benefit. "I am a double agent, a triple agent, really. British Intelligence sent me to work on behalf of Poland by becoming a Nazi spy."

Helena approached Nigel. He wasn't sure if she intended to slap him or kiss him. She did neither. She asked, "Do you know the fate of Jan, Nigel?"

Nigel bowed his head and said, "I'm so sorry, Helena. I do not know. I was busy keeping the Nazis from finding all of you here and did not get to that shed in time to save all three of them. Jan made the correct choice to run toward the east. That enabled me to lead Jozef and Piotr to you, although it did take all night to get here without being seen."

Michal ran in the back door of the barn shouting, "A Nazi! There's a Nazi coming!" He stopped dead in his tracks when he saw Nigel. "It's you! What are you, a spy or something?"

Nigel gave him a mock salute, "That's right, young man, and I have brought Piotr and Jozef with me! What do you think of that?"

Both Michal and his Papa shook Nigel's hand and thanked him. Obviously, Nigel had risked his life to save Piotr and Jozef.

Helena stood aside and recalled all the clues from the past months that indicated Nigel's true identity. Now she knew why Georg did not tell her what he knew about Nigel. But that begged a question. Where is Georg in all of this?

She did not expect to get the answer from Nigel, but she asked anyway. "Do you know where Georg is, and what he is doing?"

Nigel pursed his lips, gauging his response. "Yes, Helena. I do."

She was quickly growing weary of this charade, but she refused to show it. "Will you tell me what you know of Georg, Nigel?"

With a look that Helena could not interpret, Nigel responded, "It is best for all of you if you do not know where Georg is right now."

Helena let out a sigh and reached her hand out to Nigel. He surprised her by pulling her to his chest and whispering in her ear, "Georg sends his regards and says he will see you soon. Do not react, Helena."

She broke the embrace and said, "Thank you for what you've done for us, Nigel." Her heart was beating wildly, knowing she would see Georg soon. But it was dreadfully bittersweet knowing that her husband was likely dead.

She suddenly felt faint and sat down as she thought of what Jan must have endured to save his son and her brother.

She was in a semi-conscious state when she heard her mama's voice. "Lena, your Jan is with me. We will both help you arrive safely in your new home. Remember, I sent Georg to help you too. We will work in tandem. It will not be easy. Just go step by step and stay strong, my darling daughter."

Hanna was shaking her. "Lena! Lena! Are you alright? Can you hear me?"

"Yes, Hanna, I am okay. I just felt faint for a moment. So much excitement. I am okay now, thank you."

Helena's papa had been watching her. He seemed to know the cause of her fainting spell. Their eyes met and Jakob automatically knew that her mama had spoken to her. He had no need to make it logical. It simply was what it was. He would always be with his Marta — heart and soul.

While Jozef and Piotr went out back to clean up at the pump, the others prepared dinner.

Mr. and Mrs. Pulaski no longer felt safe in their farmhouse, so they joined the group in the barn. They arrived looking glum.

Farmer Pulaski jokingly said, "I love what you've done with the place!" His wife cheered up and said, "We are glad to be with you. You've created a festive atmosphere here!"

Farmer Pulaski saw Nigel lounging on a hay bale and shielded his wife, saying, "Who the hell is *that* man?"

Jakob explained who Nigel was and that he had saved Piotr and Jozef. He added that Nigel was part of Acorn Park and he would help them travel to safety.

"Please, sit with me while dinner is being prepared. I will tell you what I know of our plan, and you can decide if you want to join us."

Afterward, Mr. and Mrs. Pulaski walked outside to discuss what Jakob told them. Mrs. Pulaski believed they could stay hidden in the barn until it was safe to go back into their house. Mr. Pulaski was able to convince her that Poland would not be safe for a long time, and they should join their fellow Cracovians. He enticed her with the thought of starting a new farm in a free land. For her, it was what tipped the scales in favor of leaving with the A.P. group. He hugged her and said, "I'm starving. Let's join our friends for what may be our last supper in Cracow, shall we?"

As they walked back into the barn, Farmer Pulaski nodded to Jakob and gave him a thumbs-up sign.

Helena was back on her game and ready to plan. She took a head count. After adding Hanna, Mr. and Mrs. Kinski and Farmer and Mrs. Pulaski, the local A.P. numbered eighteen plus a baby and a puppy. The distant A.P. members numbered six, including Georg, Julia and Kazi, Anna Milewski, not forgetting her mama, and now Jan.

Nigel, Helena and Jozef got together in the furthest corner of the barn. The bare light bulb provided an appropriately harsh light.

Helena began. "It seems our previous planning has been for nothing."

Jozef added, "Yes, and so much for the secret Oak Code."

Nigel had a different take on their situation. "Not so fast, you two. You created a strong group that can survive because of the structure and support system you put together. As for the Oak Code, we may need it in the future, at least the guts of the code. I suggest you teach your code to Hanna, the Kinski's and the Pulaski's. And please – let Julia stay with that puppy, she keeps him content and quiet."

The three agreed on their escape plan. It was not ironclad, but they would alter their path as circumstances dictated along the way.

Next, they called everyone together and told them to be prepared to leave at daybreak.

Helena said, "Please, do not leave anything behind at all. We don't want any clues that might lead the Nazis to us. Michal will bury the trash outside, in a well-hidden place."

Jozef said, "We will pack everything up tonight except breakfast food for people and the puppy. The rest of the food goes with us and we will ration it carefully so it lasts as long as it must."

He looked at Nigel. "Will you please give us your instructions?"

Nigel had taken off the Nazi uniform and folded it carefully under a blanket. He was wearing a T-shirt, khaki shorts and a pair of sneakers. Helena remembered the bike race and thought, *He really is in great shape.*

He interrupted her thought with, "I want to assure you all that if we stick together and stay calm, we will make it out of this thing. To keep track of each other, we will form three groups of six each. I will take the lead group with Helena and Jozef, Sophia, Julia and Michal. Of course, the baby and the puppy will be with us.

"Big Jan, you will take the second group with Hanna, your wife, Doc and Mary Kaminski and Jakob.

"You will take the last group, Big Stan, with Farmer and Mrs. Pulaski, Piotr and Mr. and Mrs. Kinski.

"Big Jan, Big Stan and I will keep track of the five other members of our own group and stay in communication with each other. Don't forget the secret Oak Code. We may need it somewhere along the way. So then, I say we pack up and get some sleep, dawn comes in six hours!"

As Helena passed by Piotr, he said, "Mama, I never saw you wear a babushka before. Why are you covering your hair?"

She stopped to consider her answer, "Well, Son, I cut off my hair because I needed to appear to be a Nazi."

Piotr was puzzled. He said, "But Mama, you still have your braid. You did not cut your hair!"

Julia was listening. "Oh, Mama, just show him your hair, it's no big deal!"

Helena slowly slipped her head covering off, along with the beautiful braid that was attached.

When she lifted her eyes and looked at her son, she saw the same love and respect in his eyes that she had seen in Jan's eyes so many times. It was too much for Helena to take. She collapsed into his arms, sobbing. It was the first time she allowed herself to begin to feel Jan's loss.

Piotr said, "Mama, you are beautiful!"

Julia hugged Piotr and Julia. Soon, Jozef and Sophia joined in. It was just what they needed—to let go of the growing grief that threatened to drown them in emotion.

A few minutes later, everyone was sound asleep. Everyone except Nigel. He hadn't shared the real plan of escape with anyone. If they knew the plan, they would refuse to go. Of that he was certain. This was going to be the riskiest mission he'd ever been involved in. If it worked, it would be nothing short of a miracle!

Nigel had left Georg thirty-six hours earlier. Together, they'd arranged every leg of the perilous journey they would take with their precious passengers. The elaborate scheme would commence at precisely 0800.

When Helena told Nigel how she got Hanna out of downtown and that she'd used the disguise of a Nazi soldier, he'd been thrilled, although he did not let on. That uniform could prove to be an invaluable asset within the next twenty-four hours.

Nigel dozed off. When he woke, it was to the sounds of a crying baby and a barking dog. He did not think it was a good omen.

At 0545, three orderly groups quietly traipsed through the pig barn for the last time.

Jozef, Helena and Nigel, dressed as a Nazi, led the way. Nigel knew they would have to keep a steady pace if they were to arrive at the rendezvous point by 0800. The morning fog was a welcome ally, and they were grateful for the cool air temperature as they walked farther and faster.

They were nearing their destination when Jozef spotted soldiers on horseback on the road ahead. "Nigel, Polish cavalry! Hide yourself!"

Quickly, Nigel took off the most obvious parts of the Nazi uniform and stuffed them into his bag.

The lead horse galloped towards them and stopped at Jozef's feet. "Where are you headed? We will escort you as far as we can."

Jozef looked at Helena. She did not falter. "We are trying to get to Danzig with our family."

The soldier was incredulous. Shaking his head, he said, "That's impossible—the Nazis have invaded along our entire western border. You will never make it. You would be much better off going back to Cracow. At least there are utilities and food supplies, for the Nazis benefit, of course!"

Helena was steadfast. "I'm sure you are right, but we want to try to get out of Poland until the war is over."

He looked skeptical, but he could see by Helena's posture that her group was bound for Danzig, with or without whatever help his cavalry offered. He shouted, "Sergeant! Ride ahead of the group and let me know if you spot Nazis! Go *now!*"

The Sergeant kicked his steed into action.

The Polish commander ordered his horsemen to keep pace alongside the A.P. members.

Just then, Nigel saw the path off the road that they were to take. At the same time, the lookout ahead gave the signal that Nazis were heading toward them.

The Polish Calvary charged off to confront the Nazis. Nigel directed his group to duck off to the left into a densely wooded area on the path that Nigel knew they needed to follow.

The horsemen kept the Nazis from discovering the A.P members, but it was at their own peril. As they entered the path, shouts and gunshots were heard in the distance behind them. Some fifty yards ahead, there was a clearing and there sat a German cargo plane!

Helena turned on Nigel. "What is going on here? Are we to get on a German plane? Are you insane?"

"Helena! The others will follow your lead. Please calm yourself! Do you trust me?"

There was no time to argue, the Nazis would be coming behind them any second. "Yes! Let's go!"

Jozef and Nigel stood at the bottom of the plane's stairway, helping each person board. It was not an easy task with all their belongings.

Helena ran to the end of the line. As she ran past Big Jan, she yelled, "It's okay! We're safe—please rush everyone!"

Helena was the last to board. She looked behind her as her foot touched the top step. At the edge of the clearing, she saw the Polish Commander on his horse, alone, watching their safe departure.

She waved to him. He saluted, then vanished without moving—horse and all!

Nigel waited until Helena was on board, then closed the cargo door. Her attention was called to the cockpit. Georg stood there, dressed in a Nazi uniform. He smiled. "Hello Helena, I will be your pilot today. Please find a place to sit. It won't be comfortable, but our flight will be short."

She threw her arms around his neck, and before she could say one word, a voice behind her said, "Hey! Can I get a hug too?"

Helena whirled around and screamed, "Jan! I thought you were dead! But how..."

Jan laughed and gathered her into his arms. "I did too! Somehow, Georg found me running through the woods and brought me here."

Georg interrupted them, "Please, find a place to sit, we must go now! Tell the others our flight will be thirty minutes after I get this tin can in the air!

"Nigel, are you ready?"

"Yes, Sir, Captain!" Nigel was again in a Nazi uniform.

They watched in amazement as Nigel took the co-pilot position next to Captain Georg Stein.

There were no side windows for the passengers to look out of, so they did not have to see their Cracow in flames as they left it behind.

As promised, the flight was *not* comfortable, but it took only twenty-five minutes. Only the pilot and the co-pilot knew where they were headed. The plane made a rough landing.

With the engines still running, Georg got up and Nigel opened the main cargo door.

Shouting to be heard, Georg said, "Please, everyone stay to the rear of the plane and keep total silence. I must get clearance for our next destination. I will be right back!"

Georg disembarked and left Nigel to answer the obvious question, "Where are we now?"

He answered, "Berlin."

Horror shown on their faces. They'd landed in the heart of Nazi Germany! However, it didn't take long for the genius of the plan to shine through. They were in a German cargo plane with what appeared to be a Nazi crew.

Nigel gave them a minute to absorb the plan, then added, "Georg will bring some cargo on board and the tower will give us clearance to return to Cracow. As soon as we fly out in that direction, we will make a U-turn and get you to the safety of Paris, France!"

As Georg was bringing the last of the cargo on board, a German soldier followed him up the stairway into the plane. He looked at the passengers and yelled, "This is not cargo!"

Georg wasted no time in drawing his sidearm and knocking the man into unconsciousness before the Nazi would cause irreparable damage to their plan. He dragged the limp man to the side of the interior and said, "Now you're going with us, Mr. Nosy!"

Then he yelled, "Nigel! Close the door! We're getting out of this hell hole!"

Georg looked at Jozef. "Tie and gag the German!"

The flight took an extra thirty minutes due to the U-turn and a slight detour so as not to pass over the Berlin airfield.

Finally, they arrived at their destination. Stepping onto the runway at Paris was like stepping into Paradise. The A.P.

Underground had arrived safely, albeit weak-kneed, hungry, tired and terrified.

Jasper was thrilled to be on land, but he was barking wildly at a man and a woman running toward the plane. He knew it was Franz and Rebekka!

Helena heard her mama. "I told you I sent Georg to help you…and you did it step by step, my Lena!"

Georg came up behind Helena and asked to speak with her. She nodded and spoke first, "Dear Georg, I will never be able to thank you for saving us. You are a true hero!"

He said, "I would do anything for you, Lena. Always remember that I love you."

Helena's already knotted stomach jumped at his words. She said, "You're leaving, Georg?"

"Yes, Lena, I must — before it is discovered that this plane is not in Cracow."

Helena's hand went to her heart. "But surely you aren't going back to Poland?"

"Yes, do not worry about me. I will be fine."

With that, he kissed her. It was a lingering kiss that had to end. Letting go of her was the most difficult mission he'd ever accomplished.

Georg turned to Nigel and said, "Lieutenant Blake, you are relieved of duty. Take off that clown uniform and go enjoy your life!"

Nigel knew the moment would come when they would part company, and he'd seriously dreaded it. The two men saluted each other, then embraced. Their friendship was at its end.

Georg could not take the time to bid goodbye to everyone. He simply waved, bolted up the steps of the plane, and closed the door. His focus had to be on flying, without a co-pilot.

His plane taxied down the runway. He saw the French gunners trained on his plane. He only hoped he could get out of Helena's sight before they disabled his craft.

Georg urged the plane to go faster, faster, still faster until he got lift. Finally, he was in the sky and above a thin cloud layer. He breathed a sigh of relief. Now, to get back to Cracow.

In all the excitement, Georg had forgotten one wild card — the German soldier he'd knocked out. He heard the struggling and cursing behind him.

The plane jumped when it encountered turbulence, just as the man got himself free of the ropes.

The German charged the cockpit, forcing Georg to abandon the controls to fight him off. The plane went into a deep dive.

Finally, Georg was able to put the German out of his misery by breaking his skull against the back of the co-pilot's seat.

Georg jumped back into his seat in time to see that he was crashing into a beautiful field of flowers just outside of Paris.

Helena did not see Georg's plane go down, nor did she hear the fiery crash, but she clutched her heart at 1300 hours as she stood on an airstrip on a September day in Paris in 1939.

Nigel saw her gesture. Instantly, he knew Georg's fate. Silently, he said, "Goodbye, old friend."

Chapter Fifteen

After Cracow

They arrived at the cottage estate that Georg and Nigel had secured for them. It was within walking distance of the Paris airport. The moment Nigel showed Helena and Jan to their room, she fell into the plush comforter on the bed with no thought in her head.

Helena slept. Jan checked on her after 24 hours, 36 hours and 48 hours. When he looked in on her after 72 hours, she was still asleep.

Jan walked into the kitchen to find Nigel, who was talking to Rebekka and Franz. "Nigel, I'd like to speak with you privately. Will you meet me at the garages?"

Nigel said, "Of course, Jan. I will see you out back in a minute."

Nigel arrived at the garages before Jan. He was again relieved to see that there were two long black limousines parked there, stocked with enough food and supplies to last longer than he intended for them to be in France.

They would need to get to their next safe harbor as soon as possible. Mentally, he reviewed the detailed plan he had arranged with the help of his father and brother, and the British Intelligence, of course. They knew that there would be nowhere safe in Europe for those who managed to escape the Nazis.

By now, German Intelligence would have discovered how they'd escaped from Poland. But the trail to their current location would have gone cold when Georg's plane crashed.

Jan interrupted Nigel's thoughts. He noticed how worn and stressed Jan looked.

"Nigel, I thanked you for saving my life, and now you have saved my family and friends as well. I will never be able to thank you enough. Even after all of that, I must ask you for more."

Nigel put his hand up as a signal for Jan to stop. "I know what you are going to say and there is no need to ask. British Intelligence is already working on finding your Henryk and Jozef. I advised them that the Nazis kidnapped your ten and twelve-year-old boys. Georg was also assisting their efforts while we were still in Poland."

Suddenly, Nigel was struck by a wave of emotion. Tears dripped down his face with no warning. "Sorry, old boy, it's just that I will miss Georg. We knew the risks, he and I. But we did not plan for one of us to go on without the other. That man was like a brother to me, the best kind. Now he's gone."

Jan thought to hug Nigel, but he was afraid they'd both become blithering idiots. Instead, he said, "Georg was a friend to be proud of; a true hero, just as you are, Nigel. That kind of friendship transcends time and space. It never dies."

Nigel brightened with that thought. He said, "Thank you for that reminder. What you say is true. Georg and I were so close that I can still hear him saying step by step and we will accomplish our all-important mission.

"So then, what else do we need to discuss, Jan?"

"Well, Nigel, I was off fighting the Nazis when my boys were taken and as you know, Helena was so traumatized that she has no memory of them at all, or what happened to them. She simply went on with what she had to do to get everyone out of Poland.

"I am sick at heart, wondering what has become of Henryk and Jozef. The only consolation is that I assume they are together. My understanding of the thousands of kidnappings is that the Nazis intend to integrate them into their culture. Our boys are fair-skinned and blue-eyed, so they would be prime targets for Germanization—another small consolation. I have to believe that we will find them.

"My immediate concern, however, is for Helena. When I mention our boys, she does not even acknowledge that I am in the room. Apparently, the loss of them has produced amnesia. I would expect she might sleep for possibly twenty-four hours after what we went through to get out of Poland. But now it's been three days since she went to sleep. Did she mention the kidnappings to you, Nigel?"

Nigel put his fist to his mouth while he tried to find words that might lessen the blow of what he had to tell Jan. There was no easy way.

Nigel began slowly. "Jan, when I asked Helena to tell me the details of Henryk and Jozef's abduction, she had a mental breakdown. She called me a lunatic and told me she had only two children—twins Piotr and Julia. It took me hours to calm her. Then she slept for a while. When she awoke, she had no recollection of our discussion, or of her two youngest children."

Jan was crestfallen. He said, "Nigel, do you think we can find a doctor to help her?"

Nigel sighed and shook his head. "Perhaps after we are able to get you all settled in your new homeland. But for now, we must focus on just that. We have a great deal of work to do before you are all safe again. Then, you will find a good doctor for Helena. I'm sure of it."

Jan knew Nigel was right, but he felt defeated at that moment.

Helena's papa appeared in the doorway of the garages. He greeted Nigel with a hearty handshake and Jan with a long bear hug.

Jakob said, "Jan, our Lena is very much her mama's daughter. She is strong, willful and capable. That is how I know she will recover from her denial soon. I am also confident that my Marta has helped us every step of the way."

Jakob continued, "I know it's hard for you to believe that Marta is with us in spirit. One day you will understand as we do, Jan. Meanwhile, we will see that Lena comes around at her own pace. When she is ready, she will be able to help us find our Henryk and Jozef, God willing."

Finally, Jan responded. "I too, have felt Lena's mama's spirit many times over the past nineteen years—times of need, times of great happiness and sometimes, simply out of the blue. Those times had to do with Lena and our children, and I always felt comforted by the fleeting thoughts. I was not truly open to this until I found myself running through the woods away from the Nazis. In the deepest part of my brain, I heard '*run toward the shed, NOW!*' Without question, I ran back almost to where I'd started from, and that is where I ran smack into Georg. Apparently, he and I had heard the same voice, because Georg found me before I was captured, and well, it's just not logical. I know I was saved by Lena's mama. I know it as truth and I am very thankful."

Nigel stood quietly by, taking in their conversation. He decided not to tell them how he knew where to find Helena's brother Jozef, and her son Piotr that night in the woods, while Nazis swarmed all around.

The three of them turned when they heard a rustling at the side door.

Jan leapt toward the door and threw his arms around his wife. "Lena! You slept so long. How are you feeling?"

Helena stayed wrapped in her husband's arms. She yawned and stretched like a cat. "Still sleepy, but ravenous! I feel as if I haven't eaten for three days!"

Jakob went to his only daughter and gently turned her from Jan to give her a great hug. "Everything will be okay now, Lena. Let us rustle up food to fill your stomach!"

He looked at Nigel. "Come and join us. You can bring in some wood to stoke up the fire."

Nigel smiled and put his hand on Helena's shoulder. "Indeed, let us feed our sleeping beauty!"

They were in jovial spirits when they entered the cavernous kitchen to find golabki and fresh hot bread ready for them to devour. They were joined by everyone who had disembarked from the plane piloted by Georg days earlier, plus Franz and Rebekka.

For just a little while, they allowed themselves to forget their troubles — with the help of the wine Franz brought from the Loire Valley. And of course, dessert was sand cake prepared by Jan's mama.

By 9:30 P.M., all appetites were sated. The dishes were washed and put away and most everyone had gone in separate directions to find their beds.

Helena, Jan and Nigel were the last ones sitting in front of the fireplace. Nigel said, "I will leave you two to have some private time."

Both Helena and Jan said, "No, please share another glass of wine with us, Nigel."

"I would like that. First, I will get more firewood." Nigel walked through the kitchen toward the garages.

He was surprised to see Hanna drinking a glass of wine by herself in the dark kitchen. Had she not been wearing a white blouse, he might not have noticed her at all.

Nigel startled her. "Hanna, why are you all by yourself? Take your wine to the drawing room and sit with Helena, Jan and me. I'm just on my way to get more firewood."

"I'm afraid I would be very bad company this evening. But thank you, Nigel."

Ignoring her gloomy mood, he picked up her wine glass and said, "You're coming to the garages with me."

The wine was taking the edge off Hanna's gloom and she was not willing to give up her glass. She followed Nigel and her wine toward the garages.

They got as far as the grove outside the kitchen before Nigel placed her wine glass on the picnic table and said, "Hanna, come here, I want to show you something."

Her curiosity was piqued by this good-looking, brash man. She stood at his side in the dark and looked up when he pointed to the starry sky.

She bristled as he put his arm around her shoulders and pulled her into his side. Trying to remain calm, she said, "Nigel! What is it that you are showing me? It's cold out here!"

Immediately, she realized her error. He turned so they were nose-to-nose. He kissed her until her head spun. Before she thought to protest, she kissed him right back, matching his fervor.

Just then, Jan called from the kitchen door, "Nigel, do you need help with the wood?"

"No thanks, old man, Hanna and I are talking. We'll be in shortly with the firewood."

Jan grinned widely. "Okay, if you're sure. Don't be too long, we're drinking all the wine!"

They heard the screen door close and they were alone again in the dark grove, leaning against a giant oak tree. Nigel asked if she was sufficiently warm.

Hanna replied, "I could be warmer. How about you?" She could not believe her brazenness with a man she'd barely shared two words with.

The two lost themselves in each other until Hanna reined herself in. "I'll join the others while you get the wood."

They parted, and Hanna straightened her clothes and went to the drawing room. Franz and Rebekka were sipping wine with Helena and Jan. No one mentioned the tree bark stuck to the back of Hanna's blouse.

Nigel brought in an armload of wood and dropped it on the hearth, whistling a happy tune. Knowing smiles were exchanged all around.

After stoking the fire, he took a seat across from Hanna, so he could look at her. He noted she did not seem to mind.

Hanna was as animated as Helena had ever seen her. No one objected when Jan refilled all their wine glasses to the brim.

Nigel offered up a toast, "Here's to Georg, our hero! Without him, we would not be here getting tipsy with dear friends and family! Cheers, everyone!"

Their glasses met and clinked together. Nigel winked at Hanna. She smiled. across the room.

After a moment of reverence for Georg's gallant sacrifice, Jan suggested they talk about the next stage of the journey to their new homeland. "What do you think, Nigel, are you up for it?"

Nigel sat up a little straighter in his chair. "Of course, I'm always up for it!" He snuck a glance at Hanna to see if she caught his meaning intended for her benefit. She was talking to Helena and missed it. Just as well not to push his luck with her just yet, he thought.

Nigel continued, "Okay then, let's get down to business. I have a map emblazoned on my mind for the sake of secrecy. I will relate it to you.

"You've all seen the black limousines in the garages. They are fueled up, in excellent repair and at our disposal. I cannot tell you who owns this estate where we are, but I can tell you that those limos can travel freely in Europe with no questions asked.

"However, if Germany invades France before we get out of here, all bets are off. Therefore, we need to leave soon."

He looked around. "Are we all in agreement?"

Helena shocked them all. "What about Henryk and Jozef? If we leave Europe, we may never find them, Nigel."

Helena looked at her husband and said, "Jan, what do *you* think?"

Jan said, "Lena, I don't know what to think. It's clear that we must leave soon or risk all our lives if the Nazis barge into France. Let's hear the rest of Nigel's plan for us, okay?"

Reluctantly, Helena agreed.

Nigel said, "We are not forgetting about your boys, please hear me out. Everyone will fit into the two limos.

I believe the belongings should fit as well. We will pack smartly and sit on suitcases if we need to.

"Under the cover of darkness, we will travel one hundred and eighty miles to Calais, which is on the west coast of France. Then we will drive onto the first morning ferry and cross the English Channel to Dover on the southeast coast of England.

"By lunchtime, we will make it to Dover. We will then drive to England's naval port at Plymouth. That is about a three-hour drive south along the coast from Dover.

Now, here's where the plan gets tricky. Because many of you do not have immigration documents, you cannot travel on regular passenger steamships. However, if you know an important naval officer, as I do, passage to America on a naval supply ship can be arranged."

Nigel stopped talking for a moment and asked if there were any questions so far. Everyone was mesmerized. No one voiced a question.

He continued, "The Port of Plymouth expects a convoy of supply ships from America to dock any day. They will deliver supplies to the British Navy, then make a turnaround back to the Brooklyn Navy Yard in New York. *If* our luck holds, you can all travel across the Atlantic as soon as we get to Plymouth.

"I will not fool you; the crossing will be difficult. Supply ships are not built for comfort. The trip will be very long and hard over the high seas, especially at this time of year.

"Georg helped with this plan for the Acorn Park Underground. He also contacted Kazi and Julia and told them they should check the arrivals in the Brooklyn Navy Yard on a daily basis until your arrival.

"Kazi and Julia are so excited that you will all be arriving soon. Julia said she would work with the church and the Polish organizations to find everyone housing and jobs. She said she's sure that you will all love Yonkers as much as they do!"

Helena was reminded of the letter that Julia had written to her after she'd arrived in Yonkers. She was beginning to feel a bit better about this huge transition. She supposed that they would have moved to America sooner or later. Now it was simply sooner.

Suddenly, they were all talking at once. They agreed that the plan appeared to address every eventuality — except one — finding the kidnapped children.

Nigel seemed to read their minds. "I will go as far as the Port of Plymouth with you. Then I will drive a limo back here. Franz and Rebekka want to drive the other limo back here."

Helena glared at him.

He quickly added, "That was not my suggestion."

She sat back and continued listening to Nigel.

He said, "I will search for Henryk and Jozef. Franz wants to help and Rebekka wants to stay with him."

Helena nearly jumped out of her skin when she realized that Franz and Rebekka were not going to America with them. "I will be the one to stay and find my sons. I still have a Nazi uniform just as you do, Nigel."

Jan was truly agitated. He had no intention of leaving his wife to go back to Poland. "Stop right there! If anyone is staying to find the boys, it will be me!"

Nigel was quick to realize that the heated debate was not likely to be settled while they were all tired. He suggested they table the discussion until morning. At that time, they would also decide how soon they would leave for Calais.

Jan said, "That is an excellent idea. Shall we get some sleep, Lena?"

Silently, the couples went to their rooms, leaving Nigel and Hanna alone.

Nigel said, "Hanna, you must be very tired. You should be off to bed."

She said, "Yes, Nigel, I am tired, but first I have an idea to talk to you about."

Suddenly, Nigel was not the least bit tired. He practically stood at attention when she said those words to him. However, his hopes were dashed when she said, "I agree that someone must help you search for Henryk and Jozef. I want to go with you. I can wear the Nazi uniform that Helena has and I think it will fit me even better than it fit her as my shoulders are broader.

"The bonus is that I may be able to find my mama, if that's possible. What do you think, Nigel? It makes perfect sense, doesn't it?"

Nigel stared at her incredulously. There was far more to Miss Hanna Bjorn than just a pretty face. He stammered a response, "Well... well, that certainly puts a new slant on the plan. I don't think it's a great idea to endanger your life, Hanna. And there's Helena to consider. She would put herself in harm's way for her sons before she would allow anyone else to do so. Plus, I may not be able to protect you from being kidnapped yourself, or worse."

"Nigel, if you agree to take me with you, I promise you will not regret it. You will be surprised what a good actress I can be if I must. Working in my shop for all these years has taught me a great deal about human nature. And don't forget that I was with Helena when she posed as a Nazi soldier. I am a quick study! I can do this, Nigel!"

He had to admit, she was quite persuasive. And the bonus for him would be that he would get to know her better. He was beginning to like the idea more with each passing minute.

Nigel stared into the fire that was now dying down. Hanna reminded him that he had not answered her. Finally, he said, "Alright, Hanna, I am in agreement for you to stay with me, Franz and Rebekka to find Henryk and Jozef. We will have plenty of planning time as we drive back from Plymouth and sail away from the White Cliffs of Dover across the English Channel to Calais.

"But Hanna, I warn you that Helena will not be as easy to convince as I am."

"I know that's true, but I can sway her to my thinking...leave it to me!"

With that, Hanna gave Nigel a mock salute, a peck on the cheek and skipped off to bed. She had some serious mental speech writing to do if she was going to get Helena to agree to let her go back to Poland as a Nazi!

Absent-mindedly, Nigel added wood to the fire and watched as the flames jumped and sparked.

Aloud, he said, "There will be no sleep for me tonight."

Chapter Sixteen

LEAVING PARIS

By sunrise the following morning, Mary Jasinski and Mary Kaminski had prepared a fabulous breakfast feast consisting of bacon, omelets, sausage, pancakes with real maple syrup from the French countryside and freshly squeezed orange juice.

Rebekka pointed out that the morning meal in France would be incomplete without croissants. Mary Jasinski said, "But dear, we don't know how to make *those*!"

Pushing up the sleeves of her pink silk blouse, Rebekka said, "Never fear...Rebekka's here! I took a French pastry class at Le Cordon Bleu and croissants were the first thing I learned to make! Step aside, ladies and pass me the beurre!"

Soon, the kitchen was fragrant with the aroma of hot croissants.

Franz had discovered the cast iron bell mounted outside the kitchen door, which he rang as the croissants were put on the table in the warmer. Nigel informed him that the bell was taken from the galley of a naval ship.

Franz was about to ask how such a bell would find its way to this estate when Helena tapped Nigel on the shoulder. "Nigel, we need you in the drawing room before breakfast, please."

Nigel thought, *Oh, here it comes...I'm about to be blasted by a one-time Nazi!*

Aloud, he replied, "Sure, I'll be there directly."

Franz was left wondering what the secrecy was all about. Knowing Helena, he was glad he was not the one who was summoned.

When Nigel got to the drawing room, the scene of the previous night's heated discussion about who was going to America and who was not, he noted that Hanna looked serious and resolute, as did both Helena and Jan.

Nigel thought, *I'll be happy to get to the other side of this situation!*

He said, "Good morning! Have you all come to an agreement as to who will go back to Poland with me?"

He tried not to cringe when Helena jumped up and shouted. "No! We have not! What we *have* decided, Mr. Mastermind, is that *you* will cast the deciding vote, as we have reached a stalemate!"

Nigel felt as if he'd been hit with a sledgehammer. In his most courageous voice, he said, "Why me?"

Hanna volunteered that Nigel was the most objective on this issue because Helena thought she should stay, Jan thought *he* should stay, and Hanna thought *she* should be the one. The three had each cast a vote for themselves, so Nigel had to cast the deciding vote.

Nigel shrank into the chair he was sitting in. He thought, *No getting clear of this one, old boy! Just buck up and make the right choice!*

Looking squarely at Helena, he said, "Are you telling me that you will agree with whichever one of you I choose?"

"No!" She snapped. "I am telling you that I will go along with whoever you choose, as it would appear that I have no other choice!"

Nigel knew it was best to keep it short. He said, "Understood. Here is the unvarnished truth. Your family needs both you and Jan, Helena. It makes sense for Hanna to stay with me for at least two reasons. First, she has no family in this group who needs her, and second, she can help me find Henryk and Jozef while looking for her mama at the same time. As she pointed out, she learned a great deal from you, Helena, about posing as a Nazi. I have as much confidence in her as I have in you."

Hoping to get some help from any one of them, he said, "Jan, do you support my thinking?"

"Yes, Nigel. I do agree with you, although these days there does not seem to be any good choice. We can only choose the least risky option. I do wish I could be the one to go with you, but I trust Hanna implicitly."

Jan looked at Hanna. "Thank you from the bottom of my heart, Hanna. Our prayers will travel with you."

Looking at Helena, Jan continued, "I'm sure that Lena agrees, don't you, dear?"

Nigel once again braced himself for the wrath of Helena.

Without a word, Helena rose from her chair next to Jan and walked to Hanna.

Hanna stood as Helena threw her arms around the woman she had become so close to. Instantly, the two were sobbing.

As Nigel watched, he reflected on how much like Georg and himself these two women were. He understood.

Jan wondered how much more they would all have to endure before they reached America. His sadness threatened to swallow him up. He looked from Helena and Hanna to Nigel.

Nigel gave Jan a silent signal that they should join the others for breakfast. They left the drawing room.

Helena sat and Hanna followed suit. "Hanna, my dear friend, I'm so sorry I got you involved in all of this. I wish it was otherwise. I'm scared for you, and that is exceeded only by my fear for Henryk and Jozef."

Hanna replied, "I know, Lena. I also know that if the situation was reversed, you would do the same for me. And, you did *not* get me into this, remember—you saved me when you found me in that big old wooden trunk in my storeroom. If not for you, I'd be in a prison camp or dead by now.

"Lena, we've known each other for just a few months, but it seems like we've been family for lifetimes. I would do anything for you. I believe that if anyone can find your sons, it's Nigel because he's connected in all the right places. Why, just look at where we are now—he did that with his connections!"

Helena readily agreed. "Please wait here for a moment, Hanna. I'll be right back."

Hanna stood as if anchored to the floor. She could not believe that Helena was going along with the idea of her going back to Poland with Nigel!

Helena was back in thirty seconds. She said, "Open your hand."

In Hanna's open palm, Helena placed the matching earring to the one she'd sent to America with her dear friend Julia. She knew that she and Julia would be reunited soon. Now her hope was for Hanna to find her way to America to join Helena and Julia, with Henryk and Jozef, of course.

Helena told her the significance of the perfect little gold earring. Hanna was thrilled with the gift and the reason Helena had given it to her. She said, "Thank you so much, Lena! I promise you this earring will be back with its mate soon. And then, you and I and Julia will have many fine times with our friends and family. You'll see!"

Helena smiled. "Now, let's eat some of Rebekka's famous croissants!"

***

And so, the tides of change shifted again. Hanna, Nigel, Franz and Rebekka would head back to Poland, into the lion's den, in search of the Jasinski boys, while everyone else would ride the ocean waves and hopefully arrive in America in good health.

Jan's mama served a second round of coffee, and tea for Nigel. A momentary lull in the conversation was the perfect opportunity for Nigel to clink a spoon on his cup to call for everyone's attention.

When all eyes were on him, he related the plan of escape to the entire group. He included the most recent decision regarding the foursome that would go back in search of Helena and Jan's boys.

All parties were immediately on board with the plan and Jakob asked Nigel how soon they could leave.

Before Nigel could answer, Big Jan and Big Stan had a question for Helena and Jan. They wanted to know why they, as the elders, were not the ones to go back to Poland for the boys.

Jan answered by saying, "Papa, and Uncle Stan, thank you for offering to risk yourselves. However, it's best that you do not go because the Nazis will have your photographs plastered all over Cracow. You're high-profile citizens and there will be nowhere safe for you. Besides, we need you with us.

"I assure you that we did not come to the decision easily, to allow Hanna, Franz and Rebekka to return to Poland. We have every confidence that they are our best hope to get into Poland, find our boys and get out safely.

"We will have our fair share of challenges in front of us as we leave the safety of this estate."

Big Jan was sitting with his wife. He looked at her and she shook her head in resignation.

Big Stan, being a man of few words, said, "Jan, I trust your judgment. Enough said. I suggest we take a vote by a show of hands. Who says we should leave for Calais tonight?"

Every hand flew up in the air. It was unanimous.

Nigel took over. He said, "Very good, then we will leave tonight. Rest before dinner because after dinner we will be covering our tracks here, putting everything back as we found it, gathering all of the food and water we can carry for our journey, and packing the limos with all but the passengers."

A whimper was heard from the far corner of the dining room. It was Jasper. Julia said, "Oh, don't worry, Pup, you're coming along."

Everyone laughed as he jumped onto Julia's lap and buried his head in her cable-knit sweater.

Baby Mariola took that opportunity to make herself heard, too; it was feeding time. Sophia cuddled her close and took her to the bedroom to nurse in private. It was very likely the last privacy any of them would have for some time.

Nigel asked if anyone had any other questions or concerns.

Rebekka asked, "Since the limos are being driven back here, Nigel, why don't Hanna and I wait here for you? It will save space for travel to the ship."

Franz answered, "Bekka, although it sounds like a good idea, if we get detoured for any reason on the way back, we may not be able to get to you easily. We should stay together, even if the travel is tight."

Rebekka agreed, as did Hanna.

Helena excused herself from the table to walk in the grove out back. Rebekka asked if she could join her.

Helena nodded. "I would love your company, Rebekka." The two locked elbows and walked out to the grove.

"Helena, we have not had a chance to talk since Franz and I left for Paris. I want to thank you again for a most magical wedding. I adore Franz and being part of your family makes me very happy."

"Rebekka, you don't have to thank me. I was honored to take part in your union. It seems we've always been sisters, just as Julia and I are. And I must tell you that I thought Franz would never find someone who would make him fall in love; he was so wrapped up in his work. Did you know that he told me that he knew you would be his wife the moment he met you?"

The two giggled as if they shared a great secret.

"Well, Franz said that to me, but I didn't really believe him. I thought he was just flattering me. Before meeting Franz, I didn't believe there was such a thing as love at first sight."

Helena sighed deeply. She thought of Georg and said, "I'm so sorry that Georg is not with us. I know that you two were close, Rebekka."

"Yes, we were very close. We used to joke that we were twins born at different times." She paused to remember her brother.

Nigel and Hanna walked into the grove arm in arm. They saw Helena and Rebekka talking.

Nigel said, "What are you two cooking up?"

Helena smiled. "Oh, just a bit of reminiscing. Are you two ready to leave in a few hours?"

Hanna said, "Yes, we are. How about you, Lena?"

"Yes, but with mixed emotions. I wish my boys were safe with us."

They all nodded in agreement.

Their attention was drawn to the driveway that circled the estate. An official-looking limousine pulled into the driveway and stopped right next to where they were standing.

A young man in a British Navy uniform hopped out and approached them. He held a manila envelope in his hand.

Helena's heart dropped. She thought aloud, "This can only be bad news."

Nigel stepped forward and shook hands with the officer. "Teddy, it's great to see you, but what are you doing way out here?"

"Well, Nigel, first, your father sends his regards and well wishes. Second, I'm glad I caught up with you before you left for Calais. I have information for you that may alter your plans. Can we talk privately?"

Nigel felt Helena breathing down his neck. He took the cue properly and said, "That will not be necessary, Teddy. Whatever you tell me can be said in the presence of the ladies. Please allow me to introduce Helena, Hanna and Rebekka."

Teddy took one look at Helena's posture and could see why Nigel said what he did. "Good to meet you, ladies. Let me get right to it then."

He looked directly at Nigel and said, "As you know, British Intelligence has been assisting the Polish government since the German invasion. Well, we've just received intelligence informing us that many of the children kidnapped from Poland, specifically from Cracow, have been intercepted by Canadian troops."

Helena jumped forward and grabbed the envelope out of Teddy's hand. "What's in this envelope? What does this mean? Do you know where my sons are?"

She ripped open the envelope, but before she had a chance to read the contents, Nigel easily took it from her. He consoled her by saying, "Helena, this is good news. Please, let's hear what else Teddy has to tell us."

Helena shook with emotion. It took all her willpower to stay quiet. She acquiesced.

Nigel said, "Go on, Teddy. What else can you tell us?"

Not knowing how out of hand Helena might become, Teddy took a sidestep closer to Nigel and continued. "Canadian troops had been outfitted with horses by the Polish cavalry stationed outside of Vienna. One night at the beginning of September, some of the Canadian Calvary came upon an encampment of Nazis. They watched from the treetops with binoculars.

"What they saw was Nazi soldiers with a group of children sitting around a campfire. There were at least two hundred boys and girls between the ages of about eight and fourteen years. I will add that they were not being mistreated.

"The leader of this Canadian contingent understood most of what he could hear the Nazis saying. The children were being separated into three groups: Jewish first, then girls, then boys last. The Jews were going to be sent back into Cracow for some reason that the Canadians could not determine. The girls were being transported to Germany to be adopted by German families and the boys were going to be sent to work camps, but it was not clear exactly where.

"The Nazis troops numbered ten. They also split themselves into three groups to relocate the children. Five of them were assigned to the girls as they are considered the most important, leaving three to take the Jewish children back to Cracow and two troops to take the boys to a work camp. It was a good thing for the sixty-five boys that only two Nazis were left to tend to them.

"After the Jewish children and the girls left the camp with their captors, the Canadians easily attacked and killed the last two Nazis, thereby freeing the boys."

Helena could not stand it one more second. Through gritted teeth, she asked Teddy, "Do you, or do you *not* know where my sons are right now?"

Teddy screwed up his courage. "I'm sorry, but no. We do not know exactly where your boys are now. To the best of our knowledge, they have been taken to safety in Canada."

Nigel grabbed Helena by the shoulders. She seemed to be in a daze. He shook her out of it. "Helena, this is the best news!

If this is true, then you may be able to find your boys after you arrive in America! I'm sure the Canadians will be able to help you too! Helena, do you understand?"

Rebekka and Hanna asked Nigel to step aside so they could talk to Helena.

When Nigel loosened his grip on her shoulders, Helena said, "No need, girls. I understand, and now last night's dream makes sense. Someone in my dream told me that my boys would be found in an unexpected place."

She looked at Teddy and said, "Thank you for the information, and I apologize for being rude."

Teddy said, "I do have something else to tell you." Turning toward the driveway, he said, "See that car I came in?"

The foursome nodded.

He continued, "I have been sent here to escort you all to the Plymouth Naval Port, compliments of Commander Georg Stein of British Naval Intelligence!"

Nigel grabbed Teddy's arm. "What are you saying, Man? That's impossible! Georg's plane crashed outside of Paris days ago!"

Teddy laughed with joy. "Georg told me you would say exactly *that*! Don't worry, he'll tell you all about it himself tomorrow when you get to the base.

"Right now, we need to leave for Calais as quickly as everyone can be ready. You have extra room for passengers and luggage in my limo...chop-chop!"

The kitchen door slammed. Helena was already through it and running to tell Jan and the others the news Teddy had brought them. Their boys might be in Canada, and about Georg being alive!

Hanna and Rebekka were close behind Helena.

Nigel and Teddy stood in the grove listening to the squeals of delight coming from the cottage. The two walked into the garages where Teddy briefed Nigel on the details of all that was contained in the manila envelope.

***

The trip to Calais, then crossing the English Channel, was easier than anticipated with the extra travel space. The time passed quickly with the excitement of getting closer to finding Henryk and Jozef, and of seeing Georg.

As the three limos pulled into Plymouth Naval Base, Georg stood in front of the officer's quarters anxiously awaiting their arrival. He was thinking that this was perhaps the happiest day of his life, tempered by the fact that the entire world would likely soon be at war.

But for now, his friends would be hungry for food, and for his story. They would get both.

Chapter Seventeen

PLYMOUTH NAVAL PORT

Rebekka was out of the limo before it came to a halt. The sight of her in her brother's arms was emotional. The onlookers shared in their tears of joy.

Georg was standing behind a half wall. Nigel was next to greet him. He thought it odd that Georg had not moved from where he stood. As he went behind the wall, he found out what Rebekka had already discovered. Georg's left leg was in a cast, and his left arm was in a sling hidden by a jacket thrown over his shoulders.

The two friends embraced. The thrill of seeing each other again was somewhat mitigated by Georg's broken body.

Georg turned his head to the right as Helena approached. Nigel was shocked to see that the left side of his face was stitched up in all directions between the top of his cheek and his jawbone. Some doctor deserved an award for repairing the extensive damage. His face was swollen and terribly discolored, but maybe after his healing, only thin scars would be apparent.

Franz joined Rebekka and Nigel beside Georg. After hugging Georg, Franz said, "I'm glad you survived, Georg. You look like you could use some help. Nigel and I will assist you inside. Just tell us where you want to go."

Helena stopped when she saw Nigel and Franz all but carrying Georg.

Rebekka met Helena and said, "Helena, we've been invited to dine in the officer's dining hall. Georg will meet us there and have dinner with us."

Helena said, "Oh, Rebekka, he looks like he's in so much pain. I did not expect to see him like this!"

"Don't worry, Helena. He said the doctors are keeping him out of pain, and that his injuries will heal in time. He also said he is very grateful to be alive."

Rebekka paused and took a long, hard look at Helena before continuing. "Georg asked about you first. He is more concerned for you than for himself."

Before Helena could reply to Rebekka, Hanna tapped her on the shoulder. Helena turned toward her and they both smiled. Hanna said, "C'mon, girls, we're all hungry. Let's join our hero, shall we?"

Two by two, the weary travelers joined Georg at the long table that had been meticulously set by the navy staff. They had been told of this special occasion and spared no time or expense to make this meal worthy. There were dozens of steaming hot platters of all kinds of food from fresh hot bread to beef wellington, to stuffed baked potatoes, to minted baby carrots, to stuffed cabbage in honor of the Cracovians. It was all to be served family style, appropriate indeed.

Someone had even placed food and water dishes on the floor for Jasper, who had become somewhat of a celebrity. Jozef and Sophia voiced some concern that Jasper not look for beef wellington in his dish after this one special meal. If Jasper heard the comment, he did not care—he was eyeballs deep in beef!

At one end of the table was a big armchair for Sophia to sit and hold baby Mariola. The other end of the table was reserved for the hero who was first to be seated. Once Georg got comfortable, he was amazed at how wonderful he felt in the presence of those he loved.

Nigel sat on one side of Georg, and Rebekka sat on the other. Nigel stood. "I would like to offer a dinner prayer." Jasper yipped his agreement even though he'd not waited to eat.

Nigel continued, "Dear Lord, we thank you for all that you have given us, for keeping us safe, for leading us this far on our journey, for providing us with plentiful food and for the love of family and especially for friends—new and old."

He glanced at Hanna, who was smiling up at him as if he was a Greek god. He winked at her.

He then looked at Georg with a silly grin and added, "Oh, and thank you, Lord, for giving this big lug back to us! Amen!"

Georg basked in praise and smiled his crooked grin.

Big Stan shouted, "Amen! Now, let's eat!" The sounds of laughter, talking and food dishes being passed ensued.

A staff member delivered a drink to Georg in a tall tankard with a straw. Georg explained that this was his favorite meal: a chocolate malted shake with whipped cream fortified with mega-vitamins and minerals.

When Helena looked at Georg's empty plate, he quipped, "I have to keep my girlish figure, you know!" It was obvious that Georg could not eat solid food until his mouth healed.

Those who heard his comment laughed only half-heartedly. Helena thought that seeing Georg this way was the quintessential meaning of bittersweet. She was so very happy he was alive. But at what cost to him?

She fought hard to suppress tears until after dessert. Then she turned to Jan and said, "If you don't mind, I'll go out for some air."

Jan said, "Of course, should I come with you?"

She shook her head and went outside.

Everyone was moving around inside the dining hall and Jasper was providing entertainment by doing the tricks Julia had taught him.

Helena looked around at the concrete buildings. She wanted to walk off her nervous energy. She started walking toward the rear of the dining hall, away from the activity. She needed to be alone.

When she found a big rock outside a small vacant building, she decided it was a good place to sit for a while.

She was disappointed to see a maintenance cart driving in her direction. Then she was elated to see that Georg was driving it. This was his primary mode of transportation while he was convalescing. As it turned out, she was sitting in front of his private bunkhouse.

He stopped his cart at her feet as she sat perched on the rock. He said, "No, don't get up just yet. I want to look at you, Lena."

Helena ignored his request, jumped down and threw her arms around him. "Forget it, I need to hug you! I have never been happier than I am at this moment, Georg!"

Their embrace gave way to a most precious kiss, the kind that rings bells while angels sing.

Georg broke the spell. "Lena, my heart was broken to think that I would never see you again when we said goodbye at the Paris airport. Then, when I woke up in a naval hospital, I did not dare to think that I should be so lucky as to see you again, and yet here you are."

Helena leaned onto his lap and ever so gently pressed her cheek against his left cheek, just enough that he could feel her warmth.

"When I was told you were alive, I thought I must be dreaming; it's a miracle." She paused and spoke into his ear, "How will I leave you again?"

Georg winced and said, "Lena, I never thought I would say this to you, but would you mind getting off my lap?"

Gingerly, she complied, "I'm sorry, are you alright?"

He grasped her hand and said, "Of course, I am more than alright. So, tell me, how are you doing with all that has happened?"

Helena sighed deeply, "I simply keep going step by step. And finally, since learning that Henryk and Jozef may be in Canada, I feel like I'm headed in the right direction."

Bowing his head, he said, "I wish I could find them for you. But for the next few months, I will be riding a desk. I assure you though, I will be working day and night with my British and Canadian connections until your boys are with you."

He squeezed her hand harder than he meant to and said, "We *will* find them, Lena, I know it! You believe it too, don't you?"

She felt lightheaded as she heard her mama's voice in her head, "Keep your belief. Henryk and Jozef feel your love and they are safely waiting for you. I am with you all."

As quickly as the lightheadedness appeared, it dissipated. Georg had watched the change in her expression go from distraction to peacefulness.

He got her full attention by kissing her hand. He repeated his question. "You believe we will find your boys, don't you, Lena?"

She smiled, lifted his hand to her lips and kissed it with such sweetness that he thought his heart would melt.

He was captivated and barely heard her response when she said, "Yes." But he felt her breath on his skin.

***

In the dining hall, Nigel related the story of Georg's rescue, just as Georg had related it to him:

"Georg realized he had no time to grab a parachute as his plane nose-dived. The best he could do was to pull up with every ounce of his strength so the plane did not crash nose-first into a flower field. He was able to pull up to about a 45-degree angle. He then shielded his face with his left arm and hoped for the best before slamming into the field. He does not recall the actual impact. The next thing he recalled was waking up in the naval hospital.

"After a day or so, he asked one of his doctors how he got there. The doctor said, 'Well, Captain, that's one for the record books. You apparently crashed almost on top of a field worker who was harvesting flowers for the market. He leaped out of the way of your plane and then jumped into action when your plane stopped. He pulled you out of the cockpit an instant before it exploded. Had that man not been right there, you'd have been toast!'

"The doctor continued when he saw Georg's look of amazement. 'The field worker was an old man who looked a lot like you now that I think about it. The old man marveled at the miracle of being able to save you.'

"The doctor told Georg that the field worker said, 'That young man must be destined to do somethin' real important before he dies!'

"At that point, Georg had tears streaming down his face. He said to the doctor, 'Who is this man? I want to thank him myself.'

"The doctor scratched his head and said, 'He didn't tell anyone his name, no one had ever seen him before and he sort of, well, he…he just disappeared. It's the darnest thing any of us ever heard of!' "

Nigel stopped telling the story for a moment, he then said, "Georg thought he must have died and that the doctor's story was the wishful thinking of a dead man. He fell into a dreamless sleep and slept for a full day.

"When he woke up, the same doctor greeted him with, 'Oh, fine, you're back with us!'

"Georg rubbed his right eye, then his left with his good hand and said, 'Amazing, you're really real! Does that mean the story you told me about the old man saving me in the flower field actually happened?'

"'Yessirree, Captain Stein, you are one true miracle man!' "

The entire group listening to Nigel's story broke into laughter and applause.

Big Stan shouted, "Yeah, Georg! He's our real-life miracle man!"

Jan did not hear the last part of the story. He knew the ending. He went in search of Helena. She'd been gone for almost forty-five minutes.

As he walked around a deserted building at the rear of the base, he heard her voice. He stopped and wondered who she was talking to. He couldn't hear who it was, so he moved closer.

He recognized Georg's voice. He could not see them from where he stood, but their words painted a vivid picture in his mind.

Jan was paralyzed by the most powerful emotion he'd ever felt. He gathered control from the deepest part of his soul. Somehow, he managed to walk away.

Back in the dining hall, Jan found a festive atmosphere. He took a seat next to his Papa.

Nigel had been summoned to the Admiral's office. He told Hanna he would not be too long. She was content to join her fellow travelers for another cup of coffee.

With her acute listening skills, Hanna tuned in to individual conversations around her.

She heard Farmer and Mrs. Pulaski planning what they would plant in their garden, until they earned enough to buy chickens, goats and cows.

Although Michal and Julia were speaking in hushed tones, she overheard their plan to announce their engagement as soon as they reached America. Hanna thought how wonderful young love was.

For a moment, she mentally floated off on Cloud Nine with Nigel. Then, without warning, she was knocked back to earth by a rambunctious Jasper jumping on her lap. It was then she noticed that Michal's parents also overheard their son's plan. They kept it to themselves, but Hanna knew the reason for their happy grins.

Jan joined in the conversation between his papa and Uncle Stan. They were discussing textile production advances that could be utilized in American mills.

Big Stan went on to say it was time for him to retire from the mining business. Big Jan agreed and added that they could both find work in a textile mill in America.

Big Stan glanced at his nephew and said, "Jan! Are you paying attention? We're talking about the future in our new homeland. Or maybe you already have a job that you haven't told us about?"

Laughing, Jan replied. "No, Uncle Stan, I was listening to you and papa. I'm just a little tired and preoccupied thinking about our boys."

Jan forced himself to be more interested in the talk of mill work in America than in wondering when Helena might reappear.

She chose that moment to walk into the dining hall. Jan thought she looked quite perky for a woman whose children had been kidnapped. He wondered where Georg was.

Helena surveyed the dining hall. Her family and friends were enjoying each other. She was beginning to feel hopeful about their future and allowed herself to feel some happiness for the first time in months.

She noticed that Jan's mama, Doc and Mary Kaminski, Piotr, Franz, Rebekka and Hanna were playing with baby Mariola. Everyone was acting silly, making goo-goo and gurgling noises with the baby.

Helena joined in the fun. Jan watched her from across the room.

Teddy, the limo driver who'd delivered the happy news that Georg was alive, appeared in the center of their activities.

He looked serious but summoned a smile. "Okay, folks, we've made sleeping arrangements for everyone. There are plenty of bunks in the vacant barracks. Feel free to make your way there whenever you like."

He motioned to a staff member standing nearby and said, "Clement here will show you the way. You'll find an English breakfast here complete with gypsy toast tomorrow promptly at 0600 hours.

"We expect the first of the supply ships from New York to be in port by midmorning. The ship's captain has been advised that he will have your group as passengers on his return trip. He said his crew will need no more than three hours to offload the supplies and to prepare for the return. By 1300 hours, you should all be on your merry way to America!"

Teddy looked around and asked, "Now then, how does that sound?"

Big Stan shouted, "What in God's name is gypsy toast?"

After the laughter died down, Teddy explained that gypsy toast is also called eggy toast or French toast, and it is served piping hot with butter and maple syrup.

Doc Kaminski stood up to be noticed. "On behalf of all of us from Cracow, I'd like to thank you for everything, Teddy. Let's give him a big cheer!"

Teddy was embarrassed by the clapping and cheering. He said, "You are welcome. I will say good evening now. Georg and Nigel will also join you for breakfast in the morning."

Teddy left the group in the capable hands of Clement.

***

Helena and Jan found a bunkhouse off by themselves. They wasted no time dropping into a double bunk. As he kissed his wife and said goodnight, he asked her if she was feeling alright.

Helena said, "Yes, dear, I'm tired like everyone else. I am looking forward to finding Henryk and Jozef, and I feel confident that with the help of Georg, it will happen very soon."

Helena was instantly asleep and did not hear him say, "Yes, Georg is our hero."

Chapter Eighteen

LEAVING ENGLAND

Helena rose before sunrise. She was bright-eyed and bushy-tailed, as the saying goes. Jan did not stir, and she assumed he had a good night's sleep.

There was a light knock on the door. She didn't think anyone knew which bunkhouse she and Jan were in. Helena was surprised to see Hanna.

She whispered, "Hanna, good morning. How*ever*, did you know where to find me?"

Hanna was very pleased with her investigative skills. She smugly replied, "It was easy. I had help!"

Helena was delighted by her friend's playfulness and with a giggle, she said, "Oh, and what help might that have been, Miss Sherlock Holmes?"

From behind Hanna's back, she produced Katrynka. "You dropped your doll, Lena, right on the doorstep!"

Helena stepped outside, quietly closing the door behind her. "Jan is sound asleep and I don't want to wake him. Hanna, why have you come looking for me at this early hour?"

"I wanted to say goodbye to you, Lena. Nigel, Franz, Rebekka and I plan to leave after breakfast."

Hanna's lip began to quiver and tears welled up in her eyes.

"Oh, Hanna, I hate goodbyes. Let's just say we will meet again very soon!"

"Alright, Lena, but not before I thank you for everything that you have done for me. Whatever happens from here on, you have changed my life for the better and I promise you that I will do everything in my power to find your boys!"

She flung her arms around Helena. "We will meet again very soon."

Hanna was gone in a flash, leaving Helena looking at Katrynka, the doll that was her lifelong companion.

As quietly as she could, Helena crept back into the bunkhouse and quickly dressed for the day ahead.

She glanced at Jan and saw that he was still asleep. It was too early for breakfast, but she went in search of some hot coffee in the kitchen of the dining hall.

Helena entered through the service entrance. The cooks were busy preparing Acorn Park's last meal on this side of the Atlantic. One of them yelled in her direction, "I betcha you'd like a cup of hot fresh coffee, wouldn't you?"

She smiled and thanked him as he handed her a steaming mug of fragrant coffee. He said, "No problem, we were called in extra early to prepare breakfast for the 'big-wigs' in there." He motioned toward the dining hall.

"Oh, really...who are they, do you know?" She sipped her coffee and nonchalantly peered into the dining hall. She could hear voices, but could not see who they were. They were too far off to the right.

As she walked back out the way she came in, she said, "Thanks again, I'll be back for breakfast in a little while."

She was surprised to see Georg's maintenance cart parked just outside the kitchen door. She had not seen him come in through the kitchen. Apparently, he was part of the early meeting in the dining hall. Her curiosity got the better of her.

She walked around to the front entrance and nearly walked straight into a uniformed man. Thankfully, he had his back to her and did not see her. She backed up before being seen.

As she turned to walk to her bunkhouse, she bumped into Jan. He had a strange look on his face, and it was not friendly.

In a controlled voice, Jan said, "Helena, I don't have to ask you what you are doing because I see Georg's cart here. I know you were with him yesterday, and he came to our door this morning. I would like to know why you two have been alone together."

Helena was without words. She was completely at a loss to understand how Jan could have known she was with Georg yesterday, but she had not seen Georg this morning.

Jan stood rooted to the ground with his arms crossed. It was obvious he would wait for her reply for as long as it took.

Helena decided she had best tell Jan the whole truth. She began by confessing that she'd kissed Georg the day before. She went on to tell him that Hanna came to their door to say goodbye that morning, and she then got dressed and came over to the kitchen for a cup of coffee. She held up the cup as evidence.

Helena stopped talking. Jan broke his silence with a single word. "And?"

Helena was getting more aggravated with each passing moment, and it showed when she said, "And *what*, Jan?"

He stepped forward and grabbed her upper arms. She felt his anger and saw the fire in his eyes. "And why were you with him this morning?"

Helena angrily pushed back from him, hard enough that he let go of her arms. "I was *not* with Georg this morning! I see his cart is here, but he must be in the meeting that's going on in the dining hall. A cook told me they were called in to make an early breakfast for some 'big-wigs.' "

Jan felt marginally better about his wife's relationship with Georg. He knew Helena well enough to realize that she could get overly involved emotionally. He decided to wait for her to say what he knew she would say next.

She did not disappoint him. "I'm sorry, Jan. I suppose I let my emotions get the better of me yesterday when I met Georg by accident. How could any of us not love him and be thankful to him? Will you forgive me?"

Suddenly, Jan felt like a heel. He reached for her and hugged her so hard that she begged to be released.

Behind Jan, Helena saw Georg's cart leave the back of the dining hall. She wondered if he had seen her and Jan.

"It looks as if it will be a clear day, Jan. Should we go watch the sun come up in the east before we travel further west than we've ever been?"

"Yes, Lena, we should do that."

***

At precisely 0600 hours, breakfast was served to the Acorn Park members.

Everyone found a place at the dining table. After they had their fill of the breakfast feast, Georg clinked a spoon on his water glass.

All eyes turned toward him in anticipation of a farewell speech. He looked straight at Helena when he said, "Friends, overnight, there were some unexpected developments."

It seemed an eternity before Georg continued. No one could imagine what was coming next. They had endured so much suffering. How could they possibly bear more?

Georg drew in a long breath, even he could not have imagined this turn of events. "As you know, the Polish Government set up operations in London after the Germans attacked and occupied your country. Late yesterday afternoon, we received a message from your exiled government saying that they wanted to send representatives to our base to meet with our Admiral in charge of operations.

They would say no more. Their request was granted, and a contingent of Polish government officials arrived here at 0200 hours."

Helena suddenly realized that the officer she'd nearly bumped into the back of was wearing a Polish uniform. She hadn't given it another thought because Jan showed up just then.

Big Stan interrupted, "Georg, will you please cut to the chase and tell us what has happened?"

Georg hesitated for a moment and continued. "There is a group of approximately one hundred Polish citizens who were rescued by British troops shortly after the Nazi invasion. They were taken to London, where they arrived within the past thirty-six hours. That group will be arriving here any minute, and they will be traveling to America with your group."

Doc Kaminski said, "This is wonderful news! Where are these people from exactly?"

Georg said, "The Polish government only got information yesterday from a source in the British government that we have a supply ship traveling back to America today. Everything happened so fast that we don't know where these Polish citizens are from. My guess is that they are from Warsaw and the surrounding villages. We will be finding out very soon, though."

Georg looked out the front window. "And it looks as if they've arrived!"

There was a scraping of chairs followed by a mad rush out the door to meet their fellow countrymen.

Georg found himself sitting alone with Jasper. He picked up the pup's leash, and one of the staff members helped him outside to join the others.

It was a chaotic scene with hoots, hollers and hugs galore. In the next moment, all activity stopped as a woman screamed. It was Hanna.

She was running toward a woman. When Helena saw who it was, she was amazed. It was Elena Bjorn, Hanna's mama!

As the two groups intermingled, everyone seemed to know everyone else. Of course, it was because these people were all from Cracow. They had been discovered hiding in the church basement where the Acorn Park Underground had their meetings. Yes, Helena thought it was a secure location.

Greetings and tears of jubilation continued for the rest of the morning.

Hanna introduced Nigel to her mama. When Hanna explained Nigel's role in their escape from Poland, Elena gave him a giant hug and said, "Thank God for you, young man!"

Elena whirled around when she heard Helena. The two embraced, both talking at once. Helena felt almost as if she'd found her own mama. Elena said she felt as if she'd found her second daughter.

If tears were gold, everyone would have been very wealthy that day at Plymouth Naval Port.

Georg decided it was time to return to his office to do some work. Just then, a staff member stopped him and said, "Excuse me, Sir. The Admiral would like to see you and Nigel in his office, and he said *now*."

Georg said, "Fine, give this dog to someone and tell Nigel to hitch a ride with me. He's over there talking to those three pretty ladies, as you might expect."

The young officer complied, and Nigel joined Georg.

Hopping into the cart, Nigel said, "What's this about?"

Georg stepped on the gas pedal and spat, "Don't know, but it's probably not good for us."

***

The supply ship was being offloaded while the ship's captain met with the Admiral, along with Georg and Nigel. New orders were being issued. Nigel was ordered to travel to America with the Polish citizens. As he was about to protest, the Admiral said, "There will be no discussion, you will be our eyes and ears on the other side of the ocean until further notice. Your home base will be the Brooklyn Navy Yard."

The Admiral turned his attention to Georg and said, "And Captain Stein, you will remain here and be Nigel's primary contact until further notice. Understood?"

With a salute, Georg said, "Yes, Sir."

The Admiral looked at Nigel. "Understood?"

"Yes, Admiral, perfectly understood."

The ship's captain was next to get his orders. The Admiral motioned toward the eight young officers in the back of the room and said, "Captain Jones, these men will remove bedding, tables and chairs from our bunkhouses and place them on your ship wherever you direct them to be placed. You will now be responsible for approximately one hundred and twenty-five passengers and they will need places to sit, eat and sleep.

"My men are gathering food and supplies to be delivered to your dock within the hour. Put one of your men in charge of directing the loading of those supplies. Are there any questions, Captain Jones?"

Captain Jones was flustered to say the least. First, he was ordered to take on eighteen passengers, a baby and a dog and now he was told there were one hundred more passengers.

He said, "Admiral, I always follow orders, but just one question, Sir."

The Admiral had not sent him away, so the captain assumed he could continue. "How are all of these people going to get through U. S. Customs?"

The Admiral growled, "They're *not*! And *you* are going to make sure that they're *not*! And what I mean by that is that United States Customs had better not find out that you have any passengers on board at all! Your ship will be met by our people who will take over once you dock at the Brooklyn Navy Yard. You have a great deal of work to do. Dismissed!"

***

Outside, Georg and Nigel watched as the bunkhouses were stripped of furnishings and loaded on the ship.

Nigel said, "So I suppose you'll see that the Admiral's limos are returned to his estate?"

Georg said, "My guess is that the Admiral already arranged for that to happen!"

***

Franz and Rebekka found Helena and Jan talking with Jan's mama and papa. Franz said, "Wow! How about all this excitement! Everything's turning out better than we could have expected!"

Helena put her arm through her brother's arm and said, "Yes, Franzie, it certainly is! And I am thrilled that you two will be coming to America with us, now that we know our boys are in Canada."

Franz and Rebekka shared a look.

Franz said, "We wanted to talk to you about that. We will be returning to our Paris apartment, at least for now. We promise to visit in a few months."

Helena felt the air go out of her lungs.

She said, "But Franz, why? It's not going to be safe for you in France. Rebekka, *you* don't want to stay, do you?"

Rebekka said, "Helena, I agree with Franz. We love Paris, and Franz has a wonderful job there. Please try to understand."

Helena saw there was no use arguing. They'd made up their minds to stay.

Hanna ran to Helena and blurted out, "Lena, isn't it wonderful? We're *all* going to America, including my mama and then we will find Henryk and Jozef too!"

Nigel came up behind Hanna and put his arms around her waist. He leaned in and whispered, "Yes, Hanna, and I will be joining you in America too. If you want me to, that is!"

She jumped and turned to kiss him. "Everyone! Did you hear that? Nigel is coming to America, too!"

Jan and Helena had the same thought: *where would Georg be?*

Their question was quickly answered when Nigel added, "And...Georg will be my intelligence link on this side of the pond."

It was 1500 hours before the supply ship was outfitted as a passenger ship with everyone on board.

Georg could see the ship from his office window. He elected not to go to the dock for yet another goodbye.

There was a knock on his door. "Enter."

It was Jan. In a respectful tone, he said, "Georg, thank you again for helping all of us. Best of luck to you in your recovery."

Georg said, "You are welcome, Jan. You will be hearing from me the moment your boys are located. Nigel's help will be invaluable in America."

Georg paused for a moment. "You're a very lucky man, Jan."

Jan nodded. "Goodbye, Georg."

Jan picked up his pace as the ship signaled its imminent departure. He stopped and waved to Franz and Rebekka, who were each driving one of the limousines back to France.

Everyone aboard the ship was anxious for their journey to begin.

Georg did not watch as the ship pulled out of port.

Chapter Nineteen

AUTUMN OF 1939

It was their first Thanksgiving, a New World holiday — a time of reflection, of giving thanks, and a time to celebrate with friends and family.

Helena organized the festivities with the help of her friend, Julia. The two had worked tirelessly to situate the Polish citizens who had arrived on the supply ship five weeks prior.

Thanksgiving was the perfect opportunity to relax and enjoy a feast along with traditional music and merriment.

The Polish American Society was hosting a huge Thanksgiving dinner, but Mrs. Pulaski had insisted that the Acorn Park members come to their humble little farm on the outskirts of Yonkers for this special dinner.

Helena recalled being with Farmer and Mrs. Pulaski when they were asked by a church member if they would take over the operation of the Jenkins farm. They needed no details. They replied *yes* in unison.

Later, they learned that Farmer Jenkins was gravely ill and intended to leave his farm to the Pulaski's - lock, stock and barrel. The only proviso was that the new owners continue to breed terrier puppies to be given as pets to immigrant families with children. As it happens, that's how Julia came to adopt Buttons in 1920.

Raising puppies had been Mrs. Jenkins' pet project, literally, and Mrs. Pulaski took over the reins of that part of the farm as if she'd done it all her life. She found it a constant source of joy, especially when she gave a puppy to a child who needed unconditional love.

Farmer Pulaski got right back into the swing of delivering milk and eggs to his neighbors. He even kept the same schedule that Cracovians had come to rely on-Monday, Wednesday and Friday for milk deliveries and Tuesday mornings bright and early for egg deliveries. It was a wonderful familiar piece of home.

Mrs. Pulaski asked the best cooks she knew to help prepare the Thanksgiving feast. That meant Mary Jasinski and Mary Kaminski. They were both more than willing to assist.

Finally, the big day came. The oak banquet table was laden with a prize turkey and all the trimmings. Every chair was occupied by a special person.

Farmer Pulaski offered the dinner prayer. "Dear Lord, we thank you for all of our blessings and ask that you continue to keep us safe and productive. Thank you to all of the people seated at our table this day."

Big Stan shouted, "And thanks for the turkey, amen! Let's eat!" It would not have been a family dinner without Big Stan's special prayer. Everyone laughed and the dishes were passed, emptied and refilled.

Helena enjoyed the food and the company of those she loved so dearly. She was not overly talkative, preferring instead to relax and listen.

Her mind wandered off. She thought of those who were not present at their feast. She glanced at Nigel. He was sitting next to Hanna and her mama. He was in his glory with a beautiful woman on either side of him.

She thought of the latest reports from Georg regarding the search for Henryk and Jozef. Thus far, every lead was a dead end.

The initial reports of the Polish boys who had escaped from the Nazis and sent to Canada, proved to be false.

Helena knew in her heart that her boys were safe, but she missed them desperately and could not help wondering how it all would end.

***

Jakob Pawlowski always missed his Marta more when he was surrounded by his family, and that day was no exception.

He looked forward to days like this despite his longing. He kept himself busy. He especially loved playing music with anyone who would join him. He spent a lot of time at the Polish American Society doing just that.

Since they could not bring their musical instruments from Poland, Jakob took it upon himself to borrow violins, violas, flutes and even a set of bells for Sophia to play.

He was very pleased with himself as he surprised everyone by bringing out the instruments after Thanksgiving dinner.

It was another wonderful piece of home and it went a long way toward emotional healing after having to leave Poland.

***

Helena walked as fast as she could down toward the river to the café where she was to meet her friends Julia and Hanna.

At Thanksgiving dinner, Hanna had told her that she and Julia had something to talk to her about, so they agreed to meet for coffee on Saturday after Sophia picked up Mariola. Helena babysat on Saturday mornings so Sophia could volunteer at the Polish American Center, teaching English.

She wondered what those two had up their sleeves to talk to her about, and why they could not talk to her on Thanksgiving Day.

She burst through the door exactly at 3 P.M. The café was bustling with customers on the holiday weekend. And the aroma of freshly roasted coffee wafting through the air was intoxicating.

She heard Julia shout above the din. "Helena, we're over here!" She headed in the direction of Julia's voice and saw Hanna first.

They were seated at the coffee bar; Helena hopped up on a stool between them. She kissed Hanna's cheek and leaned the other way to kiss Julia's cheek. She noticed Julia was wearing the bracelet her Babula had given her. Helena remembered something, but her thought was interrupted by Hanna.

Hanna said, "You are probably wondering why we wanted to get together with you, Lena."

Just then, the waiter asked for Helena's order. "French roast café au lait, please."

Julia popped a small, wrapped box onto the bar in front of Helena and said, "This is something *only* for the three of us, Lena. Go ahead, open it. We are very anxious to see your reaction!"

Helena wasted no time ripping off the red and white checked paper. The gift was in a black velvet box, looking a lot like it might have jewelry inside.

Pausing before opening the box, Helena thought it did not make sense for Hanna and Julia to give her jewelry.

Hanna nudged her, "Will you *please* open the box, Lena!"

"Okay, okay...let me see what this is..." Ever so slowly, Helena opened the box. Before she could see what was inside, the hinge snapped the box shut, startling her. She giggled.

Hanna snatched the box, saying, "Oh, for heaven's sake, Lena, it won't bite you. Here, now I've opened it...what do you think?"

Helena gasped. She was suddenly crying. She'd forgotten about this special jewelry. She looked from Hanna to Julia and back at the pair of tiny gold earrings.

When she found her voice, Helena took Julia's hand and said, "When I gave you one earring, I told you it would bring us back together someday and that we would once again be a pair, just like the earrings."

Julia said, "Yes, I know Lena. But what I did *not* know is that you did not keep the other one for yourself. You unselfishly gave it to Hanna until you two were back together."

Smiling, Hanna said, "Lena, these earrings truly are a marvel...they turned a pair into an inseparable threesome, and here is the third piece that goes along with the earrings. Open your hand."

Into Helena's open palm, Hanna placed a small circle pin that truly *did* go along with the earrings. It was nearly the same size as the earrings. It was gold with a setting of fifteen small pearls.

The three held hands and formed their own circle. Helena said, "It's perfection—the symbology of the circle is everlasting love. Thank you both!" Together, Hanna and Julia said, "Thanks to *you*, Lena, we are a threesome forever!"

Chapter Twenty

MARCH OF 1940

It had been six months since the Acorn Park Underground had left for America. During that time, Georg had no time for anything other than grueling physical therapy and desk work.

The day his leg cast and arm sling were removed, he began physical therapy three hours every day without fail.

There was a method to his madness — he intended to go in search of Henryk and Jozef himself with or without permission from his superiors.

Georg knew if Nigel was with him, they'd find the boys quickly. Since that was not the case, Teddy was his next best option. He proved his mettle when he safely led the entire Acorn Park group to the Plymouth Naval Base. Georg knew Teddy was up to the task.

The two men had become close friends over the previous months, and they shared extraordinary abilities in the field of espionage.

When Georg proposed that the two of them undertake a mission to find Helena's sons, Teddy said, "Let's go!"

So every evening, Georg and Teddy sat and planned their mission. They thought the plan would likely call for going into German territory, so Georg once again became the professor and gave Teddy a crash course in German. Teddy took to the language like a fish to water.

Each afternoon, Georg made telephone connections with anyone and everyone who might have helpful information that could lead them to the boys.

He kept copious notes in a small notepad, stashed in his pocket. It was like a puzzle that he knew he would be able to solve, somehow, some way.

Georg rarely had dreams that he remembered. However, on March 9th, during a new moon, he dreamt that a woman handed him a written message about his mission. The words on the paper seemed to glow. The note read: "Go step by step, back the way you came."

He jolted out of sleep and wrote the words on the last page of his notepad. He contemplated the meaning of the dream. It started to make sense that he should take heed of those words.

He began to pack his bags, making sure he had all parts of the Nazi uniform. Then he checked the uniform that Nigel had left. It would fit Teddy.

A quick check of his watch told him it was too early to get Teddy out of bed, and he resolved to wait until 0500 hours.

He used the two hours to map out what he now intuitively believed was a foolproof plan to find the boys. Directly after breakfast, he and Teddy would drive from Plymouth to the Port of Dover and board the ferry to Calais.

He and Teddy were both overdue for some leave. The Admiral granted them leave and offered his limousine and his cottage outside of Paris. Of course, the Admiral didn't know the true nature of their activities during their R & R.

Georg marveled at how well the Admiral's generous offer fit into their plan. Georg and Teddy would follow the instructions Georg had received in his dream: "go step by step, back the way you came."

He briefed Teddy on the updated plan as they drove to Dover. However, he didn't tell him about his dream. They were accustomed to running missions based on intelligence information, not based on dreams.

Georg mused to himself, *the woman in my dream certainly seemed to know how I would find the boys.*

The ferry for the channel crossing was in port and loading when they arrived. Perfect timing. So far, so good.

Georg had never seen the cottage where the Acorn Park group stayed, so Teddy described it to him. They would not stay more than a few hours. Rather, they would use the Admiral's cottage as a transition point.

From there, they would drive to Cracow and by all appearances, they would look any other Nazi soldiers. The areas they would be passing through after leaving France were already under German control, so they should be able to pass all the checkpoints without being stopped.

The trip was long and tiring. They took turns driving so the other could sleep. When they were both awake, Georg told Teddy about the Acorn Park Underground — from its inception to their escape from Poland by air with him as pilot.

Teddy was particularly amazed by the part of the story wherein Helena disguised herself as a Nazi officer and rescued Hanna from her shop and got the Acorn Park cash out of the bank while the Nazis blocked the customer entrance.

It was not until they arrived in Cracow that Georg told Teddy exactly where he believed the boys would be found. He said, "I told you about the Pulaski Farm being the temporary housing for Acorn Park. But there was another temporary housing site that was compromised at the last minute.

"It was the crystal salt mine just outside of Cracow where Big Stan worked as a foreman for years. It was fully stocked with supplies, and there was a secret entrance made in preparation for the Acorn Park group. Somehow the Nazis discovered the entrance, so it could not be used. Everyone was housed temporarily at the Pulaski Farm."

Georg continued, "Well, Big Stan is Great Uncle to Henryk and Jozef and if they heard about the secret entrance, they could have gotten themselves to the chapel which is one hundred meters underground. If so, they will be safe from discovery. The chapel is where the Acorn Park supplies were stored, so anyone there would have plenty of food and water. The temperature in the mine is a constant 70 degrees; staying warm would not be an issue."

Teddy interrupted. "It's a long shot based on what we know about the boys' capture and escape, but it sounds like it's worth taking. I presume we will ditch the limo and walk to the mine entrance after dark?"

"That's exactly the plan, Teddy." Georg paused and said, "We will need our sidearms and extra ammo."

As they drove through Cracow, they passed some German soldiers near the Wawel Castle, where the German General Government had been set up. None of them gave a second look as the official-looking limo passed by.

Outside of town, they turned south and drove about a mile. They pulled into an abandoned driveway, past a house and into a pine grove.

"The car will not be seen here," Georg said. "I'll leave the keys in the ignition in case one of us doesn't make it back."

Teddy had not considered that possibility. He simply said, "Okay."

Georg spoke quietly. "Let's find the secret entrance to the mine. Be careful not to let the car door make noise when you close it."

They walked as carefully as they could, but the ground was frozen and twigs and leaves crunched under their feet.

Just as Georg began to wonder if he remembered where the entrance was, he saw a glimmer cast by the moon.

He motioned for Teddy to keep up. Cautiously, Georg approached the entrance and pushed the overgrowth away. It was obvious that no one had entered the mine for months. A rabbit hopped out of a hole and scared them both out of their wits.

When they realized it was only a rabbit, they shook their heads and breathed a sigh of relief.

Suddenly, they heard voices behind them in the distance. They hurried to get into the mine. They covered the entrance behind them as best they could.

Georg pulled a flashlight out of his pocket to light the way to the chapel. As they passed through the mine, they saw that it was abandoned. Apparently, no work had been done there since the Nazi occupation.

They realized that if Henryk and Jozef were in the chapel, they would hear intruders and be prepared to defend themselves. Georg and Teddy would have to be on their guard, lest they get hit on the head with a rock.

The change in the air pressure told them they were in a deeper part of the mine and that the chapel should be near. Georg heard a sound just ahead. He put his arm out to stop Teddy and turned off his light. They stood in the dark, waiting to get a fix on what they heard.

Minutes passed. They heard what sounded like rocks tapping against each other. A minute later, Teddy nudged Georg and whispered, "It's Morse code...the message is: *Stay hidden, Jozef.*"

Georg said, "That's ingenious!" He grinned and tapped out a message to the boys: *We are here to save you.*

Quickly, the response in code was: *Who?*

Now Georg knew they'd found Henryk and Jozef. He tapped out: *Jasinski.*

There was a short pause before two ragged-looking boys stepped out of the shadows and into the beam of the flashlight. They came from opposite sides of the chapel, as they'd hidden separately in case one got caught.

Henryk recognized Georg and said, "It's okay, Jozef, they're not Nazis!"

Together, the boys came forward and threw their arms around Georg. He did not want to let them go. He could only imagine what they must have gone through and how scared they must have been.

In Polish, he said, "I am very proud of you two for being so clever and resourceful. You are safe with us now. This fellow is Teddy. He knows your mama and your papa. Your family is waiting for you in America. We will help you get to them. Are you ready?"

Henryk said, "Yes, Sir, we are. And thank you for finding us." Then he looked thoughtful. "I had a dream last night that someone would find us today."

With a smile, Georg said, "You did, eh? I had a similar dream."

Suddenly, loud voices were heard near the chapel. Teddy said, "Nazis must have followed us here! What should we do, Georg?"

In an instant, Georg knew exactly what he would do. First, he scribbled something on a piece of paper and shoved it into Henryk's hand. He said, "When you see your mama, give her this note. This may be the most important mission you will ever accomplish. Promise me that you will give her this note!"

In a terrified voice, Henryk replied, "I promise, but where are you going? Why don't you give it to her yourself?"

Georg looked at Teddy and said, "There's only one way in, and one way out of this chapel. I will lead the Nazis deeper into the mine. You stay hidden here with the boys, and after they pass, get out of here the way we came in. The boys will know the way. Here is my flashlight, now go hide quickly!"

Georg disappeared into the mine. The boys and Teddy hid behind a large salt carving of the Virgin Mary.

As expected, the Nazis came running through, in search of whoever they'd seen going into the mine entrance. Georg was careful to make noise, so the Nazis would keep following him, away from the chapel.

When Teddy no longer heard the Nazis, he turned the flashlight on and asked Henryk to lead the way out of the cave.

Henryk had practiced the escape route often. He moved them along quickly. It took only three minutes to reach the exit.

Teddy stopped them to listen for other Nazis. He didn't hear anything.

When they were out of the cave, he turned off the flashlight. Urgently, Teddy said, "Follow me. We're going to make a run for the car!"

Relief flooded Teddy as he got behind the wheel of the car and started the engine. Georg had left the key in the ignition, apparently knowing how it would end.

With a huge lump in his throat, he managed to say, "You're safe now, boys. Soon you will see your mama and papa."

There was no response from the back seat, only soft sobs.

***

Within twenty-four hours, Teddy called Nigel and told him about the rescue of Henryk and Jozef. He was thrilled beyond words and begged Teddy for every last detail of the successful mission. He was jealous that he was not in the action.

Teddy obliged. Nigel was silent at the end of the story. In a monotone, Nigel said, "Georg did not make it." It was a statement. Georg had sacrificed himself for Helena and Jan's sons.

"No, I'm sorry, Nigel. Strangely, one of the last things Georg said to me was 'go step by step, back the way you came.' So, that's what I did. I got us back to the Plymouth Naval base."

"Teddy, that doesn't sound like Georg. He must have had a premonition or something."

Teddy said, "Maybe, but whatever it was, it got the three of us back to safety."

He continued, "We got lucky, our Captain Jones is leaving port in the morning with his supply ship. He's already given the boys the cook's tour of his ship, and they'll be traveling to Brooklyn with him.

"They are pretty excited to be taking an ocean voyage and to be seeing their mama and papa soon."

Nigel was still reeling from the news that Georg did not make it. He was trying not to envision what the end must have been like for him. He hoped that Georg shot himself as they were trained to do, before the Nazis got him.

He gathered himself. "I'll bet they're excited! I cannot wait to let Helena and Jan know they will soon have their sons back! Thank you very much, Teddy. I know Georg thought the world of you."

Nigel realized that Teddy must be suffering from the loss of his friend, too. He added, "Georg trusted you to get the boys to safety, and you did not let him down, Teddy. He would be proud of you."

Teddy swallowed hard and could barely say, "Thank you."

Nigel and Teddy sat on opposite sides of the ocean with tears streaming down their cheeks. Both had lost their dear friend, but Nigel had lost Georg for a second time.

Nigel recalled what the field worker who saved Georg had said. "That young man must be destined to do somethin' real important before he dies!"

***

Helena and Jan wanted to greet their sons alone. They waited on the dock, so they could see the supply ship drifting into port.

The captain had told the boys they could stand on the bridge to see their mama and papa as the ship docked. Finally, they saw two figures on the dock. They waved wildly.

Helena cried, "Jan! There they are! Our boys are here!"

Jan could barely contain himself. "Yes, Lena, it's wonderful, our own miracle!" He didn't know he was crying and wouldn't have cared if he did.

It seemed an eternity before the gangplank was lowered and the boys ran to their parents. Jozef jumped into his papa's arms, and Henryk hugged his mama with all his strength. Helena and Jan traded one son for the other. With Jozef in her arms, Helena said, "My little boy, I've missed you so much!"

Jozef proudly announced, "Mama, I'm not a little boy anymore. I was very brave! Henryk said so!"

Helena smiled and said, "Of course you're not a little boy, you're just like your Uncle Jozef. We used to call him 'Jozef the hero', you know! And we are very proud of both of you!"

Henryk said, "Mama, Professor Stein gave me a note to give to you. He said it was my most important mission." He handed her the folded piece of paper.

The four of them read the note together. It read:

With Love from Poland

Chapter Twenty-One

Epilogue

Julia and Kazi Wolowicz relaxed on their balcony overlooking the Hudson River. It was Friday evening, July 19, 1940, and they could see the brilliant full moon hanging over Bear Mountain to the north of Yonkers.

As they opened a bottle of wine, the two reminisced about their 19th wedding anniversary party the previous weekend at the new Pulaski Farm. It was a complete surprise to them. Helena had made certain of that. She had told them the gathering was a simple Sunday afternoon dinner.

Their group was so busy making a living that they didn't get together nearly as often as they would have liked. So being invited to the Pulaski farm was a welcome treat.

Julia said, "Helena puts together quite a party, doesn't she, Kazi?"

He smiled. "Yes, indeed she does. It was just like being in Cracow with our family and friends."

"Speaking of family and friends," Julia slyly said, "Helena and Jan's 20th wedding anniversary is coming up, on July 22nd. Wouldn't they be surprised if *we* threw *them* a party?"

Without waiting for a reply, she said, "Do you think we have time to put it together? We can plan it for 2:00 after church next week."

She was so excited about her idea that she didn't notice Kazi smiling and nodding in agreement.

Julia talked as fast as the ideas popped into her head. "I'll ask Rebekka and Franz to help me. I'm so glad they got out of Paris before the Germans took over in May.

Oh, and I'm going to ask Nigel to plan a special surprise for Jan. Oh, Kazi! This will be so much fun, don't you agree?"

Kazi thoughtfully sipped his wine while contemplating his response.

Finally, with a woeful expression, he said, "Jules, I don't think I'll be available that day."

Julia jumped up, knocking over her wine glass. "Kazi Wolowicz, what do you mean you don't think you'll be available that day? What could be more important than our best friends' anniversary celebration?"

He smirked and leisurely took another sip of his wine. Julia realized he was kidding. She jumped onto his lap, spilling his wine in the process. They dissolved into laughter.

Julia said, "You deserve that, you brute, for making me think you were not as enthused as I am over the idea of a grand anniversary party for Helena and Jan!"

"If what I deserve is you hopping onto my lap, then I am a happy man indeed!"

With that, he kissed his wife.

"Do you remember that morning in Helena's kitchen in Cracow when I jumped onto your lap and cheered you up, Kazi? You were feeling blue about the coming war and having to leave Poland for the last time."

"I certainly do, my dear. You always know how to cheer me up. Just your presence—that's all I need, Jules."

Julia jumped up from Kazi's lap and said, "Alright *now*, let's get planning the big event!"

Although her enthusiasm was infectious, party planning was not his plan for the rest of their evening. But he gave up his plan, for the moment, and they moved to the kitchen table to plan another joyous occasion.

***

On Sunday, everyone who was invited to the anniversary party attended 6 A.M. Mass. That is, everyone except Helena and Jan. They would be attending 9 A.M. Mass as was their habit.

When Julia arrived at the Pulaski Farm later that morning, she found everything in readiness, exactly as they'd planned. The only thing left to do was to decorate with Helena's favorite colors: aquamarine and pine green accented with ivory lace, just like the costume she'd made for herself for the 1920 Spring Social — her first real date with Jan.

***

Helena and Jan rode to the Pulaski Farm with Father Michalowicz. Helena commented that she had not seen their friends and family at Mass. Father Michalowicz was silent. He knew the reason.

As they drove onto the grass next to the big barn, they noticed that everyone seemed to have arrived ahead of them for Sunday dinner. Helena began to suspect that something was about to be sprung on them.

Jan, being a sensitive, had a premonition a few days prior. He realized that an anniversary surprise party was being planned for them. He was prepared with a special gift for his Lena.

It was customary to use the kitchen entrance to the farmhouse when visiting Pulaski's. However, today it was blocked by egg crates, so the three of them went to the front door.

Jan let Helena go in ahead of him. She opened the creaky screen door.

There was no one in the living room, but as they rounded the corner into the big country kitchen, they were greeted with "SURPRISE! HAPPY ANNIVERSARY!"

Helena was so startled that she all but jumped into Jan's arms.

She looked at Jan with tears in her eyes. "You knew about this, didn't you?"

He said, "No one told me, but I figured it out. Look, Lena, everyone is here!"

The group waited for a response from Helena. She said, "Now I know why I did not see any of you at Mass today, and *you*, Julia Wolowicz, this looks like *your* idea!"

Julia stepped forward and the two shared a long hug. She said, "Lena, you surprised us with the most wonderful anniversary party, so I wanted to do the same for you and Jan. And, I am thrilled that you really *are* surprised!"

Nigel shook Jan's hand and announced that there was some special entertainment planned for Jan, set to begin shortly.

Uncle Stan shouted from the far side of the kitchen, "Helena, come sit right here!"

Laughingly, Helena obliged. How she loved that big man. There were so many people crowded into the kitchen that Helena did not see it right away. She cried, "Uncle Stan! You fixed Mama's rocking chair! Oh, thank you!"

Big Stan's own emotions got the better of him. He had to swallow hard to get any words out. He said, "Well, get over here and try it out!"

She sat in the rocker. It seemed to wrap its arms around her. She happily rocked back and forth amid cheers and clapping. Jan walked up to Helena as she sat in her beloved rocker. The room went quiet. With tears in his eyes, Jan knelt on one knee and recited:

Lena, my love, my wife, you are the heart of my life.
When I see you smile, my life is worthwhile.
Each moment with you has been my treasure,
only my heart can know the true measure.

My joy is that you love me.

There was complete silence, and not a dry eye could be found. Helena overrode her emotion with humor. She said, "Well, Jan Jasinski, your hair is not quite as red as it was twenty years ago, and you did not accost me with a rickety cotton cart, but you are the same lovable poet! I love you, Jan!"

Nigel broke through the crowd that had gathered around the rocker. He tapped Jan on the shoulder. "Okay, old boy, time for you and me to have that bicycle race rematch!"

Jan turned to Nigel. "If you really want me to beat you again, let's go!"

Nigel motioned for everyone to go out behind the cow barn. Someone had moved the egg crates, so the path was clear from the kitchen's back door.

Jakob Pawlowski gave Helena and Jan a bear hug as they passed by. "Happy Anniversary, you two!"

Nigel ran ahead with Franz. They were each standing with a bike at the starting line of the racetrack inside the fenced area.

When Jan arrived, he said, "Wait just a minute! We're using the cow path for a bike race? You *are* daft, Blake!"

Smugly, Nigel said, "You're a chicken!"

That prompted Jozef to start a group refrain of "buk, buk, buk, buk-kaaa!"

Without further ado, Jan jumped on the bike that Franz held. Nigel hopped on his bike, and both men pedaled to the railroad tie, which was the starting line.

The path was rutted near the fence, as that was the cow's walking path. Farmer Pulaski pointed out that cows are creatures of habit and the only time they get off their path is when they go to and from the barn, or when they decide to graze.

Nigel said, "Jan, we will ride outside the ruts and go around the pasture for one lap. You go first, and I will be directly behind you. That is, until I overtake you and win the race!"

Jan looked confident, intending to win.

Helena's papa found a little Polish flag to use as a starting signal. When they all found a place outside of the fence to watch from, Jakob shouted dramatically, "On your *mark*, get *set*, and *GO!*"

Helena had a flashback to the last bike race when Georg was the starter. She knew he would truly enjoy this race. Helena mused that Georg was beside her, watching the race.

Most everyone was rooting for Jan as he had gotten hurt during the last race and had to be carried out in Nigel's rickshaw.

The two took off as fast as the dirt would allow. The crowd roared.

"Go, Jan!" was heard by all except one spectator. Of course, it was Hanna. She shouted, "You can do it, Nigel!" He grinned at her from under the racing cap he'd found in a wooden chest in the barn. She thought he looked silly, but sexy.

The fenced pasture surrounded an acre of meadow, and the path was not meant as any kind of roadway. The test that Franz and Nigel had run predicted a four-minute race.

At the halfway point, Jan was still ahead of Nigel, who was not about to lose this battle with his longtime rival!

Boldly, Nigel moved closer to the fence. Another quarter lap saw him easily pass Jan. They were both having trouble navigating the makeshift bike path.

Hanna gasped when she saw Nigel and his bike fly into the air. He'd hit a rut.

Helena screamed when she saw that Jan could not avoid crashing into the heap that was Nigel.

Everyone ran to help the unfortunate racers. Nigel's knees and elbows were bloody, mixed with dirt and pebbles, but he was standing.

When Helena and Julia got to Jan, he was also standing, a bit shaky and dirty, but seemingly unhurt.

Shouts were heard from the barn. Franz and Jozef yelled, "Stand aside, everyone, we're coming to help!"

As the crowd turned toward the Pawlowski boys, uproarious laughter erupted.

They each carried the side pole of a hay wagon normally hitched to a horse. They headed to the scene of the accident to pick up the injured.

The onlookers cleared a path for the makeshift ambulance. Franz and Jozef dropped the hay wagon poles and approached Nigel and Jan, who were now leaning on Hanna and Helena.

With great ceremony, the boys lifted the broken bicycles, lovingly placed them on the hay wagon, picked up their poles, and trotted back to the barn, leaving the injured racers in a cloud of dust.

Jakob could not contain himself. Through his laughter, he managed to declare the race a draw.

The competitors were good sports, enjoying the joke. Jan and Nigel shook hands, clapped each other on the back, and agreed never again to challenge each other to a bike race.

Hanna and Helena exchanged a relieved look.

Big Stan shouted, "Dinner is ready — let's EAT!"

The centerpiece of the dining table was a four-tier cake baked by Jan's Mama. She'd taken a job as a baker because there were few jobs for immigrants in 1940, especially for women. She was a happy baker, and all those who tasted her baking wizardry gave rave reviews. The cake she'd baked for Jan and Helena's anniversary was of course, her special sand cake.

Dinner was chicken and dumplings, fresh applesauce and green beans from the garden. Farmer Pulaski shocked the women when he described how the chickens got from the barnyard to their dinner plates.

Nigel thought he'd like to try his hand at capturing chickens. He winked at Hanna and said, "Maybe next time I will help with the chickens. Hanna can hold the chickens on the chopping block while I employ the hatchet!"

Indignantly, Hanna said, "That is not my idea of fun, Mr. Funny Man!" She was nothing if not a good sport. She kissed Nigel on the cheek and he feigned being love-struck by the gesture, much to the amusement of all.

With the meal finished and the cake served along with coffee, and tea for Nigel.

Helena asked for everyone's attention. She stood and took Jan's hand. "Jan, long ago, I made you a promise. Today I will fulfill my promise to play a song on my violin especially for you." She looked at the faces around the table and with a smile said, "But all of you may listen too."

Father Michalowicz handed Helena her violin, which he had brought from the car. Mrs. Pulaski brought out the music stand they so often used at their gatherings, and Helena placed the sheet music on it that she had hidden in her pocket.

She'd practiced long and hard to be able to play this piece to perfection for her husband. She knew he would recognize it *and* appreciate its significance.

The song was originally composed for piano, but Helena had painstakingly adapted it for violin.

She was right. When Jan listened to the first stanza, he knew it was Chopin's Fantasie Impromptu that he had practiced and played for her at the Spring Social in Cracow twenty years before.

It was all Jan could do not to jump up and wrap Helena in his arms before she finished the piece.

Watching Jan's reaction to Helena's gift was ever so touching—a moment to be remembered and cherished by every one of this proud group.

When Helena played the last note, she placed her violin in its case and walked into Jan's waiting arms. He whispered into her ear, "Lena, thank you for that. I know how difficult that piece is for the piano, but somehow you managed to play it on your violin with perfection and beauty—just like you. I love you."

She whispered into Jan's ear, "I love you too, Jan. Let's begin another twenty years together, shall we?"

As Jakob watched Helena and Jan, he glanced in the far corner of the kitchen. The rocking chair happily rocked back and forth.

He noticed that Franz, Jozef and Helena also saw the chair rock. It was a reminder that all of them had a piece of their mama's heart, of Jakob's beloved Marta, just as she promised.

As usual, there was more news from this Polish-American group. First, Helena and Jan's daughter, Julia, announced that she and Michal had set their wedding date for Christmas. They planned to start their family soon after. Michal's mama and papa were thrilled, as were Helena and Jan.

Then Nigel stood and with his usual dramatic flair. "Hanna has asked me to be her wife, and I have accepted!"

He looked at Hanna, who was aghast and said, "Oops, I think I said that backwards. I have asked Hanna to be my wife and she, for some unknown reason, accepted! We are planning a September wedding and we would love it, Helena, if you would be our wedding planner. And Mrs. Jasinski, would you please bake our wedding cake? He turned to Farmer Pulaski and asked if he would provide the chickens.

At that point, Hanna interrupted. "Nigel, you don't have to complete the planning in the same breath as the announcement. Helena and I will take care of all of that!"

As if he'd not heard her, Nigel leaned over to Father Michalowicz and said, "You will marry us, won't you, Father?"

Father Michalowicz smiled and said, "Of course I will, Nigel. But for now, you'd best consider clamming up." No one had heard the good Father talk to anyone like that, and he got a big laugh.

Nigel said, "I think you're right, Father! Who else has news for us?"

Franz stood and proudly pulled Rebekka up with him. Placing his hand on Rebekka's belly, he said, "I would like you all to meet Georg. He's named after our hero, Captain Georg Stein! He's due to make his appearance at Thanksgiving. That's appropriate, don't you think?"

Rebekka giggled with delight. She said, "Franzie, our baby might possibly be named Georgia."

Uncle Stan bellowed, "No Sir! That child is a strapping boy who will look just like his papa! I know these things, and I would be honored if you would allow me to make his cradle!"

Jan chimed in. "You can believe Uncle Stan when he says he knows your baby is a boy. Remember, he knew our twins would be a boy who looked just like me, and a girl who looked just like her mama and I'll be darned if he wasn't right on the money!"

Helena said, "I am so happy for you two! I wish we still had the cradles Uncle Stan made for the twins. They were so lovely."

Jozef said, "Hey! Maybe you will have twins!"

Rebekka said, "Please, one child at a time will be quite enough for me."

Franz agreed with a nod toward his wife and a pretend sneer toward his brother.

Sophia giggled. "Jozef, it may be us having the twins!"

Jozef's head snapped toward his wife. "Sophia, are you sure? That's the best news! Mariola! Jasper! Did you hear that? You're going to have a brother or a sister, or both!"

The baby gurgled, and the dog yipped.

Jakob said, "Well, this is certainly a day of exciting announcements. If no one else has news to share, I will leave it to Hanna to present a surprise to Helena. Hanna, dear, are you ready?"

"Yes, Papa Pawlowski, I am ready."

With that, Hanna grabbed her mama's hand and together they walked around the corner into the living room. Elena had arrived late with an apology about having to babysit for her friend's child.

When they reappeared in the kitchen doorway, they were on either side of a tall, handsome blonde man. He introduced himself as Karl Bjorn, Hanna's papa—Elena's husband.

Hanna said, "We have Nigel to thank for my papa getting here quickly. He arranged for his travel from Sweden through Plymouth Naval Port, on none other than Captain Smith's supply ship. I think Papa may decide to stay here in America and work for Volvo on this side of the Atlantic. Isn't that right, Papa?"

Karl said, "We shall see about that, Hanna. I have heard so much about all of you from Elena. I am in your debt for saving the lives of my wife and my daughter. In partial payment, I would like to present a gift to the organizer of the Acorn Park Underground."

He handed Hanna a cube-shaped box. "Hanna, would you like to do the honors?"

By way of an answer, Hanna reached for the box and gave it to Helena.

Eagerly, Helena set the box on the dining table and unwrapped it. The box did not indicate what the contents were, but it was marked "Fragile." Gingerly, she opened the top and began to sort through the packing material. She was getting more and more anxious to discover the gift.

Her hands touched something made of wood, and it felt like it had carvings on it. It was the cuckoo clock she'd consigned to Hanna's shop, "Time and Again" to raise money for Acorn Park.

Helena went to Hanna's papa and hugged him. "How did you find my treasured cuckoo clock? This is nothing short of a miracle, thank you!"

Karl said, "You are most welcome, Helena. You are a sister to my daughter, and therefore, you too are my daughter. I remember your mama. She was such a special woman, and you are so like her!"

He kissed her on the cheek and continued, "Hanna got me interested in antiques when we lived in Venezuela. On weekends, I visited shops wherever I traveled. A few weeks ago, I had a business trip to Bavaria and found a cute little clockmaker's shop. That's where I found this clock. When I heard it cuckoo, it seemed to speak your name. I knew I would be coming here, and so I bought it for you. I did not really know that it was yours. But when Hanna saw it, she knew beyond a shadow of a doubt."

The entire group got up and shook Karl's hand or hugged him or kissed him. He had not had this much attention since his marriage to Elena, and he truly enjoyed it.

Uncle Stan shouted, "This calls for drinks all around. Vodka for everyone to celebrate all of us being together!"

Farmer Pulaski found glasses and an unopened vodka bottle. Shots were poured and Nigel offered the toast, "Here's to all of us, cheers everyone!"

"Hear, hear!" sounded throughout the farmhouse.

The evening ended with Helena's clock joyfully cuckooing eight o'clock — the same time they had met Georg's plane on which they escaped from Poland. It was indeed tangible proof that "little by little, we go far."

They had come a very long way to enjoy their new lives. They had truly arrived With Love from Poland.

I hope you enjoyed this story. I would appreciate it if you would write a short review on Amazon. Thank you!
https://www.amazon.com/author/lindakeenan

About the Author

Linda Lee Keenan was born in upstate New York and has lived in the northeast all her life. She has a varied background as a business manager, a paralegal, an interior decorator, an adjunct professor, a Reiki Master, a real estate broker, a residential real estate appraiser and as a writer and sometime poet.

Linda considers herself a late bloomer as she began her college career at age 40. She earned a Bachelor of Science degree with an emphasis on legal studies at Post University in Connecticut. She minored in history and it became her passion. Linda returned to Post University as an Adjunct Professor of History after earning a master's degree in international history at Western Connecticut State University.

An innate understanding of metaphysics colors Linda's view of the world. Her writing reflects glimmers of mysticism. She naturally creates a storyline that develops in unforeseen ways and brings a plot full circle, with a smattering of humor along the way.

Linda lives in Connecticut with her husband, Bob, and twin bichon pups, Beau and Bear. When she's not writing, she enjoys watching movies, being creative at the sewing machine, interior decorating and socializing with friends.